ThunderBird Walking

ThunderBird Walking

A GRAND CANYON GHOST STORY

K e Conlon

Amokshado Press

First Edition

ISBN 978-0-9899290-0-4

Printed in the United States of America

10 9 8 7 6 5 4 3 2 1

Amokshado Press

www.thunderbirdwalking.com

Book Design by Maria Bilinski Shain

CONTENTS

AUTHOR'S NOTE

This story is set in America and draws some biographical events from the life of the author. The usual methods employed by creative writers to obfuscate time and place, tighten up the narrative and create drama are in use here. While the circumstances are possible, the characters are not real people. The main character is a better man than the writer, the motives of his adversaries come from creative imagination, and the secondary characters are fictional types based on American probabilities.

The 'thunderbird' referred to in this book is not meant to signify connection to or infringe upon beliefs of indigenous peoples or any other spiritual traditions. Rather, the ideas put forth should be considered one fictional character's perspective on an archetype. As far as accepting the dreams, visions and 'non-ordinary reality' events, I leave that up to your discretion.

May anyone who sees a political or social agenda in this story stumble off the nearest cliff.

Just looking for a balance . . .
a way back, home.

Inscription to my first journal

A man stands on the rim of Grand Canyon wondering how many days he has left. In his hands, he holds a leather journal with ragged edges. The words on those pages come from his scribe mind—notions connected to the modern world and to the whispers of other scribes from all the ages of humanity.

The man has lived his life on the edge of a paradigm shift, waiting for new insights into ancient mysteries to be accepted. Yet mostly he has walked in a dream world, alone where primeval thunderbirds dance. Words have been his only true companion on this journey. He's tried to catch it all, believing that one day he will walk on a different earth. On the edge, reliving it all again, he sets down his life journal on the rock next to him.

The book is open. Wind flips the pages, seeking a starting place for his story. The air settles, the pages fall flat, and words written at this very spot some time ago are revealed.

All lives begin and end at the same place, in the same moment, on the same ledge.

A man stands on the rim of Grand Canyon, knowing and remembering. The wind stirs again, and his spirit takes flight on the possibilities. He is alive, a survivor of a long journey, a ghost looking back over forty-seven years. He has a story to tell—and only the wind to listen. The air settles and the pages fall flat, revealing another passage.

FREE WRITING — GRAND CANYON RIM, NOVEMBER 13, 2006

She's wearing her reds today. When I look at her my breath feels shallow and tears well up in my eyes. We have a long history. She has shown me so much and yet I know I am almost nothing to her. All I can give — even if I gave all — is virtually nothing next to what she has given me. And I am but one she gives to and but one she owns by that giving. Today I sit on the edge in a place of sorrow, and she shows her reds.

I think of her depths, places she has led me to, places scattered across time and distance. Those memories massage the corners of my mind and ignite passions in my soul. I want to be in those places again. I want to touch all of them anew in the now, knowing all of her at once — or at least as much as one man can know. I want the deep reds and the pale greens, the cool magentas and the baked blacks, the soft vanilla-coloured stones and the deep chocolate-coloured water. I want the wide open places and the narrow hidden spots of her. I want to cry and hold back the tears, breathe deep and be short of breath. I want to let go of my depths in exchange for a glimpse at hers.

She's a mountain lying down and I am an explorer. Today she shows her reds beneath a blue sky, and I sit on the edge having already fallen.

1. THE SANCTITY OF FAMILY

I wrote 'She's Wearing Her Reds' on the rim of Grand Canyon while remembering my high school girlfriend a few years after she died. Long before her passing, we had gone our separate ways. We exchanged greeting cards on occasion and her last message, which arrived shortly before she became ill, wished me well on my journey. Time moved on.

In 2006, I was living a meagre life in Northern Arizona. Feeling alone, I came back to this spot on the ledge. I had said goodbye to Thérèse here after I heard of her death. She never saw Grand Canyon, never saw this spot, but when I come here I think of her and feel her presence. On that day a flock of Pinyon Jays gathered all around me, and I realized that I had found my way back to my true nature. I became proud of my choices in life even though no one else understood them. Here on this ledge that day, I felt a sense of belonging to the earth.

And then I left the ledge and forgot my true nature again.

Yes, I admit I'm in love with Grand Canyon. So much so that it takes on a persona, even a sanctity, within my mind. My relationship with nature is the number one relationship in my life. While many feel connection to their family or a supreme being, most of those feelings in me have been transferred to natural wonders. Human relationships have never been easy. The safety of family got breached in my childhood by some shadowy need for government secrecy about the generational effects of war. I became lost. I hid away my true self and the truth of my upbringing. I've lived my life on the outskirts of society looking in, wandering the wilderness and feeling free.

Nature accepts me without question. It cannot be overwhelmed by my past experiences or swayed by the subtle emotional blackmail that rises out of my years of going unheard and unsupported. The earth accepts all of me, not just the parts that people can find comfort in. I get my feelings of *sanctity* from natural wonders, but things weren't always that way. As a child, starkly opposing destinies of creativity and destruction were fostered within me, but on the surface I was a normal boy living in a typical American home.

My God-given name is Thomas Benedict WyKliffe. My mom used to say that 'Thomas' came from the great scholar Thomas Aquinas, but I've always doubted that. 'Benedict' means 'blessed,' nothing traitorous about it. I kept changing my name growing up because it didn't seem to fit me . . . Tom, Tommy, Bennie. In some of my strange visionary dreams, I got called by the spirit name of ThunderBird Walking, but I knew better than to tell people about that. An active imagination is judged either a gift or a curse, so it seems better to hide it. Friends got to calling me by my initials, TBW, and that worked for both my God-given name and the name from my inner world.

I grew up the youngest son in a large, catholic family with a strict patriarchy. My father reigned like a king, and each child eked out a role for themselves and defended their place. By the time I came along, my siblings had taken the positive archetypes, leaving me to wrestle with demons. My attempts to fit in met with ridicule, but in my time alone I developed my mind and imagination. I found alternative ways to perceive the world around me. As I grew older, I found the creative arts, and I followed a dream to become a writer.

In my childhood, I took in the world's dysfunction, and I saw how my father passed on his emotional trauma from war. Through the years, the rage and fears and inner chaos of a man who had almost died alone on a World War Two battlefield gained a place in the psyches of his children—and in me. We were supposed to be tough and silent, find ways to deal with dark emotions on our own. Being the youngest son, the sensitive one at the bottom of a heap of feigned religious purity, the *craziness* often settled on me. I had nowhere to go with it, so I kept it bottled up inside.

I'd like to wrap up my past in a nice story with scenes and dialogue. Show it and not tell it. But there are some things to be told first. *Isn't that the way of life?* You see, the events of my childhood are a secret . . . the records were destroyed by a state government under a special interest law to prevent me the psychological harm of knowing too much about myself. *Not that I care.* Honestly, it's great to be free of documents that tell an official version of some experience. Life is messy, and telling about it is like wandering around in the wilderness, hiking or rafting about, you want to clean yourself up first before deciding what makes for a good story and what is better left unsaid. So when I look back at my childhood I don't have much to show.

The others in my family were the important ones, and I stayed off to the side somewhere, rocking back and forth as if the ripples of the universe washed over me or some kind of dancing Shiva had a hold on me. And in those ripples were tides of other times, other ways of thinking, and I just knew things somehow. Things we're not supposed to talk about. So yes, I'm telling a story. I can't defend it. You're gonna want to take it this way or that way, make it agreeable, wrap it up in a nice little package for mass consumption, but my life isn't like that.

I realized a long time ago that my life and my spiritual visions were created by my imagination. I'm making up my journey out of darkness and away from the fears of the unknown as I go—I'm making up the story of my triumph in an age of terror. I sat there in my early childhood rocking back and forth, and I sit here now on this ledge defenseless in the face of your skepticism. Believing is a process, so I ask a simple favor of you. Allow me to take my journey one step and one life at a time.

You see, I need to tell you that I come from a clan of holy warriors going back maybe all the way to the Roman Empire. I suppose I could lie and say that my dad had an antique helmet up on a shelf and I asked him where it came from. "Why son," he could have said, "that's been passed down in the family since before the Dark Ages." What a nice, acceptable family moment that would have been. Except life isn't like that. The helmet, if there ever was one, got lost somewhere during the Crusades. So I got nothing to show you.

I can tell you that ideas of religious armageddon have lived in the minds of boys in my family for generations. My dad and his dad and all the oldest sons were given the name Michael—a name that means 'who is like God?' I knew from the Book of Revelations that the Archangel Michael leads God's armies against the forces of evil, so I'm sure my father as a catholic soldier fighting in World War Two believed that Hitler was the antichrist and armageddon had arrived. When the biblical peace didn't materialize afterward, he assumed another great war lay waiting—and he passed that idea on.

Growing up, I used to sneak into my parents' room and open the drawer in a dresser that stood in the corner. My father's Purple Heart medal lay hidden there. I'd take it out and play with it, secretly bring it to my room and think about all the glory held by that thing. Later, I'd sneak it back into the dresser drawer hoping my dad wouldn't catch me. I knew that he got the Purple Heart because his knee became unbendable in a great war over the future of humanity, and we were never supposed to talk about that.

As broken as combat left him, my father lived a relatively normal life engineering weapons of limited destruction for the federal government. Our family read the bible every day after dinner, and we said the rosary together at least three times a week, praying for salvation. I learned at a young age that another holy war would erupt someday soon and I would fight on the side of God.

I don't know how that led to the secret stuff that happened to me. All I know is that as a teenager I had unusual ideas and strange images all jumbled up in my mind. Remnants of things forgotten by myself and others. There's a memory I have of lying on a gurney being wheeled through a lab room, and written on a chalkboard were a bunch of big words. Being half in the dream world I couldn't make sense of them, but they stuck in my mind asking to be understood. I wrote the letters down sometimes—a bunch of 'p's and 'o's—weird words that always stayed with me because I knew they held some truth I didn't want to forget.

When I got older, I made sense of those words—*pleiotropy of phenotype*—and I realized that the phrase scrawled on the chalkboard had something to do with genetic research. Doctors were comparing me to my father and trying to answer a question. *Were we blessed in war and healing?* They wanted to find out the chemistry or psychology or magic that made my father unique so they could recreate it and pass it on to others. The idea had a noble genesis, but it went off the tracks somewhere. They left scars both physical and emotional, scars splitting apart a father and son, a chasm between and a chasm within, and I knew that to heal my own depths I had to go back and connect with my father's World War Two experience.

My dad never spoke about the war to me. It forever remained an unapproachable topic in my family. He even banned the TV show *M*A*S*H* in our house. He never said why, but I guess the sounds of explosions and laughter brought back bad memories. As a teenager, I researched World War Two and tried to get his service records, only to find out they were destroyed in the great Saint Louis warehouse fire of 1976. That search left me suspicious. I thought it meant there were generational secrets that someone wanted to hide.

Some years later, I read about my dad's darkest hours in an unpublished book my grandfather wrote. I found out my father served as a rifleman under the 84th Division in an infantry unit nicknamed the 'Railsplitters.' I did more research and came across a memoir written by a soldier from his company that included descriptions of their battles, and I pieced together a timeline.

In my mind's eye, I began to imagine my dad's war experience. I pictured him as a lucky man in combat, a death-defying soldier with God on his side. Three separate times his squad took casualties on the front lines. In one of those incidents, near as I can figure at the town of Lindern, they were cut off behind German lines for four to five days waiting for relief from Allied forces. My father survived that siege and the onslaught of the Battle of the Bulge, but those were not his darkest hours. He went on to face a more traumatic wait for rescue in the dead of winter at a turning point in the war.

In the cold and snow of late December 1944, the Allies were rebounding from the last great German offensive. By January third, they were ready to go on an offensive of their own. My dad's squad moved to take the town of Devantave, Belgium, but during their advance they came under heavy mortar fire in the woods east of a town called Beffe. The squad leader was killed, and my dad grabbed the radio to keep in contact with the American command during the retreat.

While running back through the woods, shrapnel from an exploding bomb caught him in the hip—he fell hard on top of the radio, breaking a rib and puncturing a lung. With his leg-bone shattered and his flesh mangled, he couldn't walk. Stranded in the woods alone, he waited for rescue. Three men approached but were hit by shells and killed. Three more soldiers tried to reach him and also fell prey to enemy guns. So my dad lay there with a useless leg, gasping for air, as enemy shells flew over his head and exploded around him.

Dying in a foxhole thousands of miles from home soil was a place my dad never expected to be. He had a background in engineering and got stationed at military proving grounds in Maryland after being drafted into the service. He trained in the repair of army equipment and proved lucky enough to get a transfer to a polytechnic institute to continue his studies. Academia became his haven from the cruel world of combat. My dad planned to be an engineer helping to rebuild Europe after the hostilities ended, but the war got worse, all army colleges were closed, and he was sent to boot camp. In September of 1944 he was reassigned overseas, and by December he faced some of the bloodiest combat of the war.

On that fateful day in January, the life of the twenty-three-year-old christian soldier who would become my father hung in the balance. Without luck, he would never make it home. The Company Aid Man reported the situation in the woods as *hell—intestines were hanging in trees. The soldiers who couldn't walk were left behind because of the heavy shelling. All of them were suffering from shock, and it would be hours before the last wounded were rescued.*

Pinned down in freezing temperatures under range of enemy guns, all hope lost, my dad clung to life. Air bubbled out of his punctured lung while pieces of dead soldiers lay scattered around him. I'm sure he had given up. Out of the muck, a hand reached toward him. A medic pulled him from the hole and dragged him to the edge of the woods. From there, clinging to his rescuer, he hopped on his good leg to safety.

My father never faced combat again, but the hardest struggle of his life was just beginning.

In an American military hospital in England, the doctors reset his hip bones and put both legs in a cast up to his waist, attaching a traction device at his feet so that his good leg gave support to the shattered one. They resuscitated him from death three times and gave him thirty blood transfusions. He began to get better, but something else went wrong. My dad started complaining of pain in his good leg, the one in a cast giving support to the injured leg. The doctors gave him medicine and threatened to send him to the psych ward—in those days a prison for the shell-shocked—unless he remained quiet. Weeks went by and the pain grew worse. He couldn't stay silent anymore, so he summoned a chaplain to convince the doctors to remove the cast.

Beneath the plaster on my father's unwounded leg, the doctors found an infected pressure ulcer. The tendons in the knee were rotted, and the flesh had almost gone gangrenous—only one nerve remained alive. The doctors managed to save his leg—the good leg, the one he had hopped on to get away from the enemy—but the knee became fused straight. They told him he would walk with a *bizarre gait* for the rest of his life.

After four months in England, my dad was moved to a hospital in Utah. My grandfather drove 1,500 miles across America to see his eldest son. He wrote a description in an unpublished family memoir. *He was nothing but skin and bones. His face reflected the horrible suffering of war. He said, "I am used to the pain and have forgotten how it feels to be healthy." He had seen so many fellow soldiers die, some blown to pieces, that he could not complain much of his own suffering. He felt lucky to be alive.*

My dad's war was over. He went back to college on the G.I. Bill and became an engineer, but his knee remained unbendable. He fell in love and forged a family that he ruled over like a king, but the shadow of his darkest hours in combat was always there just below the surface. After a day at work engineering weapons, he came home—always in his white shirt and black pants—and sat in his recliner in the living room until dinner. On the shelf next to him were books on religion, philosophy and health, and a few on the coming armageddon.

For my father, a hard line divided good and evil. Light and dark dueled for control inside him. For the most part the *good* side won, but sometimes an altered state of consciousness from his war trauma returned. There awoke in my dad a persona dissociated from his normal self. It wasn't who he wanted to be. He did try to change, but for me those scant moments of chaos still overshadow all his hours of love and caring.

At ten years old, I played war games with a buddy after we got home from our separate elementary schools. We made sticks into guns and hid in the woods waiting for imaginary Nazis to approach. *Attack!* Out we would jump, more often than not getting wounded and crawling back to safe ground where our injuries miraculously healed. The Battle of the Bulge was one of our favorite battles to re-enact. I didn't know that my father had fought in it—we just liked the name. We kept those games a secret for fear of get bullied for having active imaginations.

One evening, my parents got dressed in their best Sunday clothes and went to an important meeting in the city. Just after they left, the front doorbell rang. A social worker with the state government asked to come in. She said she came to meet with our parents and would wait for them to return, but that was a lie. She asked us questions about the living conditions in the home, and she left before my parents came back. My dad became irate when he heard she had been there.

I knew my family was broken. My older siblings were rebelling against religion, and my father—believing *evil* had a hold on them—turned to a psychiatrist approved for people with security clearances. Admitting he needed help threatened to open a Pandora's box on the past. As a combat soldier, he had learned that talking about feelings was a sign of weakness. He kept his dark emotions suppressed with religion, denying light and breath to the injured parts of his psyche. But the rebellions of his teenage children reflected back his inner chaos, stirred up those old demons from the war. He realized he had to face them. I was only ten, rocking back and forth in my own little world whenever the screaming and yelling started, and I couldn't unravel the complexities. I filed it all away, churned over it in my downtime, knowing that my family was broken and I should try to fix it.

My father never guessed the implications of turning to the government for help. Maybe he had no choice given his security clearance in weapons research, and maybe there were deeper secrets that eluded him. *There's no way to know, but I do know and it's more than just coincidence.* From the 1950s to the 1970s, the Department of Defense conducted a vast research program in 'behavior control experiments' that used thousands of American families as guinea pigs. People in smoky back rooms had this all planned out, and it touched everyone. If you weren't part of the experiment, you were part of the control group. Looking back, I believe my father sought integration, a resolution to his war service. He wanted to heal himself and the family, but it wasn't to be. The family was more broken than I imagined, and the secrets . . . ?

There's no one to turn to, someday you're gonna find, there's no one to turn to without them losing their mind.

Ten years old, alone, trying not to be found out. I took to writing, and that line from a childhood poem captured my sense of isolation. My true self was hidden—lost beneath the rants of my father about being betrayed, lost beneath the angst of my older siblings as they broke away from home—damned beneath antiquated worldviews about creative souls. I felt a strange darkness inside me, a chasm within, a *primitive feeling*, and I worried that the evil my dad often spoke about had found me too. I didn't know the words to express my inner darkness, and I had no one to talk to anyway. I knew to keep quiet about it.

The family was broken and a doctor arrived to fix it, but so much more was going on. New laws got passed, and government secrets were reshuffled and rehidden under the control of state authorities, corporations and individual doctors. *Mole doctors? There's no way to know.* I don't want to get all *X-Files* on you, but these things happened, and the survivors were left to make sense of their pasts on their own, watched by mental hygienists filling chasms in their minds.

I played war games, and I created a secret name for the Department of Defense psychiatrist who came into our family. I called him the mole doctor. He was a German who had his eye on us, and he had the power to destroy our home. I didn't want to ever face him, so I didn't speak about the primitive feeling or much of anything I felt inside me.

I remember another game I used to play with the kids in my neighborhood. We called it 'kick the can' and we tweaked the rules to our liking. It was a hide and seek game with a few twists. We got an empty can and put it out near the cul-de-sac at the end of the street. Someone became the seeker—the 'it'—and they were supposed to make sure no one kicked that can. The seeker closed their eyes and counted down while everyone else ran off to hide behind trees and shrubs. After they got to zero, they said "ready or not, here I come" and started looking for the hiders. If the seeker spotted someone, they ran back to the can, put a foot on it and yelled out, "I see you (so-and-so) behind the giant oak tree up on the hill." The called-out hider had to surrender and go wait on the cul-de-sac, *in the jail,* a place we sometimes called purgatory.

If the hider saw that the seeker had spotted them, they could jump out from their hiding place and run to kick the can. If they kicked it before the seeker got his foot on it, the round ended and the hiders revealed themselves. The game was stacked against the seeker because all the hiders were working together. Any one of them could jump out at any time and try to kick the can down the road to maintain the status quo. If they got there before the seeker, they kicked it with all their might and yelled some strange saying that meant 'all ye all ye all come free' but for some reason sounded like "olly olly oxen free!"

The rules for kick-the-can were tweaked in a different way whenever I played. Usually, if the seeker found one person, they got to be a hider for the next round, but I had to keep being the seeker until I found everyone. Most of the neighborhood kids were older than me, and they set the rules. They knew from my siblings that I did the rocking thing at home. Being brainier than other people, the kids made me out as awkward too. I knew my multiplication tables before some boys who were five years older than me. So they didn't like me, played pranks on me and changed the rules of the games we played so I always lost. In kick-the-can, I had to keep on being 'it' unless I caught everyone, had to keep trying to call out all the hiders who were working together to keep me unfree. They called me a dupe or a dope—or if I could persevere and catch everyone, they would dub me a genius.

So I proved myself, even with those special rules that applied only to me, and I won at kick-the-can. I found all the hiders. Everyone saw it. I made my big breakthrough, and I believed that I was finally going to be accepted by the neighborhood kids. I remember that moment, standing there with my foot on the can calling out the last hider. As he gave himself up and came toward the cul-de-sac where all the kids from the neighborhood were stuck in purgatory, I figured I had finally passed the test. *Respect. Pats on the back.* But instead of honest friendship, they bowed down to me in mock worship chanting "Om Buddha" and "Om Brahma" and "Om Shiva." I didn't know what that meant. I don't think they did either. Nothing changed, except they never let me play kick the can again.

Sometimes it seems like that game never ended, and I am the only seeker in world full of hiders.

I lived half a step ahead of the demons hidden in the chasm within my mind all through my childhood. I was a boy touched by grace in a strange way, living in what I thought was a typical American home. Years later, as I closed in on my master's degree, trifling ordeals from grade school started to well up inside me. Strange things long forgotten became as clear as if they had happened yesterday. During the week of comprehensive exams that would make or break my graduate degree, I started to picture a map of Maryland I had made in the fourth grade. We used colored sands to build the mountains and forests and waterways, and I remember being very proud of it, but I had no one to share it with. I had hidden it away somewhere, and during the last days of grad school I wanted to find it again.

Never did.

In thinking about the fourth grade, I realized that my rebellion started there. The first sign of defiance happened on school picture day. Everyone got a free comb, and we were warned not to use it in class. I used mine anyway and got it tangled in my shoulder-length hair. The teacher heard the guys in the back of the class laughing and saw the comb stuck in a knot near my ear. She came over and helped me get it untangled as she lectured the class on the wisdom of following rules. I remembered being embarrassed, but that wasn't why that moment stayed in my memory. That day I realized for the first time that I had broken free of the confines of my upbringing. I had gone from being a buzz-cut military boy to a long-haired bohemian in less than a year.

In grade school, I fell in with a group of guys with long hair. They picked fights with me in the empty halls of the school during class because they knew me as the former military kid. One guy stood as lookout while another fought me and a third acted as referee. After throwing a few punches boxing-style, we would trash-talk each other. For some stupid reason, I had to prove myself a good fighter to fit in with a bunch of bohemians. Seeking a fairer duel I could win, I started having fights after school with my war games buddy from the neighborhood—a civil war broke out in our play and we became enemies. His father, seeing my longer hair and freer personality, decided I wasn't the right friend for his catholic-schooled son anymore.

I never felt accepted in elementary school. I went to a different junior high than most of the kids I knew, and I found a group of long-haired guys to hang out with. They didn't know my past, and we became steadfast friends as we discovered sex, drugs and rock 'n' roll together. We weren't thugs. We called ourselves freaks, and we navigated along the gray areas of troublemaking that existed at that time. Recreational drugs and skipping school were considered rebellious, but there were teachers who still believed we had promising futures even though we didn't follow all the rules.

Levels of rebellion were measured in the length of our hair. My Cherokee friend Jerrold set the standard for what could be achieved in freak flags with his long locks. He lived in the neighborhood across some floodplains from mine, and we started meeting in those fields after school. We listened to music that took us on stairways to heaven and highways to hell. We hopped through misty mountains and got lost in sunshine daydreams. We flirted with sugar magnolias and got teased by barracudas. It was a time of discovery, and we found so many ideas and emotions that older people never talked about in the rebellious rock music of the day. My peaceful, primitive feeling found a haven that my parents never knew existed.

The group of us started to sneak out of our houses in the middle of the night and meet in the floodplains. We built campfires in the wilds of suburbia, escaping the unrealistic ideals forced upon us by an uptight, suit-wearing world—believing in the dawning of a better, more enlightened day. Jerrold, being more secular and likable, took me under wing in social situations, ameliorating my somewhat placid demeanor and hints of catholic piety to help me make friends. The times were good and being strange was fine, especially if you were creative.

We discovered a concrete dam in some woods back behind the junior high school and made it our destination for skipping classes. Most days it was a place of solitude—other times parties broke out. Social status didn't exist there, people could just be themselves. Freaks, geeks, jocks, auto shop dudes or school princesses, if you showed up there we were all equal beasts. You could let your hair down, whether it was long like most of the regulars or more presentable like the rarer visitors. Coming out of my shell, I liked to see who might show up on a *skip day* to smoke some pot and live a little rebellion before going back to being that person from some other clique in the hallways. *Wink, wink.*

There were a few teachers who knew about our *back behind* excursions, and we went to them if our lives teetered toward chaos. They knew what uptight administrators didn't, that a little honest rebellion prevents a violent uprising. By high school, all of these threads began to come together into a lifestyle. We were living a new paradigm in secret. We found a *back behind* for the high school, meeting there before skipping out to spend the day at secluded spots in nature. The future seemed wide open.

In tenth grade, I found my sweetheart Thérèse and lost myself in the relationship. We were like a goth couple who hadn't discovered makeup, honest with each other to a fault, two people functioning as one. Thérèse was a descendant of Bolivian mountain tribal peoples and had a mysterious way about her. We did automatic writing together, went ghost hunting in haunted houses, even had a suicide pact promising to call each other if our lives took a turn too dark—we would leave this world together. We were sixteen when we met, filled with hormones, looking at the American dream of a perfect life in the suburbs with skepticism. We both felt there had to be something more.

We made plans to *go all the way* on my seventeenth birthday—not too bad for a former catholic boy—and I worried about her seeing the strange scars on my thighs. I had convinced myself that the healed scrapes were stretch marks from being a chubby baby, but I realized they looked more like the scars on my father's leg. *War scars.* I don't know why I started thinking that way. Maybe not wanting to speak a lie forced a repressed truth to surface. I didn't want to scare Thérèse off, so I decided to tell her the fib I told myself. *They're stretch marks from being a chubby baby.*

Thérèse never asked about the scars. Many years later, she told me she had seen them on that first night we made love. Lying together after our seconds of fumbling passion, she asked where they came from and I exploded with rage at her. I became like a snarling animal, and she knew better than to raise the subject again, so we never spoke of the scars. Thérèse sensed the chasm within me better than I did and backed off when she felt close to the edge. She learned how to dance around both my external and internal scars, and she knew never to speak about the subject of war conditioning. The code of silence for generations of holy warriors got passed on down the line to Thérèse. Somehow she stuck with me through to senior year, our relationship always teetering on the edge of a cliff.

Most people considered me a malcontent in high school. My siblings had earned the WyKliffes a reputation of 'always smiling and always making trouble.' I tried to fly under the radar, live a quiet rebellion, but as graduation approached, the vice principal told me to stop coming to school because I couldn't graduate. I had too many unexcused absences. No one told me there were other alternatives, so I gave up and never got my diploma. I spent my last days of high school roaming around the floodplains not far from my house. Thérèse broke up with me, and the emotions of my military trauma from years earlier started emerging chaotically. A dropout with no prospects for the future, I fell into a deep depression.

Those weeks near graduation remain foggy to me, lost to the chasm within. One night, I took a bunch of downers from prescription bottles on top of my dad's dresser and chased them with Southern Comfort. I survived the attempt, but none of my friends could reach me for end-of-school celebrations. Weeks later, I returned to the scene a changed person—stoic and distant. I wouldn't remember for another twelve years that I had been treated by the mole doctor during my absence. The remnants of holy war conditioning—real childhood war games hidden beneath the play war games I created with my neighborhood buddy—had broken through. The mole doctor buried and destroyed the memories, deleted my emerging worldview. I went back to believing I was an ordinary boy living in a normal American home.

I learned to live in two realities. The pious surface world, the one that looks good on paper, the mendacious one. And the true to myself world, the one of caring for each other, of exploring life's mysteries for fun not profit, of expanding consciousness, of knowing that there is darkness in the world and trying to bring it gently toward the light rather than blowing it to smithereens only to have it rise again in a darker form later. I saw so many others clinging to an archaic paradigm, their defunct religion supported by retrogressive notions that propped up a military-corporate complex, a *combine* that robs us of our freedoms. My father's drugs— strong medications prescribed by doctors to put to sleep his better nature so he could go on creating weapons—were acceptable. Drugs that opened the mind to different thoughts and the heart to mellower feelings were associated with evil. It didn't make sense, just like a dam on a wild river doesn't make sense, but arguing with concrete is crazy.

There's this chasm that lives in all of us. It's dammed. We're all hiding and listening for the call of 'olly olly oxen free' said by ghosts on the wind.

A NEW PARADIGM? – GRAD SCHOOL 1992

There are those who believe that humans are born to be aggressive and warlike, but my experience tells me otherwise. The internal rage that I once believed was inborn I now know comes from the secret conditioning I faced in childhood. So much energy was put into making me a 'holy' warrior that finding peace has taken a monumental effort. It is only by recognizing the secret things I was involved in as a boy that I have been able to change.

We are not as civilized as we like to believe, and as a society we are losing our connection to mystery.

We hide in our little offices and our sport utility vehicles and tell ourselves we are big. We take all the uncertainty and wonder out of life and tell ourselves we are powerful and in control. If someone threatens our haven from the cruel world, we are ready to fight to restore our luxuries and illusions of civility. Many aspects of our lives are structured for the purpose of living safely and without challenge, and slowly the sense of shared mystery to life is vanishing. Indeed, within me, it was all but destroyed because of the warpath I was placed on as a child.

The human race has reached a turning point. We will either keep repeating the same patterns and dissolve into the chaos of a destructive holy war, a new dark ages, or we will rise to the challenge of ending major conflicts between civilizations and embrace the shared mysteries of life.

In grad school, I read books on the human mind that helped me to understand my childhood. One of them said that extreme emotional distress alters the way the brain functions. In a heightened state of fear, the beast inside comes alive and a different type of awareness replaces linear thinking. Those dark moments become an undertow in the personality, an eddy or reversal in the flow of lucidness, a chasm within. The waking mind becomes like the seeker in a game of kick the can, calling out the hidden schisms to exorcise them, to bring them toward positive flow. But the calling conjures up other emotional demons from the chasm within, and they peek out from their hiding places thinking of making a break for it, as if they can kick the can and go hide again. The beast inside lives waiting for the freedom to howl like a werewolf under the full moon. It knows the old ragman roll—the *rigamarole* list of sins that will make us give up on our better natures and let our demons run wild.

* * *

I remained silent through my childhood and here I am rambling on, trying to win my truth, but it's all jumbled up in my mind like some kind of nexus, some kind of void, a chasm within. I'm a seeker trying to work it out, unscramble it, call it out from hiding. I've been silent so long it may just flow out of me like waters breaking through a dam, like a river freed after a generation of stagnation. I may sound like some fool ranting and raving, and you may want to think this didn't actually happen, say I'm a cuckoo who flew over the nest, not a thunderbird walking on the edge of new understanding.

Kick the can. I see you hiding. I thought you flew the coop.

There is truth here. Life is a twisted game of hide and seek. I wish I could show it. There were mole doctors hiding in smoky back rooms when I was a little boy. I gotta tell it as an act of defiance. A thunderbird remembering its forgotten wings. Back in the fifties, shadowy people in the halls of power came up with the idea of having groups of 'sleeper soldiers' who would 'wake up' to re-establish a free society if the free world ever fell. So who to train? How about the sons of former combat soldiers who survived hell on the battlefield and still managed to raise a family? As a boy caught up in this, I couldn't fathom the forces that were shaping my life. My inner chaos and rage wanted to run wild, but I kept seeking the words to tame myself.

Kick the can, kick the can down the road again?

But what happens when something goes wrong in a secret backwater? What if the intended psychological conditioning of the 'sleeper' doesn't go as planned? Let's say one boy has a gift of *flow*, of making the stagnant move. He rocks to the unseen tides of the universe and keeps using his wholistic sight to crawl out of holes. What happens when this child is injured and becomes lucid of things he's not supposed to know? And what if there's a doctor—a control freak of a mole doctor—who must make sure the boy forgets? Block the flow and dam him. Isolate the memories in a forgotten compartment of the boy's mind.

Tweak the rules, go off and hide again.

I had all this stuff inside me that I was trying to piece together into a new belief system. I never became good at forgetting like most people. With each idea I learned, the whole world seemed to shift, but the primitive feeling always welled up again from the chasm within, making me dumb with disbelief.

Seeking is a process. Catch the close hiders first.

My awakening got pushed back, but the spirit of my first attempt survived in a thunderbird pendant I found at a craft festival a short time before the mole doctor's treatments. The hand-cut medallion, painted with glossy enamel, gleamed like an amulet meant especially for me. Its fiery red heart caught my eye as I walked by. I stepped into the booth and picked it up, turned it over and saw a peaceful mixture of green and gold colours on the back. As I studied it, I fancied the notion that the pendant held mystical power—its jagged wings a cutting edge for truth, its youthful heart giving way to an ancestral, serene wisdom. *It was made to see me through.* I didn't have twenty dollars to buy it so I showed it to my younger sister and left it behind. On my next birthday, my sister gave me the thunderbird as a gift.

I wore the pendant during the dark, emotional times that followed my lost visits to the mole doctor. My rage of unknown origin lived in the red-hearted side, and my hope to reconnect with spirit dwelled in the green and gold side. Over the years, I learned myths and stories from cultures all over the world about great birds whose eyes filled with lightning while their wings made thunderous sounds. The Thunderbird is kin to the Phoenix—the Egyptian Bennu bird that holds ankhs in each claw—and there are other ancient beasts of the skies like the Firebird and Fenghuang, the Simurgh and Garuda, the mythical Roc. Many of the myths describe them as ancestors of the human race and protectors from the forces of evil. For native American tribes, the Thunderbird is a beast that symbolizes rebirth, a benevolent trickster spirit who uncovers truth, and a watchful protector that brings rain. I wore the pendant all through those years I remained lost from my true nature, musing to myself in the spirit world that the mystical amulet lay in wait for the right time to return lost parts of my soul.

In the middle of my grad school days, as I ran to my truck in a thunderstorm at night, I felt my thunderbird pendant fly off my chest. It landed in the wet grass and rocks of an unlit parking lot at Seneca Creek State Park in Maryland where I worked a summer job.

I searched in the dark before bringing my truck over and searching in the headlights. The storm raged, thunder rumbled, and I got soaked to the bone. I felt along the ground, hoping to touch the jagged wings of the pendant that had been with me for more than a third of my life.

I couldn't find it. I moved the truck and kept looking. More than half an hour passed, and my hopes of seeing it again sank. Shivering cold, I told myself the thunderbird was gone, and I felt hollowness in my heart. I decided I would come back the next morning after the storm and search again, probably in vain.

As I began to stand, a glint of something shiny in the dark, wet grass caught my eye.

It's a frog hopping through the rain. I think he's an animal guide who will take me right to my thunderbird, but I also know this is just wishful thinking. I start looking over the ground again near where the frog sits. He jumps once and then is still, hoping not to be noticed. I play with him some, trying to get him to move again. He seems to be curious about where the light is coming from. It's a great mystery to him, and I again wonder if he is an animal guide for me. I look down next to him and see a shiny shape barely noticeable in the shadows. Reaching down, I feel the jagged edges of my pendant.

Back in my truck, I realized the thunderbird was cracked at its thinnest point below the heart. The break distressed me because it seemed to mirror some of my own childhood injuries. At that time in my life, I had shattered the limited prism of my upbringing and pieced together the remnants of my past, but I was still trying to accept the emotional truth of my life journey. The cracked thunderbird reflected my inner brokenness. I put the pendant away, deciding not to wear it again until I found an artisan to fix it.

I started searching at local craft festivals trying to find the artisan who made my thunderbird pendant. I didn't have his name, and so much time had passed that I didn't know if he still came into the area. I went to one of the largest festivals around, and I began searching through the booths and buildings at the fairgrounds to see if I could find him. After an hour, I was about to stop looking when I came to a tent displaying an enamel frog. It looked similar to my thunderbird, so I took a closer look, remembering that a frog had guided me during the storm. There next to it, I saw a thunderbird the same shape as mine. The vendor recognized my pendant as one his father had made many years before. He explained the process of creating it—paints were mixed with fired glass and cooled, making each piece unique. He agreed to take my pendant back home to his ailing father in Boston to see what could be done. Several weeks later, my thunderbird came back to me still broken. A note explained that re-firing it would change the way it looked, destroying the red heart in the glossy enamel.

I began painting the broken thunderbird myself, adding colour to the tips of its wings and sealing the cracks beneath metallic enamel paints. The process of preserving it and remaking it saw me though my final days of graduate school, calmed me during those times of reliving the traumas of grade school. After twelve years, I had come full circle back to my true self, once again a fledgling writer on the edge of possibilities.

I sometimes wonder if the thunderbird pendant magically held parts of my soul for retrieval, and those parts came back to me when the glass got cracked...

Or is there a sanctity of family?

I feel like I was raised by two fathers — the former warrior who controlled through intimidation and fear, and a gentler man who believed in the sanctity of family. The gentler man taught me respect for others, the bettering of oneself and faith that love could win. Over *the years, the intimidation and controlling fear of my darker father broke down, waned. The cruel king fell. Beneath that, in the shadow of the warrior, a certain sanctity held.*

I try to remember my dad as a man who instilled a sense of heritage in his children. He played the accordion and sang to us, and he took us on annual camping trips to places like Kitty Hawk, North Carolina, and Yellowstone National Park. He made the effort. When I wonder where my love of music comes from, or my creative drive, or my respect for nature, I'm reluctant to acknowledge him.

When I got my thunderbird pendant, my father was beginning a new chapter in his life. His darkest hours had passed, and he retired from the government to take a job in the private sector. At age sixty-one, he died of a heart attack while on vacation at the beach. My Aunt Gabriella, a Benedictine nun, took me aside and apologized for him. She wanted me to forgive him. She didn't know what for, but she knew my father had regrets about his relationship with his youngest son. I was eighteen, my past still lost, and I had no way of knowing that he took the secrets of my upbringing with him to the grave. His healing proved too much for him to complete in his lifetime, so he had no choice but to kick it on down the road. I guess I must admit, despite his many failings, he succeeded in bestowing a sense of sanctity upon me.

I sometimes wonder if my father, while dying in that room near the ocean, lived the armageddon he believed in. It was the night of a full moon and some religious sect had declared the world would end on that date. In my father's fading breaths, I wonder if he saw the brilliant fire of some burning city far up the Atlantic Coast. I can imagine him slipping out of this world into another reality . . . one shaped by his thoughts and fears, by a lifetime of waiting for the darkest hour. In some kind of backward rapture, I wonder if my father died in the last battle of Armageddon.

A little more than a year after my dad passed, I had a vivid vision about him.

I leave my body in my bed and head toward my childhood room at the end of the hall. Coming at me like a speeding train in a tunnel is the face of a man. It's my father. I want to dodge him in fear, but I continue floating toward the doorway. When I enter, I find myself in a square room with a high ceiling and a black and white marble floor. It's like a church with no pews, and I hear the sound of something moving on a metal track. I see the arm of a man sticking out of the floor like the dorsal fin of a shark. He is moving around the room, swimming under the floor as if the floor is water. He's attached to a metal track, and his whole life had been used up being a mechanical shark of a man. I walk on the floor worried I might fall under the surface, and I stoop down. The man grabs my arm and pulls himself up so that he is lying on the floor near me. I try to get away and start kicking at him, but soon I recognize the man as my dad. I tell him "I love you" and ask him for help. I can't say more, but I want to feel a sense of connection in my life. He does not respond. I hold him for a short time, and I can feel the intense love in his heart for me as well as the conflict in his mind over me. When I look at his face again, there is blood running from the corner of his mouth. He grows old and blood starts oozing from many areas on his face. I let go of him, and he goes back into the floor again, moving on the metal track. I turn and go up to the altar, and I see reflected in the polished gold that I am wearing a deep red, monk-type robe.

My dad never made it up to the proverbial altar. He never got off of the metal track in the marble floor, but as I held him in that vision perhaps I got the inner strength I needed to see me through. I did indeed keep the craziness of my family and, with grace of spirit, turned it to strength and understanding. Now I put the craziness back where it belongs . . . with those who would sell out the sacrifices of blood that delivered peace and homeland security to America for half a century. In the final analysis, although the colour got bled from our lives, the sanctity of family held.

LIMITED PRISMS – GRAD SCHOOL 1992

We all view the world through the limited prism of experience. Ideas are planted in our heads through education and interaction with others. It's like we are given a series of still images, and we try to fill in what happened in the off-camera moments. At some point a worldview develops, a belief in the way things are and where we are headed. We take solace in the sometimes-great notion that we figured out the truth by looking through our limited prism. We want to hang on to that worldview, believing we got it right and denying how large a role our imagination played in creating our reality.

The limited prism of my childhood left me believing in armageddon in my lifetime. That notion rested in my subconscious mind waiting to be reawakened. Fortunately, I grew up in the free and open society of America. Alternative perspectives challenged my worldview, and advanced education taught me different ways of thinking. If I had lived in a closed society, where the healing energies of spirit were suppressed and destroyed by patterns of force, I never would have changed. I never would have found inner peace. America allowed me the opportunity to learn and grow. There were college professors and unique women who were brave enough to reach across the chasm that separated me from every one else.

Those were my wandering years, a time of expansion and education, my first attempts to find my place in the world on my own. Those were the years that shattered the limited prism I once viewed the world through.

2. A SHATTERING OF PRISMS

All the days of my youth, Grand Canyon waited. The spirit of that wilderness became connected to my fate in some mysterious way. While politicians of the 1970s were thinking of flooding the Canyon with water, I was lost under a deluge of religious and military conditioning. Every Saturday morning, my parents allowed me to escape into children's television. I found a science fiction show where two kids and their dad fell through a transdimensional rift into an alternate universe known as the Land of the Lost. Grand Canyon existed on the other side of the portal between realities, and whenever the kids saw it they cried out "home." Those Saturday morning forays into imagination planted a seed in my mind. *Grand Canyon is the way home.* A simple suggestion that lay dormant within me until I began a great expansion of intellect when I entered community college.

The years after my father's death were filled with dark thoughts I didn't share with anyone. The surreal notion of armageddon still lived in a backwater of my mind, and I had nowhere to get to in life, so I bided my time taking esoteric courses at the local community college and working odd jobs. I had enrolled under academic probation because I lacked a high school diploma, and the registrar told me that to attend full-time I needed to make good grades and get a general equivalency degree. Over the first few semesters I caught onto a learning curve and aced five courses in music and the arts. Two professors recognized my talents and took me under wing, pointing me toward the study of creative writing and the humanities. That knowledge began to challenge my thoughts about the prospect of holy war in my lifetime.

My philosophy and humanities mentor, Professor Theodore Titus, told me my IQ must be off the charts. I had a very special mind and needed to organize my thinking with logic and philosophy or I'd end up off in my own little universe, maybe even helping to bring about the end of our civilization. I told him I didn't much care to get all caught up in other people's definitions of greatness. He laughed at me and quipped, "That's exactly what I'd expect someone with an exceptionally high IQ to say." A mutual respect grew between us. No one had ever treated me as an intelligent man before.

We used to sit and talk at the outdoor theatre near the arts building. Those conversations run together in my mind like one long dialogue, a dialectic on the subject of learning and enlightenment. He liked to compliment my brilliance, leaving me to deny it. He would smile and say that hiding my smarts was a good thing as long as I didn't take it to heart and glorify stupidity.

The professor's words seemed to slide out from under his white mustache. "Never take an IQ test. If you do, you'll end up on the radar of the government-military-corporate complex."

"Hide my IQ or I'll get a complex. Thanks for the warning."

"It's true. They'll lure you in with promises of money and power. You'll end up doing clandestine research on weapons—or they'll make you create a new kind of honeybee."

"But I'll never be a ladies' man."

"No, not with that nose."

"Ouch! Really though. You think I want to follow in my father's footsteps and engineer weapons?"

"If you don't make conscious decisions to take a different path, you'll end up being like your dad by happenstance."

"It's my destiny?"

"Generational memory, young Skywalker. Chances are pretty good for a son to end up doing what his father did but on a grander scale."

"Unless I take my smarts in a different direction."

Eventually, I agreed with him. At first to get him to shut up, but later on I began to think like that. I can remember those talks like they were yesterday. The professor, only in his forties, had a full head of snowy locks and a white mustache that added wisdom to what he said. He'd ramble on about the changing world, explaining that we lived in amazing times. Humans had seen our delicate planet from space, a momentous step in the evolution of humanity. A cultural explosion grew out of the realization that we were all in this together, and he believed that before our lives ended human civilization would mature past adolescent foolishness and stop making war.

"Go into humanities and communication arts, use them for healing all the war and despair, use writing to bring people different insights. It'll be a solitary life perhaps, at least in your younger days. Women fantasize about free-spirited artists and writers, but they marry corporate guys with money when they are young. You'll be poor for an American . . ."

I'd complain that I wouldn't want to be poor, but he'd go on.

". . . become a humble servant in academia. You can make a difference mentoring the fledgling intellects of impressionable college kids."

His mustache obscured the smile crossing his face as he said that, both of us aware of the roles we played. Me, the fledgling intellect being taught by him in the same way that some other professor had mentored him twenty years before. Except Professor Theo believed the great paradigm shift toward conscious evolution had been sparked when humans saw Earth from space, and the momentum of the great cultural movement growing out of that was unstoppable. The baton of knowledge still needed passing, but the maturing of humanity would be reality in my later years—humans were turning a new leaf and leaving behind the routine of war.

Idealistic foolishness.

Professor Theo often told me that people with great smarts or talents were limited in our society. They had fewer choices, not more. He found his haven at this small community college, giving up better money and prestige for some academic freedom and a chance to make a difference. He believed he acted like mentors of earlier eras, when people of learning stayed in the communities they grew up in and served as stewards of thought and knowledge. In the twentieth century that trend had changed. People went off to great institutions of learning and rarely came back to their small towns. Even when they did return, they found they couldn't go home again. After shattering the prisms of their upbringing, they felt caged in the backwaters they once knew and were unwanted by the less-educated masses. With the rise of technology and corporate-industrial competition, people who didn't fit in back home got lured into corporate labs or underground government complexes with promises of knowing secrets ordinary people couldn't fathom.

Gilded cages.

Professor Theo told me to enter academia and the arts, become a writer and critical thinker about all things pious and elitist, carve out a haven at some institution of higher learning, and hope that I could get along with the government-appropriation-sniffing bureaucrats who were nosing their way into the public funding trough of higher education. To me, all paths led toward *caught-up-ness*. I didn't want to go there, but it seemed better to get caught up in academia than engaging in the creation of secret tech or ideas that might hasten an end to the current period of stability and enlightenment.

Professor Theo served as my go-to teacher in college, a mentor who changed the course of my life, and like all special students I never went back to thank him. True thanks meant living the new paradigm and nudging others toward it, not looking back on a brief moment in the sun.

I followed the humanities curriculum, looking through all of the known history of human civilization, all the great thinking that survived from Egyptian and Greek times up through the present. I learned about the rise and fall of civilizations and utopian ideas. I saw a paradigm that lasted maybe six thousand years before Christ came along. Our current society, dubbed 'The Age of Kings,' had risen from the ashes of the Dark Ages left in the wake of the Roman Empire. I took all this into my mind, shattering the limiting prisms of my christian worldview, learning to think and reason and arrive at my own conclusions. I dealt with lofty issues of creativity and destruction, bliss and misery, the rising and falling of great notions and great egos and great civilizations of humans on planet Earth, meeting new mentors along the way.

My creative writing teacher, Professor Samuel Wellington, was another refugee from higher education institutions that wanted to shackle great minds. He had a master of fine arts degree in rhetoric and taught an independent studies program the likes of which is usually found at private colleges. A cluttered paradise of papers stacked up to the ceiling filled his office in the back corner of the English building. Those who dared to step in there had to be careful not to topple one of those towers of parchment. Every page had its place—or so he claimed—all organized in his mind. He could go right to something he needed . . . most of the time. He rambled on when he talked. He'd pause and stammer while leafing through internal clutter, flipping through the pages of a scribe mind filled like a volume of encyclopedias that couldn't be dumbed down to sound bites. He knew a hundred different ways to say anything and started three or four times before one caught the moment. A master of written expression, he could flip around anything a young writer penned till it made sense in some unexpected and genius-like way—his gift to the fledgling scribe.

I remember the first day in his creative writing of fiction class. He sat in the front of the circle of tables and told us his philosophy on creative writing, not the usual teacher stuff. We were banned from using semicolons and colons for the first semester. By his reckoning they were weak writing. "They cause sentences to lean on each other . . . put the mind to sleep. So all those tricks you use in academic writing to make your professors languorous and write an 'A' on your paper don't apply here. Creative writing is about waking up the mind, and each sentence needs to stand on its own, not lean on the one next to it."

At the urging of Professor Wellington, I began keeping personal journals of my thoughts, dreams and nightmares. And I started to write fiction, bringing some of my darkest inner thoughts to the light of word. Years before I made sense of the military training abuses I had survived in my childhood, I began writing stories about abused teenagers coming to terms with their shadow sides. To Professor Wellington, my handwritten scribbles probably looked little better than spray-painted "the end is nigh" signs, but I got to see my backwater beliefs in black and white, as delusions rooted in a strict religious upbringing. Those ideas still held power within me, but each story I scrawled weakened them. The post-apocalyptic tale became quite boring. If the world ended—if our civilization fell back into dark ages—I knew what to do. I'd assemble the survivors and lead them on a trek through the mountains. After dodging dangerous and delusional people, we would arrive at paradise and rebuild civilization. My daydreams of such a journey began back in Sunday school during my childhood. The whole story lived in the back of my mind, and writing brought it out of hiding, turned it into a boring cliché.

Professor Wellington's advanced writing students became a tight-knit group of creative minds. We developed the strange notion that if you could imagine some horror through fiction or drama, it could never happen in the real world. We challenged ourselves to go deep into our darkest ideas with glee, as if exorcising them from their hiding places and robbing them of their power to manifest in the real world. Words were my ally, like a light to shine into the chasm of my mind.

On the last night of 1984, I put pen to paper and began writing a journal I called 'Patterns of Thought and Reasons for Being.' I like to look back on those first pages and believe the words started a spiritual awakening, but I know that journeys of spirit never begin. They lie waiting for someone to pick up the mantle and move forward through the darkness. On that night I wrote about the world I saw around me, not realizing I was also describing the battle within myself. As 1984 gave way to 1985 there were two pathways leading from my upbringing into my future. The forces pulling me toward isolation and chaos were strong, but somewhere down inside I wanted to become whole again. Within me a great war raged.

It's time for the child who rumbles through the wood to become a man, to regain that which is natural to his inner peace, to find harmony with the wood.

****

One
We are one.

You and me and we are all together.
We all have the same genesis, and we have our
choice of destiny. Many see destiny as a return to the
genesis, others choose to defy this route.
Will we still be one?
Hate separates us,
but the hate you feel for another is not given to
you by them. It is yours. Your hate of yourself and the
feelings you don't accept, used not to push another
away from you but you away from all others.
No longer one,
setting out in different directions to explore and
gain knowledge, a time should come when humankind sees
itself and begins to come together. Hate and fear
cloud this realization. If they cannot be overcome the
separation will continue, people breaking up into smaller
groups, and smaller, till the point where there are only
two, and then one.
Alone forever, never to touch or feel or understand
another human again. . . .
One

Titus and Wellington gave me a starting point as a writer and thinker. On my twenty-second birthday in November of 1985, my archaic beliefs in armageddon resurfaced briefly, and I saw them as the imaginings of a confused child. I became more serious about college, working toward an associate of arts degree in the humanities, and from there I planned to continue my education at a four-year university. There seemed to be an intuitive force guiding me through three stages of growth as a writer. I recognized my *patterns of thought*, I had an *awakening* of my emotions, and I wrote about a sense of *rejuvenation*.

I went on to earn all the credits for an associate of arts degree *with honours* and that opened me up to a different set of life possibilities, but I had one bureaucratic hurdle to overcome before I could get the piece of paper acknowledging all my learning. As I signed the graduation form, I asked the registrar about taking the general equivalency test to get my high school diploma. The man behind the counter looked at me over the top of his glasses and turned to another man trying not to laugh. They both smiled and said in unison, "You don't have a high school diploma?"

I shook my head 'no' and stammered to explain how I started going full-time without taking the test. The men laughed as one of them inked my graduation papers. "It doesn't matter now that you have an associate of arts degree." Ever since that day, transcripts from that college have been stamped with the word 'official' over the word 'non-graduate' printed under high school status. It never made a difference.

The summer after graduating community college felt like my last gasp of youth. On June first, I set out with two of my brothers in a four-door Dodge Dart. We were spending thirty days on the road traveling to the Smoky Mountains, Yellowstone National Park, California Redwood country and Grand Canyon. I saw the trip as more than a journey of miles. I believed it was a turning point in my life. During my days in the small college I dreamt of standing on the rim of the Canyon as a thunderbird ready to fly, but I always startled awake from my perch feeling empty and depressed. Still, I knew I wanted to go there for real and live on the edge of the chasm. I had already applied and been accepted into Canyon State University for the fall semester. Excited about the road trip and the prospect of my new adventures in learning not far from Grand Canyon, I started keeping an on-the-road journal. After hiking the Smoky Mountains for a week, we headed to Yellowstone. I had been there with my family as a child, and I wondered how seeing it again might stir up my past.

I have been here before, Yellowstone, but long ago
as a child — as someone else. It's recorded in here,

my mind, but I do not remember most of it. What trace elements will be triggered to consciousness by sites I've seen before? What feelings will be unburied? One can only wait and wonder how the future shows the past. The occurrence that has happened most recently is out of proportion to past occurrences. Perhaps something new can make us see more clearly some outmoded notion in the landscape we left behind.

I will re-travel the ground of the past in the future to find out what both mean.

As I traveled, I started writing about ghosts—not departed spirits, not apparitions, but ghosts that roamed my psyche. There were feelings that haunted me ever so rarely but cast a shadow over my world. I believed everybody had metaphorical spectres inside them, dissociative moments that spooked them. I wanted to piece my haunted moments together to come to know *the true nature* of myself.

The 'ghosts' I captured in my on-the-road journal were faded and lost remnants of the military trauma from my childhood. As a young man, I was filled with naive notions about the world, and I feared I would fail to find a sense of purpose for my life. I saw other people becoming trapped in lifestyles without real choices, and I didn't want that. I wanted to do something of meaning, not waste away behind a desk engineering weapons like my father. This road trip was a turning point. I was either going to become ordinary or I was going to find my way back to my true self. I was a trauma survivor searching for meaning, as if there was some accident where others died and I survived, but only echoes of that past remained—and these ghosts in my psyche needed to tell their story before they could find peace.

After hikes in the backcountry of Yellowstone and walks beneath the Redwoods on the 'left coast,' we drove that old Dodge Dart toward a big hole in the ground. The car died in the parking lot of the Flagstaff train station, and we replaced the broken starter before making our way north to the national park. At first glance, I wrote that Grand Canyon was "impressive but not spectacular." I had stalked her in photographs and the written word. I knew lots about that ditch, but at first sight I didn't feel deeply in love. I got to know the Canyon the same way I get to know a woman. I start from the top down. *Show me you're intelligent, show me you can affect my heart, then let me into your depths.* Most women have moved on before I get to the depths, but Grand Canyon wasn't going anywhere.

On a hot morning late in June, I showed up at the backcountry office in Grand Canyon Village with my two brothers looking for a camping permit. The rangers laughed at us for not planning ahead and put us on a waiting list. The next day temperatures in the inner gorge hit one hundred ten degrees and lots of people cancelled their trips. We got a permit and hiked the South Kaibab Trail to the bottom of Grand Canyon, making our way through the tunnel and across the black bridge. By the time we threw off our backpacks at the boat beach and jumped into the forty-five-degree Colorado River, I knew I had found a place I wanted to visit often.

On the last day of that first trip down into the Canyon, a feeling of *home* took hold. I wrote in my journal how my generation had to stop that monstrous ghost eating away at nature. I imagined what it would be like to live near Grand Canyon, to escape into the wide-open wilderness whenever life closed in on me. The Canyon had gotten into me, like a good woman lingers in your mind after she has walked away. I felt I had found something to live for, something that reached inside me and touched my soul. As the road trip wound down and my youth slipped from my grasp, I tried to sum up what my first Grand Canyon encounter meant to me. I used the metaphor of walking a trail.

The trail winds up and about and you always wonder where it leads. Indeed, you wonder if it leads anywhere. You're sitting there out of breath, tired, half dead and thinking "This had better lead somewhere." You forge on and look ahead trying to see where it turns, and if you can't see you guess. You get tired out again and stop and rest and turn around and see it all beneath you. And then you understand. The trail leads to a better understanding of self. It leads to where you can see the beauty of where you have been, and by recognizing the beauty that you've been through, you are able to recognize the beauty closer and closer to yourself. Soon there is no reason to look ahead wondering where you are headed because the beauty is all around you and you feel it inside. And you know that where you are going is beautiful because you are bringing it with you.

There is a feeling of history and destiny here and marvel of nature. It clears your head and uplifts your spirit. The Canyon serves no practical purpose. Even if he could, mankind would not think of engineering one. He would seek to put a bridge across it to conquer it, but really it can't be conquered. It serves no purpose, but the wonder of why it is here fascinates, uplifts the spirit. To know that mysteries remain and always will, Grand Canyon stands for that.

Spirit called to me, in simple ways and in unusual ways. I was seeking a sense of *home*, and I found it where creative writing met Grand Canyon. I left there knowing I would be back soon with time to hike the trails and find places that tourists never saw, but I didn't know that those two years at the Canyon State University far away from where I grew up would wake an inner conflict that shook me to the core of my being. As I explored the Canyon wilderness, increased my knowledge of communication arts, and found a woman to stir my wild side, the ghosts of my past kept rising toward the surface.

* * *

DAMMED BE ... — GLEN CANYON DAM OVERLOOK

The water yearns to break free — to live in the old, natural way. My emotions do too. When I believe that I can break free of the damnation of my upbringing, I feel the rage build till my heart must hold it back. I cannot let it go because the flood would sweep me away, but I know too that to live fully, to restore the sandy beaches and revive the true nature of the surging rapids, I must un-dam my heart.

I don't.

I calm the rage, pretending that cold, clear, green water is more beautiful than true muddy red. I tell myself that restoring my true nature, like tearing down giant dams, is too much.

Behind the wall, emotions still yearn for freedom. My body aches and my heart grows lonelier with each passing day. The dam within weakens and seeps of betrayal. I worry one day it will give way, that I will break and express myself in some flood of horror that tries to set things right all at once. Or I will run back to doctors who lurk like engineers waiting to refurbish the dam within that blocks my true nature.

Dammed be my heart like the dam at the head of Grand Canyon that turns the muddy red muddy river to frigid green, killing the Canyon day by day, taking away the sandy beaches, drowning the rapids, sullying my spirit with a rage of unknown origin.

I met Devi in the back of aesthetics class during my second semester at Canyon State University. She was a svelte woman from India—her skin glowed like midnight and her beauty mesmerized me. On that first day, she caught me staring at her during class and told me to pay attention to the lecture. I replied with a wink saying, "I am studying aesthetics and beauty . . . yours." She smirked and rolled her eyes, but later as we walked out of class she said we should meet for study sessions in the library.

We were both far away from our hometowns, losing our religions and discovering different ways of thinking. Devi nourished ideas of rebellion from a hurt-no-living-thing Eastern philosophy while I explored bohemian peacenik modes of relating. We spent long hours studying the myths of the ancient gods and goddesses, talking about what it might have been like to live in those times. We became inseparable friends testing the limits of modesty together. Our closeness annoyed some of my other friends at the university. They joked that we looked like John and Yoko, and they warned me that hanging out with a woman like her could only lead to a broken heart.

One day in the library, Devi took me to the stacks in a remote corner of the building and starting pulling books off the bottom shelf. I sat down on the floor collecting the dusty volumes and noticed they were all about sex. *The Ancient Art of Sensuality*, *The Kama Sutra*, books probably last read by hippies from the sixties. I carried them to the checkout for her, smiled at the girl behind the counter who glared at me with a look of concern, and I took them to Devi's car.

We never acted on those notions of alternative sexuality. We flipped through the pages together, talked about sex but never took the next step. We studied in her private apartment, ate dinner and watched movies, but she said she had a boyfriend back home that she visited on weekends. She couldn't have sex with me. Denied a real-world connection, I started to have intense nighttime dreams about Devi. We met on some other plane of existence and lived out unspeakable fantasies. She mesmerized me as a dark goddess, a destroyer of the ego, a dam breaker of all my patriarchal constructs, a Kali enchantress. She touched both sides of the chasm within my psyche, diffusing the pent-up energies between my waking reality and the dream world.

In the few months I knew Devi, she provided me the encouragement I needed to jump up the ladder of responsibility in the student-run television station at the university. I found a strange balance between the fantasy world inspired by her and ordinary living. We were growing closer, yet somehow her presence kept the ghosts of my psyche in check. I never got to find out how staying with Devi would have shaped my life because she disappeared one weekend and never came back. I learned she had withdrawn from the university without a reason. Whether family tragedy or the rigors of her religion, I never knew why she left and never said any goodbye. She was out there somewhere living her life, leaving me to live mine alone.

With Devi gone, I couldn't find anyone to match her intelligence and intensity. The feelings she stirred up now went untouched. I began to feel lost among people, and I soothed my loneliness with solo hikes deep into Grand Canyon backcountry. My future seemed full of prospects, but I felt blocked from them, disconnected. I sensed a psychological dam within robbing me of my vitality, weakened but still holding.

One day while researching graduate schools in the Canyon State University library I came across the question "Where do you see yourself in ten years?" My first thought was that our civilization would be in ruins—the ghosts of my holy war conditioning resurfaced—and I realized the absurdity of believing in those ideas again. Visions of possible futures rushed at me in the same way that remnants of my past did. I felt lost and fragmented. I couldn't find my bearings. I couldn't find the flow, the balance, the natural inner peace I knew existed somewhere.

Feeling troubled about the future, I took a nighttime drive out of town to clear my head and parked on the side of a desolate cinder road somewhere east of Flagstaff. I left my truck and went for a short walk over a little hill in the light of the full April moon. I sat down and stared out into the stars above the Painted Desert, feeling insignificant in the grand scheme of things. After a while I got up to go home. I walked back over one hill and saw another hill. I went over it expecting to see my truck, but no truck or road appeared. I knew it couldn't be far. I had only walked five minutes. *Or was it ten?* It's just right over this hill, I thought. *Or is it over that one?* I soon realized I was lost and alone in the desert at night.

If you've been lost, you know the questioning of self. In the desert, where everything looks the same, it's especially tough. I tried to retrace my steps. I tried to find the road, and finally I admitted to myself that I didn't know which way to go. I knew my truck was parked nearby and I wanted to find it, but I didn't know what to do. When you are lost, all you can do is take in your surroundings and head the direction that *feels* right. After a while of not finding, the doubts creep in and you stop. Again, you take in all your surroundings and head the direction that *feels* right. As you move on that new heading, the sense of *lostness* disappears yet with each step it eases its way back in.

I wandered around going this way and that way, following one four-wheeling road and another, searching the unforgiving desert for the vehicle that would take me home to a peaceful rest. The desert loomed larger and larger. Each crossroad or fork offered hope because my *lostness* told me that all roads led somewhere. I believed that one would take me to the road my truck was on. But doubts set in and my *lostness* told me that every road leads to a dead end. I thought of abandoning my truck and heading toward the city, but I didn't much relish the thought of wandering across someone's private land in the middle of the Arizona night. Besides, I knew my truck—much like the inner peace I sought in life—lurked somewhere nearby and I didn't want to abandon it.

After five hours of wandering unknown terrain, of contemplating my insignificance and my mortality, I stumbled upon a cinder road. I remembered parking near a closed gate so I searched for it—going one way, back the other and turning around again to go further the first way. I found the gate and walked toward my pickup. The golden truck glimmered in the fading moonlight, but I remained unsure. *Was this the wrong road, the wrong gate? Did this vehicle belong to someone else?* I approached with caution, not believing the truck belonged to me till my key opened the door and I sat in the familiar seat. I felt smaller and more insignificant than ever because I couldn't claim to be lost anymore.

After being lost in the desert for hours, I knew what being lost for years might be like. Doubt would rule my mind. *My truck, a mirage of a memory. My former self, a ghost telling me that the life I once knew never existed. Lostness, a familiar friend providing me comfort and acceptance.* And when I stumbled upon that old cinder road—a road leading back to truths long forgotten—how spooked would I feel? If I dared to walk that road and I found the gate, could I handle the rage of all those lies welling up inside me? If I crept up toward the truck and those strange keys in my pocket unlocked the door, could I handle the feelings of insignificance as I sat in the familiar seat?

BEFORE THE FLOOD ...
– PENNED AFTER THE FLOOD

Looking back on my days at CSU, I see that my haven from the cruel world was academia. I was fulfilling my dad's expectations of getting an education, picking up the mantle from where the war interrupted his life, but mostly I felt lost.

All those little moments moving me toward knowing. Sometimes they feel like small miracles, an improbable series of events being guided by some supernatural force. Other times they feel like craziness, like being lost in a desert, like nudges toward isolation.

Every now and again a person or an idea or even a 'ghost' breaks through and points me toward a spiritual realization, a deeper kind of knowing, a shattering of prisms. Larger and larger cracks are created in the psychological dam within ...

The world feels brand new again just before the flood sweeps me away and down into the chasm within.

After graduating with my bachelor's, I moved back to my childhood home in the Maryland suburbs and started attending classes in the master's program at American University. The privileged students whose parents paid their way saw me as a maverick getting by on a student loan. I felt no sense of working-class camaraderie there, so I used it as a time of deep, independent study. There were professors who tried to mentor me, people who tried to befriend me, but I didn't respond to their reach-outs. I went through the motions of getting my degree, turning into something of a loner and misanthrope—no one could live up to my expectations, least of all myself.

I made it through the first year, exceeding my doubts and surpassing the lower half of first-year students not invited to return. About one hundred of us moved into the second year, knowing that only fifty would survive to get our diplomas. I handled the academic pressures with ease, but I began having terror-filled dreams where an evil presence held me down on my bed not allowing me to move. Visions of persecution haunted my nights while memories of the fights in the hallways of my elementary school filled my waking thoughts. My symptoms mimicked schizophrenia, and fearing I was losing my mind, I went to see a counselor in the university's health office.

When I told the counselor my worries about the onset of schizophrenia, he became irate. He thought I was trying to trick him into a diagnosis as part of my research for a thesis paper. He lectured me on the seriousness of schizophrenia and threatened to take me to a locked ward to see patients in the throes of the disease. He went on yelling about how life didn't happen like some Hollywood movie with a woman to sacrifice her freedom and take care of me, anchor me into reality. As a graduate student at American University passing my classes, my mental clarity and awareness were enviable, and there were no signs of schizophrenia or mental disease.

After yelling, the counselor realized that my self-diagnosis, though foolish, had been sincere. My fears grew out of a film history course on Ingmar Bergman. I had been researching a thesis comparing the portrayal of schizophrenia in his films to the real-life version of the disease, and like a med student studying an illness I saw all the symptoms in myself. The counselor concluded that the dreams were consistent with sleep paralysis, a rare type of disorder that pointed to some kind of minor schism working its way up from my subconscious. I couldn't face a deep-seated truth from my childhood days so my mind repressed it, and a brief course of associative therapy would allow it to emerge safely. We talked about how the academic pressures were forcing many of my fellow grad students to fall by the wayside, leaving only the most dedicated for an even tougher second year. I had survived but I felt unsettled. My doubts had me rethinking my whole world and peering into deep dark caves in my psyche not visited since grade school. Old haunts awoke, and I believed that long-held family expectations were proving true—I had labeled those feelings *schizophrenia* by mistake.

I believed I was the keeper of the craziness gene in my family, and my siblings seemed to play that to their advantage because they didn't want to face their own feelings about the chaos of our upbringing. So anything I said got filtered through a way of thinking that allowed them to keep their internal schisms intact. My want of truth-telling pushed me toward becoming a storyteller, a revealer of secrets, a scribe who nudged people toward integrating their scattered parts into a whole. I thought I had walked away from those retrogressive notions that creativity and craziness were connected, but the echoes remained and remnants of those fears hidden deep inside of me were re-emerging.

The long-ago feelings of my grade school days had attached themselves to my situation in graduate school, or so the counselor thought. I didn't tell him the whole truth because I knew it went much deeper than that. Spooks from my past were running loose again. I kept thinking of my dad as a shark in the floor of my childhood room, that vision where his face turned to blood. The closer I got to graduation, the more I felt like I was outdistancing my father and surpassing all those notions about being the keeper of the craziness, opening the door in my psyche that the mole doctor had sealed long ago. I saw myself in the deep red, monk-type robe and likened it to the blue graduation robe I would be wearing after one more semester. The antiquated patterns of thought were falling apart, but the ideas taking their place were not fully formed yet. *Could it have been back in the third grade, when I had a military buzz cut, that the first trauma occurred?*

I couldn't accept the truth—fear stopped me from shattering the prism that defined my father as a noble, truthful man. I was spiraling downward emotionally, and one night I felt a falling sensation along with a deep anxiety bordering on panic. Feelings of emptiness attacked me, forcing me to check myself into a hospital for observation. On the full moon of December, I ended up in a locked psyche ward of a university hospital because all the beds in the free wing were filled. Near midnight, another man suffering from emotional exhaustion and anxiety was put in the room with me. We recognized each other. He was the father of a childhood friend from my neighborhood, and we started to rehash some of the old times. The talk soon turned to some of the spookier aspects of the nearby Maryland backwoods, and we started laughing about how we had both checked into the hospital under a werewolf moon.

From there, Mr. BeLlyall ventured into a heart-to-heart talk with me. He said that other parents in the neighborhood thought my father was a scary man, and they were worried about how he treated his sons. Some neighbors talked of the need for an intervention, a call to social services, but no one wanted to violate the great American notion that a man's home is his castle. Outside of proof that he sent his sons off for some kind of militia training, nothing could be done.

It seemed like a miracle of chance that I ran into old man BeLlyall there that night. Our conversation shifted my perspective. I had never assessed my father as a man with flaws before, a man with secret worries that he needed to pass on certain thoughts about the art of holy war to continue a long-held family tradition. I thought my relationship with my father had stopped growing when I turned eighteen, but it was still changing. Death ends a life but it doesn't end a relationship. Freezing it in place had made me ill, and now the time came for the thaw. I knew I had laid something to rest before the fourth grade, before I let my hair grow out. It boiled up once before high school graduation and got locked back down by the medical procedures of the mole doctor. As I approached my next graduation, this one for my master's, I had another shot to find the truth. I needed to re-examine my life from elementary school and destroy the beliefs that were keeping me frozen in place.

AWAKENING, DREAM JOURNAL, MARCH 20, 1992

Things are boiling just beneath the surface and I need to get them out or I'll go mad.

I want to be strong — I want to get this over with
and get on with my life, but it seems more and more like
this will always be with me. I am scared of what lurks
within me — it makes me into what I don't want to be. It
seems I should at least have a chance to be happy, but
happiness laughs at me.

There's a hurt and burnt boy I want to run away
from and forget but he keeps following me. This hurt
and burnt boy who needs to be taken care of but I
don't know what to do. A hurt and burnt boy who keeps
beating me up. My life is such a sad thing and I don't
think I deserve this.

This is a time in my life when I should be moving
steadily toward my future and finding pride in myself
and my abilities. Instead I fight each day with feelings
coming out of my childhood, feelings that weigh me down
and cloud my future. It seems I will never rise above what
lies hidden in me and there will forever be the question
in my mind "What could I have been if I didn't have to deal
with this?" No matter where I get to there will always
be that. Things look so bleak and I haven't dealt with
anything yet. I'm so wrapped up in negatives that no light
reaches my soul. I'm alone and any attempt to reach me
makes me realize how alone I am.

Sometimes rage or tears seem my only choices. . . .

On the right road but moving in the wrong direction, heading
toward a life with a dresser top full of prescription drugs new and
improved over those like my father used. I needed to accept some hard
truths about my past to stop moving back and forth over the same
wounded ground. I began a journal called 'Awakening' that year, and on

February 19, 1992, at the age of twenty-eight, I wrote that I had been involved in some kind of secret militia program as a child. With my realization, things became more complicated and dangerous. Denial and dissociation had been my allies. They kept me from connecting with feelings of loss that were too overwhelming, but now I wanted to do away with my best allies and stare down my demons.

I took this idea that I had faced military exploitation as a child and went the direction that *felt* right. My dream about a hurt and burnt boy who came out of my past pointed the way. I was dancing on the edge of recall. I needed to decipher what was real, what was symbolic, what was memory, and what was dream.

In graduate school, I learned that the stories we create to describe our experiences shape our outlook on life. They also shape the outlook of others around us and create a ripple effect through our friendships and society that reinforces our beliefs. In this way, we create the prisms through which we view the world. If we focus on helplessness or disempowerment, we will feel paralyzed and depressed. If we focus on growing and learning, telling life events from a place of freedom and emotional strength, developing a backstory for our actions, we transform ourselves and the world.

Unfortunately, the mole doctor knew the power of storytelling too. His medical treatments during high school created a psychological dam inside me that lasted twelve years. The mole doctor left me isolated in a stagnant backwater unable to connect with others. He created phantoms and ghosts inside me that spooked me away from understanding the trauma at my inner core and discovering my true self. Whenever I started to become whole, I felt the overwhelm of the past weighing down upon me, drawing other people's dark sides toward mine. But the mole doctor didn't count on the power of imagination and creativity. He must have thought that there was no way a son of a war veteran would end up pursuing an education in the arts. My knowledge of writing and storytelling proved to be like fuel for a lantern I carried in the darkness. I stayed one step ahead of those ghosts and phantoms inside me and made my way through that dark chasm within. And on that winter moon when I talked with old man BeLlyall in the locked ward of a hospital, a bit of luck came my way. I rebounded and earned my master's degree that spring, graduating in two worlds—the academic one in my blue robe and the spiritual one in my deep red robe. I saw a new path, a brighter vision of the future, but the shadows were still there trying to snuff out the flame.

After graduate school, I turned my attention to finding the road toward inner peace by searching my parents' house. I found an unlocked lockbox with my father's Department of Defense documents, and I went through boxes of papers hidden away in the attic. I felt like a man taking a pickaxe to a giant cement dam holding back a great body of water, every piece of parchment another futile swing against the psychological barrier in my mind. I kept at it, swing after swing, believing that one document could start a crack that broke the dam wide open, shattering the false prisms of my upbringing. After months of looking over my dad's mundane dossier and finding little of worth, I came across a medical notebook hidden in the attic with words written in my mother's hand.

5-21-81 — Began treatment by family Doctor - psychiatrist on 6-10,
7 sessions till 7-31-discontinued . . .
7-31-81 — Complete Physical exam - Sacred Christ Hospital . . .

The entries puzzled me because I couldn't remember the treatments. I knew the mole doctor as a man who oversaw the troubles of our family, but I couldn't remember meeting him in person. He existed as a shadowy figure in the corners of my awareness, and the sessions where I met him lived repressed behind the psychological barrier in my mind. When I tried to recall his face, I pictured the melting Nazi from *Raiders of the Lost Ark*. Nausea overtook me and a heavy sense of darkness and doom rushed at me like a great deluge of emotion sweeping me away. To quiet the feelings, I began sending letters to the mole doctor and the State of Maryland asking for my medical records. I was naive to the implications of my experiences, not realizing that I was following in my father's footsteps of turning to the government for help. The doctor wrote back to acknowledge that the medical treatments took place, but he stonewalled me about why they happened.

I didn't need the mole doctor. Asking the question proved to be enough, the psychological dam inside me began to give way.

Over the next months, a flood of wreckage from the depths of my being broke free. I felt like I was being swept down a wild canyon by a raging torrent of memories. Dammed emotions, dark currents and angelic voices swirled all around me. Somehow I knew the truth didn't lie in the churning chaos—darkness can only be escaped by seeking light. I longed to be free and calm, clear of the emotional deluge. I wanted to climb out of the muck and be whole. I wanted to make love with the angelic creatures of the light, but all seemed lost. I felt I could never escape the raging waters of the chasm within.

I began having visions of suicide. I saw myself at Apple Orchard Falls, a place near the Sunset Fields pullout on the Blue Ridge Parkway in Virginia. I had visited there with a friend some months earlier, and we hiked the trail to the precipice. In the vision I stood on the edge of the cliff in the woods, trying to get my courage up—and I jumped. The fall brought a rush of emotions, tears and regrets until I hit the ground—only to find myself standing on the cliff again. I didn't want to be there. I didn't want to die, but that might be better than reliving a nightmare of death I couldn't escape. Sometimes I dreamt of running through the woods toward the cliff and grabbling hold of a tree to stop myself, only to find myself running toward the cliff again not in control of my own body. It seemed like a nightmarish glimpse of a possible future, like a madman running toward an unwanted suicide. I knew I needed to do something drastic. I needed to face my past or I might keep running into the sunset of my life. I decided to try hypnosis to get to the root of the visions.

I had been reluctant to try hypnosis before because I figured that whatever needed to be recalled would surface naturally in its own time. But after contacting the mole doctor, the emotional pressure of my memories trying to break free forced me to take action. Hypnotherapy made rational sense, yet I feared the treatments would spark a stir of echoes, a deepening of the horror that I couldn't turn off. And I had no one to turn to or confide in, so I kept it all a secret. I found a private hypnotist in a suburb of Baltimore miles from where I lived. We took things slow, and I didn't tell her about the remnants of military memories rising out of my past.

One of the first things we revisited was a map of Maryland that I had made in fourth grade art class. All through my final exams in graduate school I had been thinking of that map lost in the basement of my parents' house. I went searching for it but never found it, and the hypnotist saw it as a good starting point. I remembered making the map with coloured sands, creating the brown mountains and green valleys and the blue Chesapeake Bay. I was very proud of it, but there was no one to share it with so I hid it away. Thinking about it all those years later under hypnosis brought back a flood of emotions.

The feelings weren't about the map of Maryland. I knew that the memories recurring to me were like the tip of an iceberg, hinting at hidden things that happened in my childhood. My knowledge of storytelling and the arts learned in graduate school was fighting the military conditioning from all those years ago. It was a battle between expression and secrecy, light and shadow, and expression finally had the skills and power to shift my inner paradigm. When I hid the map away in fourth grade, I laid to rest a bunch of feelings and memories too. They boiled up once when I was seventeen and got suppressed back down by the mole doctor. Now twelve years later, truth reasserted itself and I listened. I knew that the story of my life needed to be torn apart and retold.

So I went further into the mystery of my past under hypnosis. We scheduled more sessions, working our way deeper into my mind and stirring up ghosts.

And there, down deep in my psyche at the end of a surreal waking dream, I found the mole doctor on the edge of a blast zone in my mind. He had been there long before, apparently had hypnotized me in some of the forgotten sessions noted in the medical notebook. In my waking dream under hypnosis, he stood next to me as we looked at the hanged body of a dead slave who tried to escape. Everything I needed to know about *the chasm within* was hidden within that vision. It took years to unravel the truth of the messages—those ghosts would haunt me in the depths of the Canyon years later as I walked to find peace—but in the surreal waking dream under hypnosis, the dam in my psyche broke wide open.

I could go on a rant about what I found in the chasm within—how bigger events lined up with my research into government secrets, how a matrix of awareness reversed a never-ending negative spiral, and how once I made sense of that I could let it go. The short of it is that I opened a door of perception and stepped into a deeper knowing of myself and the world around me.

I was able to screen out mental illness and brain abnormality as the root of my troubles. I got into a research program at the National Institute of Mental Health and received PET scans of my brain that showed no tumors or degenerative diseases. The young doctor leading the study told me they were developing a revolutionary way to diagnose mental illness by mapping the brain, and a specific pattern had been linked to schizophrenia. Strange as it sounds, the childhood map that got lost and forgotten led me to get my brain mapped, and 'craziness' as an explanation for weirdness took a holiday in those days. I got lucky.

I don't know what became of that doctor or his revolutionary research. His new paradigm seemed to vanish—but listening to people passing through my life giving me better answers to old questions saved me. If not for that fortune I might have become a conspiracy theorist lost in confusion, unable to make sense of my feelings.

As the dam broke open and I wrestled with the lost truths emerging from inside me, two women showed up to see me through my darkest hours. Devi, the Kali enchantress from my college days, emerged in my imagination like a benevolent goddess keeping vigil over my destruction and re-creation, and another woman entered my waking life and started to invade my dreams.

When I think of Ally, I see her taking off her motorcycle helmet and letting her long, sandy-blonde hair fall around her shoulders. She often peeled off her leather riding gear near the equipment vault of the cable access station where I worked. She was an intimidating presence— beautiful, tough and smart all rolled into a divine feminine form. She showed up in my life at the same time that the visions of jumping off cliffs at Apple Orchard Falls darkened my nightmares. I wanted to keep my inner chaos hidden from Ally, but getting to know her stirred me up inside.

Past and future seemed to fall away whenever Ally arrived. I felt so in the moment with her, believing fate had led us to each other. I asked her out on a date, and she gave all the details as if she had already planned it out. I showed up at the place—a dance club with a trendy, urban, biker atmosphere—and found my way to her table. Her friends seemed disappointed that I didn't have any other guys with me. I peeled Ally away from them, danced with her even though I don't dance, and we shared a couple of drinks. I felt like I had found my soulmate and I hoped she felt the same, but at the end of the night she disappeared leaving me no chance for a try at a goodnight kiss.

The next time I saw her, she walked with crutches. She had wrecked her motorcycle on the way home from our date, only remembering flashes of the accident. She was heading out of control straight for a road sign and laid the bike down in front of her to take the impact. When she came to, the sign was demolished and her bike lay totaled, but Ally got up and limped away with only a sprained ankle.

Her wreck led us into talking about memory. We felt like we knew each other from some other time and place, and we wondered if we had met in childhood. There seemed to be some kind of kismet between us, an energy that threatened to overwhelm us. We were locked deep into each other's psyches, haunting each other, and she didn't know how she felt about me. I still wanted to go out, but she wanted to take it slow because our feelings for each other were so strong. After not seeing her for a few days, I phoned and found her sick. I felt ill too. Both of our inner worlds were in upheaval and the next day she disappeared for good without a word. She abandoned her projects at the television station and stopped returning my phone calls.

I searched for her as if seeking an anchor to keep me from falling into the dark recesses of my psyche, but it was too late. The chaos of the past was upon me. I needed a savior and one arrived. Ally took the form of an Anima spirit and protector in my dreams. She became an embodiment of balance and completion, calming my nightmares and dark visions by telling me what they meant. She took me places and showed me amazing sights. Sometimes we flew like birds to a beautiful canyon lake beneath a sky filled with rainbows, and we had dream sex. She kissed me gently all over. Our auras turned into twisted rainbows and our energies mingled together. It was the deepest spiritual connection I've ever felt, more real than dream. The horrible nightmares from the chasm within and the visions of suicide at Apple Orchard Falls were balanced by Ally's presence and an unspoken promise of finding love in the real world once I made it through the dark times.

Trying to track down where the real Ally went, I stole a look at her paperwork in the files at work and found an address for her mother. I wrote a letter and sent it to be forwarded to Ally. Weeks passed with no response. I began to feel foolish and even a bit creepy. I wondered if I put too much detail in the letter by asking if we could have known each other in elementary school and shared a secret first kiss in the sixth grade. I knew so little about the real Ally. I didn't even know her age. We only had one date, but I felt like I knew her intimately because she visited me in dreams.

After my darkest hours passed, the visits with the dream version of Ally faded. The stir of echoes left me feeling compelled to find her in the real world. I got an address for her on the West Coast, and I wrote to her. After a while not hearing back, I called long distance. Ally said she got my letters but didn't know how to respond. We couldn't have kissed in sixth grade because she was a few years younger than me and went to a different school. We spent the next few months sharing phone calls. She was happy in California, living with her boyfriend and riding in a motorcycle racing league. We saw no future together for us. Our conversations became more awkward and we faded from each other's lives.

In many ways, comparing the Ally spirit in my dreams with the real-world woman ended practical relationships for me. Integrating reality with the fantasy archetypes inside me seemed impossible. I knew I was touched by strangeness—it had been labeled 'craziness' in my younger days, but now I knew it as 'creative genius' or 'eidetic imagination' or even an ability to 'conjure avatars' in my mind. Crazy in a good way, as long as I didn't take myself too seriously.

A life has many pathways, many meetings and partings along the way. I captured those moments in writing, pushing back the darkness and triumphing over my inner chaos and terror. In the primordial funk of my mind, I met spirit guides who gave me insights and took me on journeys. From the shark in the floor of a church becoming my father to the women of my dreams pointing me toward a healing path, those visions changed my fate. I caught up to *the keeper of the craziness*—that role assigned to me by family for having creative imagination—and I pulled off the mask to find my true self. I had been placed on a warpath, given a holy warrior mission, but somehow I avoided my own personal armageddon. In one sense I felt angry and used, duped by the mole doctor, but I focused on trying to become a writer, a creator rather than a destroyer. I knew finding peace was the ultimate victory over the forces of chaos that interrupted my childhood.

The Ally and Devi in my psyche were light and dark angels who shattered the prisms of my militant upbringing. I sometimes wonder if the strange visits from these Anima spirits were just a trick of the mind, a balancing of sanity and shadow. *Or were there real beings that took Ally's and Devi's forms in my dreams?* While the Anima spirits faded after I calmed the dark times of my soul, a simple gift from the real-world Ally shaped my life for years to come. She gave me a blank book with wild animals on the cover. On the first page she wrote her last message to me.

Write it down. Capture the 'voices' from the wilderness. Shatter the prisms of upbringing. Let go of trying to prove to others what you know in your heart to be true.

THE MISTRESS OF LIGHT IS
JUST PASSING THROUGH

I have experienced a kind of spirit recall. Lost parts of myself have been released from their hiding places to meet up with images in my mind. They take the place of foreign entities with craven faces hiding in my tissues. Through that process I have become more grounded.

I have become an ethereal being at times under the hands of a mistress of light. I can feel emotions hiding in me. A happy giddiness in my chest, a brooding darkness in my gut, fear in my lower back, sexual craving in my loins, all trying to hide from my awareness. I am told this is a quantum level of experience. These emotions are just passing through but rigidity traps them . . . pushed out of mind they lurk in tissues. They must come back into our minds before they can be released.

There are dark mistresses and masters who would manipulate these hidden energies for their own ends. They take our longing for belonging, our desire to please, our want for meaning and twist it to their own ends. They see these pent-up emotions as things to be teased and toyed with and played against each other, but never released. They see a person as a thing to be manipulated into servitude for their own profit, their own pleasure, their own vanity. They can own you through this manipulation if you let them . . . but they are blind to the light.

Indeed, it is the Mistress of Light that scares me the most. She uses no restraints, no whips and no paddles. She needs them not. She can stir these things up without even a touch sometimes — with energetic techniques these emotions are forced into the open. And it's not for Her to play with, it is for release . . . to be sent on their way. Sure I try to hold on to them. They have been there a long time and it is almost like losing a part of myself — but the Mistress of Light says it's time for them to go so that I may live in the Now.

The Mistress of Light is the scariest of all because She does not want. She could have me completely and totally and unconditionally in those moments after if She wanted . . . but She is above that. She is selfless and just passing through. I may wish and fantasize — and, given the chance, beg — for Her to be gray or black with me, but Her magic is white light and She is just passing through my life like a haunt of my deepest wants and desires.

3. VOICES FROM THE WILDERNESS

The vignettes I wrote in my 'Voices from the Wilderness' journal were *free* stream-of-consciousness writings. They materialized whole from the dark void inside me that I called *the chasm within*, and I wrote them down. The first entry came to me during a road trip into North Carolina. I had visited Fort Bragg Military Reservation and other places I remembered through hypnosis and dreams to see if any truth lived in those messages from my subconscious. I validated so much for myself as I confronted my visions of suicide at the cliffs near Apple Orchard Falls in Virginia and traveled the backroads of the military reservation. The writings in my 'Voices from the Wilderness' journal served like a lantern shining light into the chasm within. I felt more alive in those days because of a sense of inward and outward movement toward understanding myself and the world, but I also felt isolated—words were inadequate to capture my journeys unless they came from that ghostwriter in the dark chasm.

TROUBLED VOICE

Where all this leaves me is utterly alone, isolated in the middle of a vast wilderness. Occasionally, ravenous beasts stir the brush looking for their next meal, looking for something that won't or can't defend itself — they are bad-hearted beasts who need to feel powerful and dominant.

So what can I do? Cry out is about all.

Cry out for no one to hear because it interferes with who they are and where they want to get to. They don't want to know my past because they don't want to believe that someone could come into their lives and set them off course into the shadowy wilderness.

And that's why my heart is bad — I block people from their hopes and dreams, from where they want to get to, because it happened to me. My own sense of direction was crushed and now I am alone . . . a voice crying out in the wilderness, a voice that no one wants to get near because they fear it's a beast looking for its next meal — a beast that will drain their energy and turn their heart bad.

My heart is bad and I am that beast. I sneak up on you with grace and charm and drain your heart of hope and dreams. Some are drawn to me just for the thrill of it, to see how long they can last or how close they can get and still get away. All leave weaker, not knowing what they got themselves into or why they ever listened to that troubled voice from the wilderness.

I had always equated a part of myself with the beasts of the wilderness, not in a positive way but as an uncontrollable force bent on sabotaging any progress I made toward happiness and fulfillment. In 'Voices from the Wilderness,' I began to question my long-held beliefs about the 'beast' lurking inside me. The writings were grim and necessary, capturing thoughts and limiting beliefs that split my reality into good and evil. I became an alchemist in that journal, transforming dark synergetic ideas into ink upon the page and creating a different way of looking at the world for myself.

I wanted to live my life as a free spirit, but the State of Maryland had other ideas. In my naiveté before breaking the dam in my psyche, I confronted the mole doctor and the State of Maryland in writing, and I told my story to others, sending letters to activists and public officials including the long-serving federal senator from Maryland. I thought of it as a grassroots effort to be heard, but instead I got caught up in bureaucratic rigamarole—that ritual of confused and meaningless talk pretending to be discourse of great import. The senator told me she forwarded my letter back to a Maryland official, assuring me, "I am sure you will be hearing from him soon." No written response ever came, but a few weeks later a five-ton box truck rear-ended my pickup at high speed.

Sitting on the side of the road after the wreck, I wondered if the totaled truck belonged to me. The pickup's bed was smashed into the passenger door and one side of the front end was flattened. The mangled heap sat in the middle of the road facing the wrong way. Looking at it, I recalled an earlier moment of wondering if that golden truck belonged to me. I remembered it parked on the side of a cinder road at night out near the Painted Desert. Dazed, my head bleeding, realizing the totaled truck was mine, I heard a familiar voice yell my name. I didn't see who called out, but responding, "Don't worry, I'll be fine," brought me back into the moment.

I knew that the wreck served as the response the federal senator had promised. I had asked the wrong questions of the powers that be in America. *They* destroyed my truck on my dad's birthdate—by intention or strange coincidence did not matter. The ambulance arrived, and I got carted away strapped to a gurney. While waiting for a head scan at the hospital, I thought about the prayer card hidden away in my wallet. It had been given to me by my counselor. She worked for the State of Maryland and had helped me write the letters to the mole doctor. She was puzzled why he cited legal loopholes to block me from getting my own medical records, and she couldn't believe that the state bureaucrats backed him up. When we pushed harder, *they* transferred her to a location near the mole doctor's office not far from the naval warfare complex where my father once worked. The new psychiatrist overseeing my counselor was trying to push drugs on me despite my objections, and I knew I was being played. *They* were trying to force me to an emotional breaking point.

My rage began boiling up into the spectre of an armed siege to get back at the rigamarolers, and I told my counselor that. She claimed I was delusional, creating drama where it didn't exist, processing my reality through ideas in movies. She said she would quit her job if she ever thought she was being lied to or manipulated by her bosses. Her pleas didn't sway me, and I told her I had decided to leave the counseling program. I was forced to attend an exit interview with the head psychiatrist, and it ended up being like a scene from *Total Recall*. The shrink tried to convince me I was *delusional, lost in a fantasy, in need of help to get along in life.* People in suits could spoon-feed me reality and make sure I digested it properly. But I knew they had no hold on me. This was still America before the fall. So I bid my counselor fare-ye-well and a few weeks later she sent me the prayer card with a note saying she had quit her job and taken another position clear across the country in Seattle.

In the hospital on truck-whacking day, waiting for my head scan, I thought of that prayer card hidden in my wallet in the envelop of personal effects in the other room. After everything checked out okay and my scrapes were bandaged, I got the wallet back and pulled out the card. Dog-eared and worn, kept for no good reason, I read the prayer for protection and placed it back in hiding.

A policeman found me walking out of the hospital and asked me to sit down for a brief interview. He wondered if the name Augusto Giani meant anything to me. I said 'no' but felt a twinge of remembrance. Later, when I got the accident report and saw the address, I realized that I had met Augusto Giani when I was seventeen. My dad took me to his house to buy my first car. I believed there must have been other connections—I figured he knew the mole doctor and the wreck was meant as a message for me to be silent. Or maybe they thought I wouldn't remember, that the wreck would stir up the *ghosts* of lost memory in my psyche. I was beyond that but it didn't matter. I got the message to keep quiet, and I realized turning to government or lawyers for help meant hanging out with people in suits. I wanted to be free, not caught up.

I had thousands of words in journals. I had scars on my body and fragments of traumatic memories trapped in my head. All the remnants of my experiences lived like separate souls lost in the darkness until the wreck knocked them together and I arrived at knowing. *Knowing* is an inexplicable thing. It's not a rationalization. Words cannot express it. *Knowing* is an echo of truth. Perhaps the loss of my truck put me in touch with the losses of my childhood. Perhaps the moments of dissociation after the accident connected the scattered parts of myself— stirred up those voices from the wilderness of my psyche. Maybe trying to communicate my past pushed me into believing. Somehow, I came out of the wreck with a new sense of knowing myself.

The bureaucratic rigamarole was an attempt to keep me in denial. Doctors, lawyers and politicians wanted me in situations where they were in control of the outcome. They wanted me caught up in their legal system, fighting to prove to skeptics what I knew in my heart to be true. The more they rigamaroled me, the more I recognized the reality of my past, so I walked away from the feeble clamouring. I didn't let them make me into a keeper of their craziness. The rigamarolers were bent on keeping secrets and intimidating me into silence to stay in power. I didn't want to be like them, disconnected from my heart and spirit . . . lost from all sense of mystery . . . *caught up.*

I stepped out of the cage they were building around me and headed out into the chaotic wilderness of thinking for myself in non-government-sanctioned ways.

VOICE OF THE SPLIT

There's a dubious goal I've been trying to achieve — integration. It's dubious because, what the hell is it good for? It's telling the split it isn't needed, telling this part of me to go away, but isn't it an essential part? Where would I be without the split?

It's there to protect me from the overwhelm of my experience and doing away with it is foolish. It's a necessary part of me, and I wouldn't have survived without it. But now I want to get rid of it in the name of integration, in the name of being whole so that I might find intimacy with another, so that I might become more sensitive to myself and others. It seems like a good idea, but the problem is that the road is way too long.

I think I know why human spontaneous combustion occurs — because the split suddenly disappears and the overwhelm is too great. This goal of integration cannot be achieved when the emotions are so great. The whole of me is less than the parts of me I have now because the beastly part tears me down and trips me up.

Instead of trying to do away with the split, I should thank it for being there, for keeping me sane in the face of insanity, for letting me forget the pain and enjoy some happiness. I should thank the split for containing my darkness and for not allowing others to see it. That has afforded me more genuine closeness than I would have achieved otherwise. But what thanks do I give? I try to do away with the split in the name of healing, but all I achieve is people seeing my pain, being overwhelmed and splitting on me.

Should I hide the split inside of me or bring it out and force it on others?

Hungry for something new, I quit my job and moved to North Carolina. Leaving Maryland was like setting out into the wilderness. Nothing so friendly as a natural wild place but rather the wilderness of human society without a safety net. The denials of the State of Maryland about my past still weighed heavily upon me. I was torn between feelings of running out on a fight and following my bliss. Good job prospects that included health care always evaporated in the eleventh hour, and I suspected it was because I had been red-flagged in secret medical files that state governments share with corporations, but I didn't care too much. Western medicine didn't interest me. I was turning to alternative healing practices that wouldn't be covered by insurance anyway. I worked whatever jobs I could find, grateful that I wouldn't be trapped in a three-piece suit for the rest of my life.

Two of my high school friends had migrated to the Chapel Hill area for the music scene, and I got temp jobs that allowed me freedom to hit the road with them. There was a network of music festivals emerging in the Blue Ridge Mountains and all along the East Coast. Up in the North Carolina hills where bootleggers once ran moonshine, I found a music scene sometimes called 'Americana' and other times called 'pickin'-in-the-woods.' It was where all the best aspects of rock 'n' roll had gone, real American songwriters backed up by musicians who could set their instruments on fire.

In April of 1995, I went to my first Merlefest. At one point, I woke from a deep sleep on the back of the lawn and heard music followed by jubilant applause off in the distance. I headed toward the sound and soon arrived at the 'little pickers' tent. Lively rhythms flowed into my ears and I peered through the crowd. On stage, four women were playing upbeat 'old-time' music. I was still a bit dazed from my deep sleep in the bright sun, and they seemed almost divine. Soon I became a bit fixated on the fiddle player. Her name was Evia—that was it, she needed no last name—I liked her songs and felt inspired by the music. Like Ally and Devi, she seemed to tap into that archetypal woman in my psyche.

Back in the real world, my life wasn't going so well. I was living in a bug-infested rooming house that used to be a church in the North Carolina town of Saxapahaw. Still unable to find employment in my career field, I continued to work temp jobs while trying to get established as a freelance writer. I was getting better at writing spec scripts for television shows and fleshing out feature film ideas, but whenever I made cold calls to agents or producers, a state of near panic overtook me. After about six months with no psychological counseling I convinced myself I needed it again. I thought of going back to Maryland to resolve the past and set things right.

I didn't realize that I had discovered one of the keys to deeper happiness—following bliss, focusing on activities that bring connection. I had spent so much time and energy worrying about armageddon and trying to prove holy war abuses to others that I never much enjoyed the simple things in life. I didn't recognize that not having a counselor to talk about the tactics of rigamarolers could be a blessing. The lack of ruminating created a void that was filled with the sense of community at music festivals.

I once had a dream that my mom was a beached whale as big as a high-rise and completely immovable. Strange, because my mom is a five-foot-four Irish woman, but I knew what the dream meant. My father died in a high-rise at the beach and my mom is an immovable presence when she wants to be. I headed back to Maryland to try to move her and bureaucrats in government to see my truth. I flailed, flipped and floundered like a fish out of water as I worked to bring my intellect and heart to the same place.

I arrived back in Maryland on my dad's birthday a year after truck whacking day, losing more of my life to the rigamarole tactics of the powerful. I soon became tired of taking on the establishment, and I decided to head out to California to create a future as a screenwriter. After a week in Hollywood I was depressed. I couldn't get into an apartment, and the dreariness of the city seemed to weigh down on me more each day. In the afternoons, I drove away from the concrete and camped on the coast near the ocean. One evening at the beach camp I declared in my journal that the idea of moving to Hollywood was a foolish mistake. I couldn't pretend that I could have a 'normal' life, and I was running away from what I needed to do. I wrote, "I need to stand up and tell my story, not in some esoteric way, not through a fictional screenplay, but to the people. My life isn't about settling down and living happily ever after. All that is secondary to pursuing the truth-telling about my childhood. That is and will be the predominant story of my life."

Broke, feeling I had failed, I headed back to North Carolina to begin building a sustainable shelter yet again. Over the next several months I worked toward a truce in my confrontations with my mom. Sick of the arguing, we agreed to disagree. Still, I needed a story that would explain the split between us and allow me to let it go. I told myself she had made a promise—my mother vowed to my father before his death to never reveal what she knew or suspected. It may not have been true, but it put our discord into a context I could live with. She knew I wasn't a liar or delusional, but she had also seen my father fight a similar battle with the state. I think she understood the rigamarolers better than I did and wanted me to let it go and get on with my life. So I created this idea in my mind that my mother held back the truth out of caring and that she had made a promise to my father, and I was ready to pick up my life again in North Carolina.

In the months away from north cackalacky bouncing around America, I freed myself from many of my archaic patterns of thought. Nothing worked out, but deep down inside some essential changes started to root. I realized again that instead of asking rigamarolers to validate my experience, I could simply live life as a survivor of things kept a secret in America. I had my writing and the music in the hills of the Blue Ridge to soothe and enlighten me, and I was casting off my black-and-white way of looking at the world.

I moved back to North Carolina with an insurance settlement from the wreck that destroyed my truck. With that money, I took a break from working and started writing a memoir about my life, figuring that I could get a publisher interested someday soon. Little did I know my spiritual journey was just beginning. An entry in my 'Voices from the Wilderness' journal captured my state of mind.

VOICE OF ESSENTIAL FORCES

I will no longer listen to that voice implanted in my head as a child that speaks of the world in terms of good and evil. It is a confused and confusing voice, perhaps even a deceitful one, and the end result of listening to it is always intolerance for someone or something. So I will no longer listen to that voice.

I will now strive to hear a different voice. One that does not judge, one that speaks of the world in terms of forces that are either within your grasp or out of your grasp — forces that are the essence of things — forces that work for you once you have mastered them or work against you if you haven't mastered them.

Dividing the world into good and evil is archaic. It does not work. It needs to be silenced.

It is like a storm that blows in from the sea. A man on a boat is following the stars home when the storm comes up behind him and the clouds soon block out the guiding points of light in the sky. He curses the storm as evil because now he will certainly be lost at sea. Meanwhile on shore, the woman farmer welcomes the storm as good because it brings much-needed rain for her crops.

So the same storm is labeled good and evil, but actually it is neither. It is a force that is destructive to one and beneficial to another. Furthermore, its destruction of the man is the result of the boat master's lack of mastering the storm. While he cries out that it is an evil that has descended upon him, he does not realize that all he needs to do is hold his course. Since the storm came up behind him, it should carry him with haste to the shore.

So I let go of the good and evil voice, and I grab hold of the rudder and the voice of essential forces.

In spring 1997, I staked out a spot in front of a stage at Merlefest and waited to see a band named after a wild beast of the American plains. The lone woman in the group, Evia, had become connected to my ideas of an archetypal soulmate. After first seeing her at the festival two years before in an all-female band, I became a bit obsessed with her—so I waited alone at the Americana Stage to see her new incarnation. From the first notes, I got the band's groove as an eclectic mix of old-time music and psychedelia. Evia was a diminutive woman with a voice both childlike and self-assured. Her songs merged an innocent view of the world with touches of counterculture wisdom, a mixture that seemed to pull from both ancient and modern notions. The band wasn't flashy or imposing—no one stepped out to scorch the stage with a solo—the players shared the sound in a selfless way that seemed to say the whole world can live in harmony. It was exactly what I needed to believe.

Early in the set, Evia sang a song that felt like an epiphany to me. It hit upon ideas I had just written in a voices-from-the-wilderness piece about *the rise and the fall* of the human ego. I felt like Evia was speaking directly to my life, that we had a deeper connection that transcended the ordinary, and I wanted her to know that. I started following the band to other gigs, talking to Evia as a fan, and I decided to ask her if I could use a line from one of her lyrics as an epigraph in the book I was writing. I printed up a page with 'The Storm Within' and took it to a street festival her band was playing in Asheville, North Carolina. Between sets, I cornered her near the stage. Evia smiled as she recognized me, invited me to sit and chat. Having grown up in a militant male-dominated milieu, talking to her always felt like a battle won in the revolution toward female equality. I believed that the two of us were ahead of our time, that we had made the shift to a different way of thinking about the roles of men and women, but as I handed her my words I realized something was amiss.

The injured part of me wanted to believe that my life was coming together and that Evia was destined to be a part of it, but I had never applied rational thought to the situation. Perhaps my longing for connection created my delusion, or maybe the unspoken idea that the two of us had shared a first dance together as children at a wedding in New York long ago fueled my infatuation. Whatever the truth, Evia's music bridged the emptiness inside of me, so I gave her words no one had ever seen before, a piece of eclectic free writing that mirrored notions from one of her songs. As soon as I handed her the pages, all kinds of hidden feelings rose up inside me and I wanted my words back.

VOICE OF THE STORM WITHIN

I sometimes wish I was young again, reinvigorated, rejuvenated, naive. The more I know, the less meaning there seems to be. Sometimes it seems that all the meanings I've ever believed and all the words I've ever used to describe my life are merely attempts to define chaos. I fear there is no meaning to anything, no place to get to. I don't want to know myself any better than I do today.

I'd like to live in the moment like an oak tree does. It doesn't worry about the struggles of the past and has no hopes for the future. It stands tall, reaching for the light and casting a cool shadow beneath it. There is nothing for the oak tree to explain or make sense of. If storm winds blow too hard — breaking a limb — there's no heart to sink and no anxieties that well up the next time the wind blows. There is no war within itself over what happened when the limb broke. For that ageless oak tree, it's all part of the cycle of life. It creates no stories of its rise and fall.

Human beings are different than oak trees. We define ourselves in the stories we tell. We rarely live in the moment. We all came from somewhere and we're building for the future. It's a constant battle to define ourselves as winners or conquerors or at least survivors. We create shelters from the storms that would wash us clean or test our mettle. We hide from things that would make us know ourselves. Illusions are all we know, and we strive to make those illusions real.

There's a struggle within each of us to create the story of our rise.

Once something rises we know its fall is inevitable. The story of the fall licks at our heels. It's a dark undercurrent that seems to create itself, an alternate illusion that tries to define us as losers or the conquered. The story of the fall rips down the shelters we have built and laughs as the storm has its way with us, but still we refuse to live in the moment. We're busy trying to build a new shelter, trying to calm our broken heart with a story of rebirth and rejuvenation.

We rise and fall on the 'shelters' we build around our experiences. Was it a defeat or a learning experience? Were we a helpless victim or a cunning survivor? Am I kin to an ancient warrior or a bird of prey learning to fly? Every moment is another page of our story, another chance to define ourselves as on the rise or falling.

Somewhere between the rise and the fall is a place of oneness with the moment. It holds no doubt or certainty and feels no strength or weakness. It's just a moment, nothing more and nothing less. Once you realize you are in it, it's gone. But it also becomes a part of you.

She took my printout and thanked me, said that her husband was waiting on stage and she ran off. Hearing that, I fell into a void, feelings of loss, thoughts that the world had passed me by. Minutes later, the music faded behind me as I walked away from the festival.

In those years that I faced down the rigamarolers about secret events in my childhood, other people had been living their lives, following their callings and building sustainable shelters. In that moment when my illusion of possibilities with Evia shattered, I was feeling all the emotions still trapped in the chasm within me. The world didn't wait for me, and what was worse is that I felt that people were scared of me, saw me as *not-all-there*. I had missed the starting gun and the snickering laughter after it. I came-to as the *oh my gosh what's wrong with the guy* hush swept through the spectators. I couldn't blame myself or anyone else because nothing was wrong with me or them. I hadn't hurt anyone or done anything unforgivable. I had overcome impossible odds just to make it this far. Dealing with the rigamarole had set me back in life, all of it made sense.

I knew I wanted to be a creative writer, an artist with words, but I also knew that for every one of them that got heard, a thousand more were crushed underfoot and made silent or trite. Many voices from the wilderness got lost because the masses didn't relate to their enigmatic struggles, and some voices rose high only to be cut down, making the struggle all the more bitter. If creativity lurks inside, letting it out is happiness. It's the whole reason for striving to make sense of our experiences and finding a way to pass on moments of clarity. I knew all this and I wanted to be one of those timeless voices. I wanted to believe my life was coming together, believe that my bliss was not an ignorant one, but I also wanted to believe I had arrived at a place of coziness.

There is perhaps nothing worse than becoming comfortable with your place in life. Yet comfort is something you can't help but try to attain. Whenever I got to a place of calmness and connection in my life, whether real or imagined, the ghosts of my past rose up to destroy the shelter I had conjured into place. This time I felt like I had risen higher in building a life than ever before, and I believed I was on the verge of success in so many ways, but I didn't realize my foundation was built on smoke and mirrors mixed with wishful thinking. I had fallen into the calm muck that was taking over America.

VOICE OF THE CALM MUCK

It is easier to hide in the hand-me-downs of a lost society than it is to break the patterns and follow a spiritual journey. So I ran and hid and a year slipped by and now I'm trying to climb out of the muck and pick up where I left off.

It is easier to be a spiritual searcher when you're in the middle of a raging storm. Spirituality is about calmness, and a storm lets you know you don't have it. When the rain beats down you look for shelter from it. You are active in your search.

But calmness doesn't mean the journey is over. Perhaps what it means is that you've gone and hidden yourself away. It's easier to believe in yourself when you're not being tested, when you are safe in your shelter and the storm isn't raging against you. But are you getting anywhere?

So I retreated, lived in calmness, worked the hand-me-down patterns of a lost society. I let go of good and evil and didn't grab hold of anything. The storm is still there with its essential forces, holding my destiny, but I know how to find calmness now and it is easier to hide in that. Sink into the calm muck.

And yet it seems somehow that hiding from the storm, hiding from the wilderness only makes the voices from the wilderness howl louder and demand more attention. I'd like to hide, but there is something calling. The storm is rising and threatens my shelter. I need to fix that, deal with that, but I don't know what to do or where to go.

All creative souls seek bliss in their lives, yet the bliss turns into a calm muck. There is both bliss in knowing and bliss in ignorance, and what once seemed to be a bliss in knowing, if you cling to it too long, becomes an ignorant bliss. Many seek the 'now' moments and call that enlightenment, but there is a deeper bliss beyond the darkness. It's not never-ending, calm muck returns, but having someone to share that knowing bliss with is happiness for a creative soul. . . .

Sink into the calm muck.

I wrote 'The Storm Within' about the rise and the fall of the human ego—and I thought I found someone who might understand. In the hometown of Thomas Wolfe—writer of *You Can't Go Home Again*—I gave those words to Evia and realized I was stuck in the calm muck of delusion. The scars of the past told me that I wasn't ready for a domestic life with a woman. I was a generation removed from war, but the echoes passed down by my father lived within me—and even if some might believe, most would say that my mind had conjured up those false notions of a secret militant childhood. I couldn't disprove that, and I knew I couldn't explain my life to anyone in America because the shadows of government secrecy hung over me. Fear would lead people to attach me to the stereotype of possible shooter or terrorist even though I was more of a peacenik. Any woman I might love deserved better than to be trapped in that life with me. I knew I couldn't sink into the calm muck of peaceful and polite society without falling into unhealthy and abusive patterns of secrecy and intrigue built up over the generations of holy war believers in my family.

Coming out of those lost moments in Asheville, a new clarity gripped me—blissing out reached its end. I believed I had to go back into the chasm again to face my demons. I needed to take an activist approach toward understanding my early years or I wouldn't find true happiness or fulfillment in anything. There was no other life for me to live. Time came to get real about my future.

I could no longer afford to be young and naive.

Away from festivals, I worked in the printing department of the University of North Carolina at Chapel Hill. They paid me $25,000 a year with full benefits, the best job of my meagre life. I organized a file room in chaos, making order out of the scattered remnants of twenty years of print jobs, and in my spare time I began to learn about printing. The work didn't fulfill any life dreams, but I liked my boss and I lived a free-spirited lifestyle. As I got further ahead of the curve in keeping the file room organized, I got access to a work computer. I began to build a website after hours, presenting excerpts of my life story to average Americans in a time when internet pioneers were still respectful of the medium. People were curious and supportive, and I had a small following as a writer for the first time in my life. I also earned enough money at my job to begin exploring alternative healing modalities that balanced my energies and relieved stress. I began to believe I had found a place where I belonged and that my life, as meagre as it was, might eventually work out.

After a year of outstanding performance reviews at the university, I received a raise and took on duties involving digital scanning. My 'hippie' boss retired and a different set of bureaucrats took over. Soon my workload tripled—I gained an additional job title but my wage stayed the same. When I complained about my job description not reflecting my duties, coworkers laughed at me and bosses didn't care. No one's job description matched what they were doing. Everyone had given up trying to be recognized for all that they did—advancement was based on kissing the right asses in the right ways. My work kept piling up. I felt like a rat on a treadmill covering two jobs for one wage. After weeks of complaining with no response, I filed a formal grievance.

I didn't understand that only fools file grievances. I had been reading Martin Luther King, Jr.'s idealistic writings, and I believed I would be treated fairly. I soon realized that the university's grievance policy was a mockery of Dr. King's *Letter from the Birmingham Jail*. The rules forbade all the forms of protest he wrote about. I couldn't understand why the university wanted to limit employee input or stifle nonviolent approaches to change.

My new boss earned more than the salary designated by the state, yet she made stupid mistakes that wasted thousands of dollars. She bullied employees into covering additional duties without pay for their overtime. I didn't understand why people put up with it, and I figured that if I made a stand and took the higher-ups to task, the rank and file would come forward too, or at least have my back. So I took to my grievance with vigor and got the attention of the vice-chancellor. In the first meeting with all the bigwigs, I told them "If you want to use my master's degree skills, you have to pay for them." They replied that they didn't care about my student loan debt and that whatever pay the university gave me entitled them to all my skills and education. They said I couldn't negotiate a raise, and if I didn't like that I could quit my job.

I pressed onward and wrote a letter to the federal senator from North Carolina—and he said he would look into the matter. I got some traction against the bigwigs after that, and they asked me to write a description of my extra job duties so they could petition the state to create a new position. Upon receiving my write-up, two lower supervisors among the rank and file sat me down in a room and shoved a piece of paper in front of me, pointing to the bottom of the page trying to get me to pen my name without reading it. I ignored them and started reading.

Hoodwink. Hornswoggle. Bamboozle. I stood up, ripped the page in half and threw it across the table. The paper said I agreed to go back to being a file clerk at my previous wage. The position that I created and defined was going to someone else. By signing I agreed this was okay, a resolution of my grievance.

I should have walked out of the building and kept going, but I had nowhere to go. I returned to my desk and refused to do any of the duties of the new position. I went back to being a file clerk and didn't speak much anymore. About a week or so later I got a package at my home address with a stick of deodorant and a note inside that read, "You better clean yourself up." The postmark showed it came from the university mailroom, and I traced it down to the printing department—sent by the rank and file who I thought might stand up with me. Everyone kept doing their same routines, kowtowing to the system, wasting away their lives. No kinds words ever got spoken to me again there.

I saw that I was reliving many of the frustrations I had faced when I fought with the Maryland bureaucrats over my medical records. I wondered if the higher-ups were trying to trigger the trauma of my childhood military conditioning to get me to back down. It was a game to them, another person to crush underfoot. I felt betrayed. People in suits were rigamaroling me again, stealing from me before the paycheck and leaving me unable to pay back my student loans. They acted as though the university belonged to them, not the community or the public or the future of America. They didn't care that there had been a shooting rampage on the streets of the town by a student from the university—the rigamarolers thought that was all part of the game. They either didn't see or didn't care how the military conditioning in my background might erupt upon their institution because they lived in communities with gilded gates and were set to retire wealthy.

I had fantasies of walking into the printing building with guns and blowing away the lot of them, fulfilling a twisted desire to rebalance the present and make up for the past. All my education denied, all my knowledge of nonviolent philosophies thrown aside—letting the amok shadows inside me run loose for a minute or two.

I saw my sustainable shelter in Carolina evaporating. The used Opel Kadett that I had bought after the destruction of my truck was dying. I poured money into it but it gave up the ghost anyway, leaving me facing a wintry January with no ride. Unable to afford another car, I bought a bicycle and rode it four miles each way along a snowy highway to get to the closest park-and-ride lot to catch the bus to work. Rent went up so I started looking for a different place to live, and I no longer had money for the alternative healing work that relieved my stress.

I began to look for work elsewhere and turned to my alma mater in Arizona. Canyon State University had plans to open an interactive classroom site in a building about a hundred yards from the rim of Grand Canyon. They needed someone to live there and be the caretaker of the place, working with people in the park to create educational videos to share with the world. I figured I could move to Flagstaff and take a job as a part-time, non-benefit employee while I waited for the job on the rim to get funded. It seemed like the perfect way to escape the cage being built around me in North Carolina.

I contacted one of my former professors who was a proponent of this kind of virtual university. Dr. Grey Vonsousa, a teacher of humanities and religious studies at my alma mater for over thirty-five years, told me that we were witnessing the "beginning of the end" of the traditional university system. Maintaining infrastructure was getting too expensive, and the culture shock of people from remote areas and foreign countries moving to universities to face different belief systems led to violence on campuses. Too many new ingredients had cooled down the American melting pot. Affordable, quality education for the world would die unless this idea of presenting classes over long distances to remote locations succeeded. Dr. Vonsousa saw a way forward to keep American universities in the forefront of learning. He was enthusiastic about it, passionate, and I believed there could be no better job than working for Canyon State University and bringing stories about Grand Canyon to the world.

Idealism coloured my worldview. In reality, the State of Arizona faced a massive budget scandal, and politicians would soon be targeting education to pay for their mistakes. The planned distance learning system would be downsized, and a major restructuring of the entire higher education system loomed on the horizon. Rigamarolers were invading, plotting to kick all the aging hippies and progressive teachers to the curb. The first set of budget cuts hit my alma mater while I was contemplating my move. The job that I had my eye on got delayed but remained on the books. I had second thoughts about going to Arizona. I felt trapped in a life I didn't want but escape seemed impossible.

Looking back, I see my days in Carolina as a time of integration, of trying to build a sustainable shelter where my dreams of being a writer could live. I wanted to believe, but the chaos of the past kept rising up within me and sullying my world. My voices-from-the-wilderness writings gave me a foothold on understanding my true nature and kept me connected to my inner writer, but the connection was fleeting, tenuous, like a narrow pathway along the edge of a cliff. The cruel world of a dying university set me off balance, but at least I never bought guns or learned how to make bombs. Some kind of Irish luck from my mom's ancestry held, but I knew that I needed to change my life if I wanted to keep the writer voice alive.

My friends were getting married, moving up in their careers and leaving for greener pastures. I was alone and women didn't 'get' me. I tried to find gratitude for the calm muck supporting me—I applied the usual platitudes that sustain mediocrity—but I didn't believe my own mutterings. Even before filing the grievance at work, I began to feel like my attempts to create a writer's life had stalled. There was no simple highway to my dreams, and I wondered what to do.

Find a new religion.

Many friends got born again. Whether following a new age notion of 'rebirthing' or falling back into christianity, they had decided to control-alt-delete their current selves and find their inner child. I knew I could never go back, so I looked for a spiritual path to take me further. Back before the upheavals started at work, I came upon an advert by a woman offering a class in shamanism that included *journeying* into the 'spirit' world, and I decided to take a chance on that. The visions I had as a child and the dreams that helped me through my darkest hours seemed to fit with notions connected to the ancient practice called shamanism, but coming from a catholic background I had doubts about the authenticity of anything in the 'new age' realm.

I signed up for a weekend getaway to learn about shamanism, never thinking it might throw my life into chaos. On a Saturday morning in October, I drove out a backroad in my Opel and crossed a mossy, stone bridge shrouded in mist, finding my way to a white brick house up on a hill. The place held the spooky charm that older houses do, hints of history and spirits. I joined the group gathering outside, both intrigued and skeptical with what might follow. A woman in a purple stole soon came from the house and welcomed us. After the hellos we went up into a second floor loft that served as the place to journey between worlds. The scene seemed surreal, and I mused to myself that the 'shaman' might be a suburban housewife with a little practice on the side. I stifled my negativity and found a spot near the back of the room so I could keep an eye on everyone.

I learned that through a process called 'shamanic journeying' a person could enter an altered state of consciousness and have lucid dream-like experiences. A vision quest into an 'upper' or 'lower' spirit world could be brought on by listening to specific percussive beats. The concept interested me because during the most intense part of my trauma recall period I had experienced lucid dreams and visions, and I had visits with 'spirits' or 'avatars' or archetypal mentors. In some ways I missed the intensity of that time, but I didn't want to relive the nightmares from the chasm within. I wanted to reconnect with the Anima spirit and have visions that would help me find a new sense of purpose and direction in my life.

After several hours learning the principles behind shamanism, I was ready to try a vision quest for the first time flanked by other members of the class. The woman shaman told us not to expect much, and I was sure that would be the truth. We were taking a journey to the lower spirit world to catch a glimpse of our power animal or just to remember anything we saw in our creative imaginations. I took a spot on the floor, and she began beating a rhythm on the drum. Patterns like those on Indian blankets danced before my mind's eye. They moved faster and faster and gave way to green swirls of light, a vortex. Soon I found myself more than two thousand miles away.

CANYON CALLING

I am standing near Lookout Studio on the rim of Grand Canyon in Arizona. I jump off and soar down into the great chasm. I feel like a powerful bird as I wing over the Indian Gardens area. Within seconds I swoop down across Tonto Plateau and fly into the tunnel at South Kaibab suspension bridge. I turn towards the solid rock wall where I see clockwise green swirls of light and enter a different kind of tunnel. I emerge awkwardly feet first into a plush jungle. I know I've entered the lower spirit world.

There, I see four manifestations of birds.

First, a huge raptor with thundering wings swoops down over me. I duck out of the way, but the image of a great wing imprints in my mind.

Next, I am on Plateau Point overlooking the Colorado River. A Hopi native wearing wings is dancing. An ancestral Thunderbird Kachina joins him — modern and ancient dance together.

Third, I am back in the jungle where a raven is eating bugs off my bare feet as I stand on sand. I know this means that I am regaining power and grounding.

Last, I am high up on a cliff sitting on the edge of a huge nest. There are four eggs in the nest that represent power areas of my life. Then I notice a fifth egg. It's unexpected and unwanted. I feel overwhelmed by the power there at the nest. I spend time trying to become comfortable. Eventually I do, then I am being called back to the surface world.

I visit each of the four incarnations again and fly back to the Canyon rim.

In the class, after we were called back to ordinary reality, I spent about ten minutes writing down what I remembered. Other people started sharing their visions while I kept writing, not listening to them. When it came my turn to speak, I read out my experience in all its detail as a hush fell over the room. Being so caught up in my own reverie about what I just envisioned, the feelings I sensed from others didn't sway me. *Skepticism, whispers of skullduggery, feelings of inferiority?* I kept reading. When I finished and looked up, no one said anything.

In a meditation later in the class, I visited the upper spirit world to ask a question. *"How do we hatch these eggs?"* There's a response, but I can't hear it. I ask again, but the beating of the drum back in the surface world drowns out the reply. Then I hear laughing, and I understand that this is my answer. I have too many distractions in the *ordinary* world to hatch the eggs of the spirit world. A flood of information follows the answer. The basic message is that I need to go to Arizona and live near Grand Canyon. Things will make more sense after I arrive.

Back in the ordinary world, it seemed impossible to move from Carolina. I had a job and a network of friends. I was discovering shamanism, and I was earning the best salary of my meagre life. I managed to visit Grand Canyon for two weeks as the millennium changed, but whatever there was to discover in Arizona would have to wait for a more lucrative time of my life. I made arrangements to do solo work with the woman shaman in Carolina. She wanted us to take a journey to find out if it was right for us to go further together. When I touched her hand, I sensed an ancient, African spirit there with us. We journeyed together, so many new ideas coursing through my mind. I felt there was much to learn, but at the end of that first session the shaman said it wasn't right for her to work with me. I needed to follow my earlier vision and go to Arizona.

Cut loose, dislodged from logic, cast into the murky waters of following my heart. Over the next few months, the rigamarole at work boiled up and my life in Carolina disintegrated. I came to wonder if the young, woman shaman and the ancient, African spirit had cast some kind of malevolent spell on me. First my car died, then my work situation soured, and one by one things both real and imagined that kept me from leaving for the desert southwest near Grand Canyon fell away. Moving to Arizona felt like a fool's errand in some ways, but in inexplicable ways it made sense.

I remember the looks on my coworkers' faces when I announced that I was quitting. By then I had cooled the tensions in the workplace, made nice with the dimwits. They were surprised and puzzled, and perhaps envious, wondering how I could just walk away from my life and head to a small town without any prospects. But the decision to leave them was easy. I was no longer going to be subject to unfeeling bureaucrats or the foolish rank and file, playing the game of get kicked or canned. I couldn't stay at an institution that looked on its workers as slaves who must kiss dumb, privileged ass to get ahead. The call of the Canyon in a shamanic vision gave me a direction to go. Without it, I might have given into my deep-rooted rage and carried out those fantasies of blowing the lot of them away with automatic weapons.

So I listened to those voices from the wilderness of my spirit—my now constant companions—telling me to go to Grand Canyon. I had no car, no solid job prospects and about three thousand dollars to my name. I rented a moving truck and left Carolina for Northern Arizona, where I would do a lot of walking.

4. THUNDERBIRD WALKING

Get up! Get up NOW and WALK or you'll die here!

Not exactly words, more like an urgent message screamed from the core of my being. I lay shivering cold on the side of Hermit Trail in Grand Canyon—not a good thing because the sun was scorching the rocks around me on a one-hundred-degree day. Just up the trail a short way, I hoped, was the Santa Maria shade house and spring where I could rest my weary body and fill my empty water bottles. I needed to get up and walk to live another day.

My hike began at Monument Creek campground that morning. I overslept, so instead of a break-of-dawn start to my nine-mile trek out of the canyon, I faced the heat of day. I had planned to get more water at Hermit Creek camp, but that meant more time in the hot sun of the inner canyon. I wanted to get out of there, get up the steep trail to the next water source and rest there through the afternoon. I figured that my two litres of water would sustain me. The shade house waited about five miles away, and given my usual uphill pace with a thirty-pound pack, it would take about three hours to get there. I didn't know that a rockfall had changed the trail, made it tougher and longer. I also forgot there were few shady places to rest along the way. I was hiking solo, breaking the rules, with no other soul to warn me of my dangerous plan.

The ghost of a hermit that lived on that trail had become a nemesis of mine. Each time I hiked there, I left with a deeper haunt in my memory and a desire to go back to set things right. On my first trip to Grand Canyon in 1986, I startled a pink rattlesnake sunning itself on one of the stone steps up near the rim. It coiled up, shook its rattle and jumped under a nearby rock. Maybe I should have taken that as an omen warning me never to return. Instead, I came back over and over again with the idea that I could conquer the trail—and that's the worst mindset a Grand Canyon hiker can bring to the backcountry.

By ten o'clock my water was gone and the heat of midday set in. I had been hiking for three hours, and the first signs of exhaustion were slowing me down. I figured the shade house with the spring couldn't be far. I expected to see it around each new turn of the footpath as my mouth grew dryer and my nausea grew worse. I stumbled as the voices of hikers coming down the trail echoed off the Canyon walls. *Water!* I hoped they had some extra from the spring not far away. They spared me a litre and told me that the shade house was still two hours uphill. I thought they were wrong. *My pace couldn't of been that slow.* I sat down in the waning shadow of the Canyon wall and drank the water they left for me. Feeling rejuvenated, I soaked my shirt with the last drops of moisture and stepped back out onto the trail. The shade house would save me if I got there quick enough. After about a hundred steps, I threw up the water. My body didn't accept the moisture. *Heat stroke.* I knew that meant serious trouble and I needed to get to a place where I could rest, a place near where a helicopter could land if needed. *The shade house.* I walked alone, a dying man in the burning sun.

The ghost of the hermit began haunting me, whispering ideas into my mind, enticing me to join him as another spirit forever roaming the Canyon backcountry. I walked Hermit Trail in the early days of a new millennium, a man a few years shy of age forty. My life didn't add up. I lived a humble existence in Grand Canyon Village, and I wandered off alone on long hikes into the wilderness trying to piece together the craziness of a world that didn't need me. There on Hermit Trail with the sun beating down, the patterns of denial about the secrets of my childhood were imploding within me. I thought I heard a ghost whispering to me. Louis Boucher, gone now some eighty years, trying to convince me I had found my purpose in life—to die forgotten on a wilderness trail. *As good as any purpose I suppose. Better than living a meagre life as a near-minimum-wage servant to the tourists on the South Rim while being mocked in legal briefs by wealthy government attorneys.*

Twelve forty-five in the afternoon, July 1, 2001. *Only stupid people hike this time of day. All moisture gone. Cold and clammy skin, not a drop of sweat. Evaporation wins.* I couldn't go on. The latest mirage of the shade house ahead was not enough. I didn't feel myself fall. Time skipped a beat . . . on the ground convulsing and shivering.

It's okay. It's only death.

Get up! Get up NOW and WALK or you'll die here!

The next few moments are a series of disjointed images interrupted by nothingness. I remember my feet walking a cold and dark trail. There were ominous clouds in the sky, a threat of snow, spirits laughing and reminding me of other moments in my life lost in the depths of forgetfulness. I was a man out of time and my confused and forgotten past whispered into my consciousness as I stumbled toward dreams of shelter. In reality, it remained sunny and hot, of course, not a cloud in the Canyon sky. I should have died, but somehow I made it. I got to the shade house and collapsed while a kind soul—perhaps the ghost of the hermit himself—pumped me water out of the spring.

I slept away the heat of the afternoon thinking about my first year in Arizona. I was facing down another nemesis in my life, one much more indifferent to my pursuit of happiness than Hermit Trail. I had gotten myself caught up in the de facto terrorist-making machine of the United States' federal court system.

One year earlier, just past midnight on July 2, 2000, I pulled into the Interstate 40 rest area on the eastern Arizona border. Music written by my childhood friend Jerrold played over the speakers in the rental truck. I had looped his song called "Arizona" dozens of times on my drive across the country, believing in the message of the lyrics. *"Come with me. I'll show you something you need to see. If you don't, you'll never know what I was going to show you. I might go, or will I stay? I don't know . . . Arizona."* As I drifted off to sleep in the desert air, my move from Carolina to Flagstaff felt like the right choice even though I didn't have a job or a place to call home yet. On July fourth, I settled into a one-room apartment with no kitchen and went to see fireworks.

For the first month I had a lot of free time on my hands. I began spending long hours at the Canyon State University library researching how to get information from the government. I had fallen into forgetfulness, gotten caught up in the odd notion that people in power had answers for me, and I planned to send out more requests seeking clues to my past. Trapped amid the unnatural pillars of parchment in the library, I didn't realize that the truth lived inside me, ready to rise to the surface as I walked on wilderness trails near natural pillars of stone. My heartfelt requests to bureaucrats couldn't bring real answers because too many in my generation had picked up the hand-me-down patterns of government denial. I got stonewalled again, but I also discovered a direction to go. I found mention of an initiative by the Clinton administration designed to make it easier for citizens to file legal complaints against the government on their own behalf. That idea inspired me, filled me with foolish hope. I envisioned standing up and speaking my truth in federal court.

The rules and procedures for filing a civil case were complicated, and the pitfalls of entering the legal system seemed endless. I needed to write a formal complaint and submit it to a district judge in Arizona through a summons process. By going on record, opposing lawyers could say that my claim amounted to perjury and ask the judge to throw me in jail. My doubts grew when a legal aid organization rejected my request for assistance and several lawyers refused to take my case. By September I thought of giving up the effort, but a simple experience came along that felt like a reward for following my heart to Arizona and daring to speak my truth.

While doing the legal research, I took a part-time job in the television services department at the university. It was an entry-level position working on academic television programs and teaching students how to use television equipment. After a few weeks on the job, my boss asked me to be part of a crew for a special project delivering satellite internet technology to remote tribal lands. We did video shoots on the Navaho reservation and the Hopi Nation in eastern Arizona before heading to the Havasupai reservation down in Grand Canyon.

We flew into the village of Supai in helicopters, landed and unloaded the equipment. The corporate sponsor wanted a faked video of their satellite dishes arriving by mule, so we staged the shot on the dirt trail in town. As the dishes and computers were being installed, my boss asked me to be his assistant cameraman while he got aerial shots of Havasu Canyon. We removed the door from one side of a helicopter and climbed into the back seat as the pilot got ready for the flight. The mechanical bird thundered to life, and I grabbed hold of the back of the camera and held the clasp of my boss's seatbelt so it couldn't pop open and send him falling. The ex-Navy pilot took us up over the village and headed down the Canyon toward Navaho, Havasu and Mooney Falls. After one pass, we made a sharp U-turn and went lower, flying down below the rim of the narrow chasm. The helicopter swerved between the cliffs just above the treetops, allowing us to capture shots of the blue-green waters meandering through the gorge.

Looking down, I saw my friends from work swimming in the creek below Havasu Falls. We were close enough that I could wave and smile . . . and catch the pangs of envy on their faces. Soon they began ignoring me and went back to swimming. I worried I had acted too arrogant by smiling down on them while enjoying a once in a lifetime experience. Flights below the rim were restricted on federal lands because sudden downdrafts could sweep a helicopter into a cliff wall, but we flew over tribal lands and I didn't think of those negatives. I remembered my shamanic vision back in Carolina where I jumped off the rim and soared through the Canyon as a thunderbird spirit. Human technology had created a thundering bird that gave me a similar feeling, allowing me to fly free between the cliff walls. I believed this proved I was on the right track in life, fulfilling my destiny. Spirit had gifted me this flight through the Canyon because I had answered the calling to stand up and speak my truth in federal court.

When the helicopter landed, I went to join my friends for an evening swim below Havasu Falls. I wanted to tell them about my adventure and allay some of their feelings of envy. The trail was short and easy, but when I got to the falls my friends were nowhere to be found. They had already made their way back to the village. With twilight setting in, I went swimming alone in the flowing pools of blue-green water. The cliffs glowed in the setting sun as the peace and quiet of the Canyon settled around me. I sensed something mystical happening, and I saw my reflection in the water surrounded by rainbows. The blue-green pools shimmered with life-force energy. I swam in the heightened awareness of that moment till daylight faded, then I headed back to Supai village as the dark of night set in.

As I hurried up the trail, I heard a voice call out to me. "The Wigleeva were watching you." I turned to see a Havasupai man in blue jeans standing near some green brush growing alongside the cliff next to the trail. He smiled and pointed up the Canyon. "The Wigleeva."

I knew that Wigleeva referred to the red sandstone pillars with natural faces that stood looking out over the village. In Havasupai legend they are the protectors and watchers of their lands, and when they fall the time of the people of the blue-green waters will come to an end in Grand Canyon.

I smiled back at him and asked, "The sandstone pillars, what did they see?"

"They saw you swimming in the healing waters at the magic moment between day and night."

"Is there any meaning to that?" I asked, wondering if I was missing something.

"They were laughing at all your worldly worries, all those big plans you got." He said with a stone-faced smile.

"I'm glad someone finds humour in it," I said.

The man stepped back and seemed to disappear into the dark green brush. I didn't follow. I pulled out my flashlight and made my way up the trail back to the village.

I felt the Wigleeva watching over me as I set up my sleeping bag in the daycare building that night. My bond to Grand Canyon became stronger on that trip. Those two days below the rim and that swim in the twilight hour—a short slice of time out of my life—became like pillars in my memory. I had learned the value of contributing to others by helping to bring satellite internet technology to a daycare center in a remote tribal village, and I saw the grateful smiles of the Havasupai children who followed us around curious about why we were there.

Something deeper lived in those smiles, something I made sense of as I pursued my legal case in federal court. The kids gathered around as we arrived in the helicopters. They had seen the flying machines before, but so many arriving at once made it a special day. When we pulled out the cameras and started to shoot, they approached us with both intrigue and fear. Many tribal peoples have a belief that photographs steal a part of the soul, each image freezing a moment and taking it out of the flow of life. Too many stolen moments can keep a spirit stuck in the past, unable to move forward, unable to have new feelings. And yet a self image is intriguing, beguiling, proves that we have lived and laughed or cried. So these kids approached with curiosity, and we had power over them with our technology and knowledge. We could spook them or calm their fears.

And I realized that the mole doctor and others in my childhood had held that same power over me, and they chose to use my childhood beliefs to create a holy war mentality. They conditioned me for violence, probably invested their money in the military-industrial complex, then abandoned me to my own devices—destroying all memory, all documentation, all photographs—leaving me searching for truth, convinced that a fulfilling life somehow dwelled beyond restoring lost scraps of days gone by rather than living free in the flow of each moment.

In the court case, I was chasing a dark spectre from my past, a short epoch that had eroded away from memory. I needed to stand strong for myself, to stand strong for justice even if no one else stood with me. I may fall. I may be laughed at or washed away unknown, but I thought of my two days in Havasu—those notions attached to the smiling, curious faces of the children and the Wigleeva watching over me. And later on, when the stresses of presenting my sketchy past to government lawyers got to me, I remembered the feeling of swimming beneath the mystic waterfalls of Havasu Canyon. I felt like part of something bigger than myself—and I believed I was fulfilling the promise attached to one of those *eggs* in my shamanic vision back in Carolina. Playing a small role in the ongoing rejuvenation of southwestern tribal peoples made my complaint in federal court feel insignificant.

With every moment of connection inviting us to community, there's a nemesis pushing us toward isolation, trying to make us a hermit lost in the wilderness devoid of human contact. In Arizona, I was walking back toward humanity, returning to the surface with word of what I had found in the depths. The trail back proved rough, obstacles were being put in my way. I found solace in the mystic waters of Havasu Canyon and harshness in the burning sun of the desert. Ally and foe soothed and challenged me.

On the twenty-eighth of November 2000, I signed my name to a federal civil complaint against the State of Maryland, the United States Department of Defense and their unknown 'mole' doctors. I had finished writing it on my thirty-seventh birthday, and I filed the case on my own behalf without a lawyer. In my time researching the law, I became grounded in understanding what happened to me in my childhood. I knew there would still be setbacks, but a certain spiritual resilience dwelled inside me. Living on the edge of Grand Canyon seemed to put everything into perspective. I thought of some lines from the film *Grand Canyon*, the part where the Simon character talks about how *when you sit on the edge of that thing you realize what a joke people are*, and I imagined the ancient rocks laughing at my feeble attempts to know myself. Making a federal case out of my life felt real humorous next to the nothingness of Grand Canyon.

If I learned anything from my dealings with people in power suits, it's that some folks and their underlings only laugh when the joke is on somebody *less* than them. From the get-go, the State of Maryland played games with my legal filing. When I phoned their attorney general's office to see if they had gotten the waiver-of-service summons and other legal papers I mailed, I found an intern on the other end of the line—a young man from the sound of his voice—and he started to laugh at me after I asked my first question. He had already learned that 'pro se' citizens were to be mocked and ridiculed, were not even worthy of the decency of a cordial phone conversation. Some privileged-class twenty-something boy working the phones in an office sworn to seek justice for American citizens knew the disenfranchisement game. He told me that after opening and reading my complaint, the lawyers decided not to honour my pro se waiver-of-service summons. They could have accepted it if they wanted to—the mailed waiver of service had been created to allow poorer people access to the summons process—but the state was not required by law to follow it so they declined acceptance in this case. I knew they were using a delay tactic because they wanted to locate and destroy any remaining medical documents before becoming legally bound by the court, and it made me irate.

As I hung up the phone, warpath rage erupted inside me. The healing path activity of expressing myself got denied, ridiculed, blocked. I thought of calling back this foolish and smug boy—this underling pucker-er to Maryland state lawyers—and asking *What if I had gone away for six years and come back not with words but with a bomb? Would you have listened to me then?* I knew the idea was just a metaphorical expression of my anger, a movie in my creative mind, not anything to make real, but I wondered why such a calculated tactic to create rage in a person seeking justice seemed to be the norm of the State of Maryland. *Something bigger to hide?*

After being served the papers, one of the state's female lawyers mocked me by phone saying that their board of physicians didn't investigate truck accidents—and noting coyly that one of the judges on the federal bench in Maryland is the daughter of her boss, the state's attorney general. After she failed to get a dismissal on legal grounds, other Maryland lawyers attempted to lure me back east to face their notoriously corrupt court system. The federal judge in Arizona, seeing all their rigamarole, dismissed them as a defendant, writing that it didn't "serve the interests of justice to transfer the case to the State of Maryland."

For all the loathing from the rigamarolers at the state level, the United States Attorney's Office of Arizona proved even worse. According to the procedure rules, copies of complaints against the government could be delivered by certified mail to the local U.S. Attorney's Office. I prepared all the paperwork and sent copies to the Flagstaff address. I got a letter back stating that they couldn't receive my complaint locally, and it had been forwarded to Phoenix, but I still needed to do it over to be legit. I thought that officials of the federal government should follow their own rules and accept service at their local office, but they didn't care about that. Small-town folks were not allowed a voice. People in positions of power were not even pretending to play fair and it enraged me.

I sent a letter expressing my anger to an assistant U.S. attorney in Phoenix. In those more innocent days before 9-11, I wrote, "Perhaps the cost of service doesn't mean much to members of the privileged class in America, but to me it is a meal or two—or perhaps an afternoon movie or two to escape the stresses of life for awhile. As someone not poor enough to proceed 'in forma pauperis' yet not rich enough to achieve equal justice under law, it is truly disheartening to see privileged-class government officials play games on this important matter. When I lose on this matter in court—and especially if I should not get my day in court—I hope you will remember your actions here. Next time someone blows up a federal building or walks into an institution with guns blazing, I hope you will remember your actions here. Honestly and fairly dealing with this complaint might plant seeds that would show people a different way to address grievances." I concluded the letter by saying that I would effect proper service as soon as my funds permitted.

Some weeks later I received a visit from a special agent of the FBI and a United States marshal. They had been looking for me at the request of the U.S. Attorney's Office and managed to find me at work during a studio production. When they said they needed to talk to me, I tried to schedule an appointment for later that day after I finished my shift. Of course, they couldn't wait or come back. They had commandeered a conference room from my boss to interrogate me, causing a stir throughout my workplace. Closed up in that room, the special agent pulled a copy of my letter out of a thick file and asked me about the line with "federal building" in it. I referred to it as "provocative in response to a provocation" and pointed to the next line about planting seeds to show people a different way. They proceeded to ask a series of questions about group affiliations, military knowledge, body modifications and my current life situation including if anyone close to me had recently died. I realized they were doing a terrorist threat assessment and looking for trauma-triggering events.

When we were done talking at work, they asked to see my apartment. I didn't want to get into a car alone with armed federal agents, so I hesitated. They said that if they made sure there were no bomb-building materials in my apartment, they could report back that I had cooperated. I knew this meant that if they didn't see where I lived I could expect future visits from government agents. So with no 'patriot act' to worry about, where they could take me out to the desert and hold me for days or weeks without notifying anyone, I went with them to my apartment.

Once inside, the marshal—who stuttered and carried a gun on his belt—spotted the book *From Freedom to Slavery: The Rebirth of Tyranny in America* by attorney Gerry Spence. He commented that the author had never lost a civil case, and I replied that Mr. Spence had declined to take mine. The special agent called me into the bedroom, and I saw him standing over a bunch of small plants I had grown from seed. He asked me if they were pot and assured me he couldn't arrest me for that, only the federal drug cops could and he wasn't going to call them. I replied that they were coleus plants, the painted nettle, my favorite tropical plant because of its vivid colours—and so far as I knew smoking it did not get a person high. He laughed and the tension evaporated from our encounter. After looking around for a few minutes, the two seemed satisfied I wasn't a terrorist and returned me to work. My shift had ended and I lost a day's pay.

The visit by armed federal agents seemed stupid to me. At one point, I asked them about the hundred-some letters I had sent to all kinds of government officials about my childhood, and they replied that all issues related to my past were classified by Congress as outside the investigative jurisdiction of the FBI. While the agent and the marshal were courteous and professional, we all knew by the end of the apartment search that they had been used to intimidate me during a court case.

This interrogation with the FBI occurred in February of 2001, about two months after filing my civil case. According to the *The 9/11 Commission Report*, Hani Hanjour—pilot of the jetliner that crashed into the Pentagon—was training on a Boeing 737 simulator at Pan Am International Flight Academy in Mesa, Arizona, from January through March 2001. The FBI interviewed me as a possible terrorist while a member of Al-Qaeda was preparing for his September 11th suicide mission about a hundred miles down the interstate.

It's strange how life works. You ask questions one place and get answers from another. That's because the answers were already there, living inside you and working their way to the surface. They arrive right on time—if you take care to remember life as it happens, to write it down by hand on pages blank with possibilities—you can look out over a natural landscape and see truths that rose over all the times you set foot there.

I learned more about my past walking the Hermit Trail area over a period of twelve years than was ever revealed by government bureaucrats. In 1990, ten years before my move to Arizona, I took a hike alone to camp next to Hermit Rapid on a backcountry permit issued by a ranger named Moses. I got heat exhaustion about a half-mile short of the river and swore to never hike there again. In the last days of 1999, I took a change-of-the-millennium trip from Carolina to hike Hermit Trail. Again, I was defeated just short of the river. I'm not sure why I kept going back, but in my mind those Hermit hikes are forever connected with the denials of state and federal bureaucrats about the events of my childhood.

On my change-of-the-millennium hike, parts of the trail were washed out. I had to climb over and around huge boulders with my backpack. I strained tendons in the top of my foot and the injury slowed me down. By sunset, I had made it only as far as Tonto junction two miles short of my destination on the river. I continued on by flashlight, got a bit lost, and found the trail again with dumb luck. I made my way through the narrow-gorge canyon down toward the camp at Hermit Rapid. With my strained foot and now my leg hurting too, my mission to get to the river became doubtful.

A fool in the dark, exhausted and getting cold, I kept going. Every one hundred yards or so I found a large rock where I stopped to sit and rest with my pack on. Trudging onward, I could have fallen in the night to lay injured for hours or days before discovered by another hiker. I came to a rockfall in the narrow gorge and got stuck as I tried to squeeze through with my pack. I jerked myself forward free of the rocks and fell to the ground. I noticed a flat area sufficient for a camp beside me as I struggled back to my feet, but the mission to the river still beckoned like the ghost of some lost love. The lost trauma of my past loomed in my mind as if I would find new answers somewhere down the trail.

Exhausted and cold, one flashlight dead and another fading, I decided I was lost and should wait till morning to find myself. I made for a flat area in an alcove and set up an impromptu camp for the night. The next morning, I walked down the rest of the trail without my pack and discovered the river campground a short distance away. After watching the rapid for a while, I went back to get my pack and had breakfast on the beach. Later that day I hiked back up the gorge I had traversed in the darkness. There was no mole doctor to steal my memories from me as I made my way over the eerie ground and through the rockfall. My strained leg and foot slowed me down for the rest of my trip, but I made my itinerary, finding each campground in the light of day, remembering that my pain came from that night wandering the narrow gorge above the river—and from a mostly forgotten night long ago.

A few days later, while camping at Monument Creek, I looked back on that first night of my hike. I realized the same feeling of déjà vu had come up on my previous two hikes on Hermit Trail. I began to see a repetition of things from my past that were foggy or forgotten. Unprovable but real, the remnants of a story from my past came together for me on that Hermit trip. I remembered that at some point in my lost childhood I became lost on a training mission. I got injured and failed to reach the goal. After medical evacuation and trauma treatment, the darker mind games to confuse my memory began. How that happened, I'll never know for sure. There's no proof but the beating of my heart while walking alone on a healing path.

I spent the millennial New Year's Eve at Monument Creek. When the moment of midnight came I listened. *Nothing.* Not a sound from humanity. A gentle wind swept down the wash and I thought of it as the Canyon laughing at the passing of time. I had the feeling of being in the womb of the earth, protected from the harshness of the world of humans. Two days later, I hiked up into a new millennium. I noted in my journal that I wanted to come back and live right there on the rim. *Life is a journey, and there's no way to know how hard or long it might be.* Adversaries wanted to keep me a hermit devoid of connections to humanity, but I could make my way back, return truth to the world. As the millennium began, I fancied myself an ancient thunderbird walking out of a chasm into a new epoch of life.

During my first nine months in Arizona, I filed my civil case, wintered through in Flagstaff and began searching for a full-time job as spring approached. A pall hung over the university. The visit from the FBI made people wary of me, and budgets cuts killed off most prospects as brighter minds left looking for greener pastures. With the atmosphere at Canyon State University feeling poisoned, I applied to the corporate concessionaire in Grand Canyon National Park, believing it would be a great honour to live and work there. The housing was meagre and the wages were low, but I could sit on the rim and wait for the ruling on my legal case.

As I prepared my application, I began to doubt they would hire the likes of me. I figured my desire to live in a place known around the world as a natural 'crown jewel' would lead to rejection. After I mailed one application, I realized I had forgotten to include the employer reference page. To make up for my mistake, I mailed a second application to the South Rim and a third to the North Rim. A few weeks later I had three separate job offers. No one checked my employment references, let alone did a background check. I should have seen that as my first hint that things were less than ideal.

In April 2001, after planting my coleus in inconspicuous spots around Canyon State University, I left for a job at the retail distribution center on the South Rim. Being at the Canyon every day felt great, and I excelled at my job. The manager of the distro center had lost a lot of battles trying to make things better for her employees and needed to fill positions the corporation didn't recognize. Soon I began to drive a box truck around the national park—no raise, no change in position— they needed a driver and I stepped in. We worked out of an awkward historic building that once served as the power-generating station for the village. The Park Service had elaborate plans to make the area into a heritage education campus for tourists, but the project date kept getting pushed back as the powerhouse building fell into ruin. Carpenter bees bored into the ornamental eaves of the roof, and most of the first floor was blocked off as unsafe. We worked up on the third floor. Getting merchandise down to the truck required sending packing crates down two conveyor belts. The longer one outside the building didn't have any cleats so we slid them down to the bottom where someone stood waiting to catch them. A warning of "this one's super heavy" informed the person below to brace for the catch before lifting the crate and placing it in the truck. Things could have been easier, but I liked the sense of community required to get things done. It made me think of how the pioneers of Grand Canyon Village must have struggled two hundred years before.

The corporation owners, rumoured to be unnamed senators and other hobnobbers, had begun taking decisions out of local hands and shifting them to far-off penny-pinching overlords. The executives didn't know that Grand Canyon National Park was different than other federal lands. A community of people lived in the village on the rim. Many had made their homes there for twenty years or more, inheriting them from the previous residents. The locals knew the history of the area and took pride in their community, adding a certain ambiance. Times were prosperous, but the overlords announced additional cutbacks every few weeks, besmirching the name of the family company they owned. The money taken from the village went to line already-full pockets. Many longtime employees became fed up and began an exodus from the park, their wisdom replaced by a blank stare or the broken English of a foreign college student working for one summer.

The corporation also owned the employee housing and used it as a bargaining tool in hiring. Local Americans who had nowhere else to go were kind of stuck with what they got. They told me up front that I would be sharing a dorm room for the first summer, but if I stayed on until winter I had a good chance of getting into an apartment. Later, I learned they promised that to everyone but never made good. Many Americans were housed in dorms for years while foreigners on temporary visas took the community apartments.

When I first arrived, I shared a Maswik Lodge cabin with two roommates. My total living space measured forty-nine square feet. I looked around me and saw decay, a waning of spirit, and I began to feel more and more like a wage slave. I kept reminding myself that my tiny living spaces were just temporary and Grand Canyon waited less than five minutes from my door. I took to walking the rim and hiking into the depths while I waited on the ruling from a federal judge about my life experience growing up in America.

A letter arrived that set a date for a preliminary hearing that I could attend by phone. Cell service hadn't reached the village yet, but there were house phones in the dorms for employees to use. I found a landline in a wooden booth in the lobby of one of the rustic dorm buildings, and I figured that box would offer enough privacy if I kept my voice low. I prepared myself for the hearing by going over my complaint and trying to guess what questions might come up. When the time came, I squeezed myself into the booth and called up the number given to me by the court. Someone hooked me in and asked me if I could hear. Before I could answer, I heard an announcement welcoming the judge into the courtroom. The phone then seemed to drop out. The voices from the courtroom sounded muddled and the judge said that he couldn't hear me at all.

I spoke up louder and the judge complained that he could barely make out what I was saying. Fumbling sounds occurred on the line and a voice came through telling me I needed to speak up. My voice already carried out of the phone booth into the hallways of the dorm, and people in the common room were looking my way. I turned toward the corner of the booth and yelled into the receiver. "Is this gonna be loud enough?" The judge said it would have to do.

He asked me to restate my complaint in plain language, and I started to yell into the phone. I thought of how this was symbolic of the distance between the average citizen and the government, how the lines of communication were antiquated and failing, how shouting seemed to be the only way to get heard. I also wondered if the government defense lawyer had paid off a technician to mess up the phone call. The shouting could have made me sound angry, even made me feel angry, made me give up on trying to communicate. I pulled back on what I planned to say, became a man of a few choice words, and after about thirty minutes of shouting and struggling to hear, a tentative date for an in-person court session was announced. I had passed my first test, but it still felt like losing. I hung up the phone and stepped out into the hallway of the dorm, other people looked at me with a mix of consternation and puzzlement. I didn't try to explain.

In July of 2001, not long after my near-death experience in the heat on Hermit Trail, my day in court arrived. In the prior eight months, I had traded legal motions back and forth and somehow held my own against the best lawyers tax dollars can buy. For my trouble, I earned the right to travel over two hundred miles to Phoenix to face the suited bureaucrats on their turf. No attorney went with me, no sibling offered me support in person or by phone, and I told no one at work about the reason for my absence. I went alone. I took a shuttle to Flagstaff and boarded the early morning Greyhound headed for a city in the Sonoran desert named for a bird of rebirth.

Once in Phoenix I took another bus and got off downtown near the courthouse address. By design, I was arriving about two hours early—time enough to get through security, find the layout of the place and collect my thoughts before appearing. As I rounded the block on foot, I found a construction site surrounded by a fence. The empty shell of a building stood at the address given to me by the government. *Was this some government trick? They gave me the wrong address?* I bothered some construction workers who told me that the courthouse had been moved to another part of the city, and they helped me map my way to the other location. An hour and forty minutes later, after two bus transfers and worries I wouldn't make it on time, I had the ritzy Sandra Day O'Connor courthouse in my sight. I went through security and jogged up the steps to the second floor. A group of attorneys came walking down the hallway toward the same courtroom I had my eye on. One of the guys stepped over toward me and asked if I had a pleasant drive down from the northland. I lied and said yes and we entered the courtroom together.

The Department of Defense lawyer argued for dismissal on sovereignty and liability shield grounds. After he finished, I stepped up to the podium ready to deliver a heartfelt plea for openness. I planned to claim that the burden of government secrecy on my family had been too great, and it only served to allow other people to live their lives in ignorance of the generational effects of war. I stood at the podium waiting for acknowledgement to proceed with my argument, realizing that the judge's bench was thirty feet away and an armed guard filled the space. I wondered how fast the guard could draw and if one of his ancestors had ever fired on an Irishman with a maniacal look in his eye rushing across the great divide between citizen and magistrate. The space seemed symbolic of the distance between the ordinary man and those who worked in shiny white buildings—between families that made sacrifices in war and families that lived on hand-me-down fortunes. I waited until the judge glanced up and saw me at the podium. A look of annoyance crossed his face.

"Why are you standing there?"

"I'm ready to give my response to the motion," I said.

He sighed. "You have thirty days to respond and I prefer it be in writing."

Not wanting to defy the judge, I gathered my papers and stepped away from the podium. I didn't get my Gerry Spence courtroom moment, and I left feeling like I had just played one of those games of kick the can from my childhood. I realized no ruling was coming that day or any time soon. We were never going to be arguing what mattered, and I was never going to see my childhood medical records. The fourteenth case filed against the U.S. Department of Defense for military abuses would end like all the others—with no secrets revealed. As I left the courthouse I began to see the foolishness of my idealistic notions. Haughty lawyers with a bottomless taxpayer-funded trust account could play kick the can forever and manipulate the rules however they wanted. I congratulated myself for making the stand and decided on the ride home that I would write a final argument and be done with the case. I would leave it up to the judge to award me some money so I could pay back my student loan held by a Department of Defense credit union. I wanted to move on and rebuild my life.

In answer to the defense motion, as my last statement of fact to the court, I wrote, "I don't think my father sacrificed his blood against tyranny in World War Two so that privileged-class lawyers could construct statutory schemes that keep secret the military exploitation of his child."

On the nineteenth of August 2001, I set out on a day hike along the rim of Grand Canyon. I left from Yaki Point east of the village, the opposite direction of the Hermit area, and headed toward Shoshone Point. Monsoon clouds were building off in the distance, but I dismissed the idea that a bad storm was looming. As I approached a rock ledge where I often sat to write, thunder rumbled and drops began to fall.

Not knowing what to do, I headed down below the rim and stepped into a narrow alcove under a huge rock.

The previous two weeks had been full of emotional turmoil. Three days earlier, I submitted the final argument for judgment in my legal case against the government. Before that, I attended a 'pitchfest' in Hollywood only to realize that a career as a screenwriter had passed me by. As I walked the rim, I felt lost in another personal obsession for some unattainable woman musician I had just seen at a gig in Flagstaff. Many things were stirring in me. The negatives were high, and I was thinking of my mortality.

The storm set in over the side canyon next to me. Lightning hit and thundered five seconds away. I kept dry with my back pressed up against the rock that covered me. I didn't know that an alcove was a stupid place to be in a canyon thunderstorm. The lightning came closer . . . thunder followed, two seconds . . . one second . . . BOOM! A blast struck two hundred feet away. I hid under the rock as the wind blew rain on me.

I became aware of asking the Great Spirit that I not be struck. I decided that if my hair stood on end I would jump out of the alcove and grab onto a tree below me. I felt like running out of there, getting away from the Canyon, but I didn't want to give up my little spot of shelter against the storm. I heard an electrical crackle followed by lightning about one hundred feet to my right and another strange crackle as lightning thundered down and struck below me. A third crackle sparked close above me. BOOM! Lightning struck the rock I leaned against. Electricity tingled in my back and shot down my legs, pushing me toward the ground. I crouched away from the rock and grabbed hold of my sandals in deference to the power of the storm, feeling grateful that my feet weren't melting into the ground. The wind blew harder and cold hail pellets whipped at me for about ten minutes, but the lightning moved off. After the storm, I crawled out of the alcove. Looking under my shirt, I found a welt on my back where the electricity had burned me.

Some twenty-three years earlier, a different kind of lightning struck me. I met a young woman who became my first lover. She saw me through the storms of my troubled times. When we were seventeen, she asked about my scars and learned there were places not to tread and questions not to ask. Still, she cared and tried to understand.

Like all friends and loves, Thérèse began as a reflection of my aspirations and through time became a reflection of my better self. While she looked back with fondness on our years together, I could not. She tried to build a sustainable shelter for the both of us, but I was never comfortable with that. I backed away. I took that reflection of her with me and held it up against other women, distant and impossible women, seeking to recreate the familiarity I once knew but had let go of—seeking a reflection of who I might become rather than who I am. There on the Canyon rim with lightning striking all around me— twenty-three years after I met her, ten years after our last breakup and months after our last contact—I thought of the last words she wrote to me. "I am watching you on this journey. May you continue toward the sun."

Out there under a rock on the edge of the Canyon, I didn't know that Thérèse had died three days earlier from a rare disease. Upon hearing of her death a few days after the storm, I walked out to a ledge near El Tovar in Grand Canyon Village to write a eulogy card for her family. A flock of birds gathered all around me.

For Thérèse . . .

Through a time when I was troubled and not understanding of myself, she gave me care and understanding. I am sure that support blossomed in me in ways I don't fully appreciate. I was glad to see she had a daughter and continued to pursue her dreams — things which proved impossible to capture with me as I went through my troubled times.

In our last contact she wished me peace and said "I am watching you on this journey . . . may you continue toward the sun." I feel she is watching me still and that her strength, caring and understanding lives on.

*And as I write this on the Canyon rim four days
before what would have been her 38th birthday, a flock
of dark-winged blue birds has gathered all around me.
They jump from rock to tree and soar down and back up
on the canyon updrafts, calling out to each other with
fun. In the small tree above me, not knowing or caring
I am so close, these Pinyon Jays call out over Bright
Angel Canyon — mere voices from the wilderness that I
cannot understand.*

I like to think that Thérèse visited me that day as I wrote about her, saying a goodbye carried by a flock of birds, and that she also saw me through that lightning storm on the edge of the Canyon three days after her death.

On September 11, 2001, I was working at the distro center. I went next door to get something and heard the news on television. When I returned and told my coworkers we were under attack, no one believed me till they turned on the radio. I thought at first that it was domestic terrorists. To me—perhaps because of my state of disempowerment—the attacks seemed to symbolize something very basic and archetypal. The World Trade Centers were *ivory towers* and the message to the government was that they had forgotten about working-class Americans. When I found out the truth, I wondered about the sophistication of the terrorists. *Did they know that such a split exists in America? Were they trying to exploit it?* The luckiest thing on that day is that the Trade Centers were not true ivory towers and working-class firefighters came to the rescue. If it were not for that—if only the rich who take advantage of the poor were in those buildings, or special interest lobbyists—the feelings after that attack would have been much different.

I thought about the letter I had sent to the U.S. Attorney's Office with the words *the next time someone blows up a federal building, I hope you will remember your actions here.* Would there be any reconciliation after 9-11? Would there be any kind of apology from the government for coming after me and missing the real terrorists? Fall edged toward winter and no word came on the fate of my case. As the cold weather closed in on the South Rim, I took a position as lead sales associate at a gift shop. The job included a small bump in pay and an elevation in housing status. Without other employment prospects, I thought that by the end of winter I could get better housing and make a long-term go of life at Grand Canyon. I became satisfied with writing in journals for myself, and I learned to have fun fitting into the strange world perched on the edge of the nothingness.

My job involved counting the daily take while overseeing a few employees, and I began noticing some odd corporate practices. We carried a lot of foreign-made products such as cheap leather change purses and shoulder bags from Mexico with "Grand Canyon" burned into them. They didn't sell well, but every few months the price would go up ten cents, twenty cents or even half a dollar. I wondered about that. We had thousands in inventory and every one of them would get retagged. A few weeks or months later they got retagged again. I figured that changing the price shifted the bottom line so the company could say their assets were greater, but they were still the same unsellable items.

We also sold rocks. A sign said that picking up rocks from the national park was illegal and that these were collected from private land. I noticed some of them had stickers on the bottom that said "made in Afghanistan." After September eleventh, the store filled up with American flags and t-shirts. We were selling patriotism while placing price tags over the "made in Afghanistan" stickers. I always thought of asking people who came up to my cash register with their Old Glory t-shirt and a flag on a stick, *Would you like a rock from Afghanistan with that?*

One day I was working alone on a slow winter morning. An unassuming man came into the gift shop and when he saw my name tag he did a double take. He asked if I was the one who wrote "the letter." I didn't know what he was talking about until I remembered I had written a letter to upper management after September eleventh. The corporation had used the attacks as an excuse to freeze the wages of employees in the park, citing the potential downturn in tourism. Fed up, I wrote a letter to management saying that the salaries of the top-earning executives in the company should also be affected. A few weeks later, there were some firings of top management people working in Grand Canyon Village, but all that seemed to accomplish was to further deplete the level of connection between regular workers and the far-off overlords. Soon after that the corporation announced that they were changing their name effective April Fools' Day. The made-up name and logo got painted onto the side of every company truck, but the wage freeze was still in effect. I never heard mention of my letter again until this man walked into the gift shop where I worked my meagre job. So I smiled at him and acknowledged that I did send that letter. He said he was pleased to meet me and that I was lucky to still have my job. He knew the people who ran the place and he was surprised I had not been fired for speaking out. He winked at me, and I wondered if this was finally a response from upper management to my private letter.

With winter winding down, I had risen to number three on the apartment waiting list. I talked to the apartment manager and was told with a wry smile that the rules had changed again. Seasonal hires with status and foreign students on summer work visas would be arriving shortly, and I wouldn't get another shot at an apartment until next winter. I never got the call and my name started moving back down the list. Not willing to go through another summer like the previous one, I decided to leave Grand Canyon Village before someone arrived to share my seventy-square-foot living space.

With hints of spring in the air, I got word on my legal case against the Department of Defense. I opened the envelop to see that the decision had been written on February 19, 2002. In filing my complaint, I had let the judge know that the day of my awakening to the realization of having been a survivor of holy war abuse was February 19, 1992. By signing his final judgment on the same day ten years later, I surmised the judge was telling me that truth takes time—there was some merit to my complaint, but he was bound by law to dismiss the defendant even though he believed my story. I didn't get any money to make my life right, and I still had to repay my student loan.

I had battled the terrorist-making apparatus and won my soul. In the court case we never talked about anything real. The government lawyers threw legalese garbage in my path, hoping to obscure truth, kicking the can down the road again, but their maneuvering allowed me to see all the truth I needed. All paths to nonviolent revolution had been bottled up again in America and that left one way to speak to government, a way that I would never follow. Getting my story out of darkness into the light of public record would have to serve as my only victory. My student loan was now accruing about seven hundred dollars a month in interest, and my whole future would be lost if I didn't find some means to increase my income. As spring set in, I headed back to Flagstaff, found a job as a driver and tour guide, and once again looked to the ever-increasing long shot of selling a book or script as my only way toward a better life.

On a crisp morning in May 2002, I stepped out the front door of my trailer village room with a backpack on and walked toward the Canyon. My plan was to hike rim to rim the hard way, south to north, and continue on to Cape Royal. With no campsites available below the rim, I needed to complete the whole twenty-plus miles of a forty-six-hundred-foot descent and fifty-six-hundred-foot climb in one day. I had thoughts of a victory over the elements, but I once again learned that Grand Canyon can't be conquered, only experienced.

The descent down the South Kaibab Trail proved easy. I made the familiar seven-mile hike to Phantom Ranch in time for a nine o'clock breakfast, and I started my ascent. The long trek up the North Kaibab Trail took its toll. Rest stops at Ribbon Falls and Cottonwood camp helped to rejuvenate me, but the hard part lay ahead. Just below the Supai tunnel, I hit a crisis of body and will. It was six o'clock in the evening, and I had less than two miles left to go.

I lay on a rock yelling to the Canyon spirits to *give me a break*. After a few minutes my will returned, but I moved on slower than before. My energy waned as darkness set in. White rocks loomed above me, glowing like ghosts in the shadowy twilight beneath an almost full moon. Around each corner I looked ahead, hoping the top would come into view. Feeling loopy, I cried out, *Are new layers of rock being added?* I waited for a reply. *No response is good. It's only craziness if the rocks talk back.* At eight twenty I reached the trailhead, gave a weak yell no one heard and held my hiking stick over my head in triumph—living a moment of personal victory. I felt I had connected distant parts of my psyche by hiking Grand Canyon from rim to rim.

The next day while resting at the North Rim, I wrote about my hike in my journal.

> In life too the 'going up,' the rebounding, is the hard part. Retreating was easy, but my frustration followed me. It's been a good year here at Grand Canyon, I found my spiritual center. I know who I am and I'm ready to emerge from the shadows with my story. I've done the hard work. I've lived through the crisis, now I must bring it home. All other options are closed to me.

After another night of rest, I continued my journey toward Cape Royal overlook about twenty miles away. The trail was flat, and drought had left the forest dry. It seemed a warm thought could start a wildfire. In heading toward the point, I cut too far to the west and ended up on the wrong mesa. I started to backtrack as the sun hit the horizon. I had half a quart of water left when I stopped for the night and set up my tent next to a fallen tree in the middle of nowhere about two miles from where I wanted to be. Lying there alone, feeling silly after my long journey, I started laughing as I talked to the dead log.

I told that dead wood that I had stepped out of my tiny room on the South Rim two days earlier and started walking. Now forty miles later, my whole hike seemed improbable and ridiculous. I laughed with the ghost of some tree once living and now worthless like me. We knew I was never supposed to get this far, never supposed to fathom what had happened to me as a child. Yes, I admit it—there on Cape Royal next to a fallen tree, I went a little crazy and laughed with Canyon spirits and dead wood at the ridiculousness of it all, about my foolish walk and my unbelievable journey in life too. Though my prospects to pursue happiness were meagre and probably always would be, in that moment I knew that I had won on everything that mattered. If no one but me and some dead log in the woods ever knew that, at least we could have a chuckle out where civilization couldn't reach us.

I laughed too because I understood the true depth of my victory. Everything was in place so that I might become a terrorist, yet I saw all those patterns clearly. Six months to the day after being struck by lightning on the Canyon rim, the court had dismissed my case saying it was *not in the interests of justice* to pursue it further. I was free. I had faced down government lawyers who chose to play a role in creating a terrorist rather than in seeking truth and justice for an American citizen. Thérèse, one of the few people I had formed a bond with as a young adult, had died a sudden and unfair death, and I was cut off from most prospects to build a future for myself. And of course there was the chasm within, the depths of chaos, despair and rage swirling around the lost experiences of my past. Despite all of that—because of the walking I did at Grand Canyon in those first years of a new millennium—I believed a brighter future was possible.

The Hermit area of Grand Canyon is still connected to those struggles of the past. I go back sometimes but not out of any compulsion to conjure the ghost of the hermit or reclaim parts of myself. I like to take a simple walk around Hermits Rest, visiting the historic building or making my way down to the always elusive bench of Mary Colter. I've taken day hikes to the Santa Maria Shade House, dropped in at Dripping Springs and found reclusive spots for some alone time overlooking the Canyon. I have no need to push it there anymore or to add another layer of aggravation to my thunderbird walking experiences. I'd much rather take a simpler trail without a pack, like hiking up to Thunder River Falls from a raft trip on the Colorado. These days I prefer a gentler Grand Canyon experience than what the hermit has to offer.

Looking back on this time in my life, I think of the four manifestations of birds from my shamanic vision in North Carolina. The great raptor that swooped down and left an imprint in my mind was symbolic of my childhood conditioning and the fear instilled by the government. The thunderbird dancers symbolized the meeting of ancient and modern taking place on the Colorado Plateau, that ongoing rejuvenation of native spirit that I played a small role in. The ravens eating bugs off my feet represented the grounding I found by walking the Canyon. And I equate the nest in the cliffs to lessons learned on my Boucher hike . . . success was coming but it had been delayed. I was living an improbable, fragile life, and I needed to become comfortable with the precarious dynamics of my experience.

And what of the fifth and final egg? *The unexpected and unwanted one.* It was the turn my life took after leaving Grand Canyon. The once simple highway to a better life in America was crumbling beneath my feet like some forgotten bridge. There seemed no way to capitalize on the sweat of my efforts. I continued to believe in a brighter future, and I thought that the road would get easier, but all my efforts amounted to nothing more than arriving at a different vista from which to look into the depths of *the chasm within.*

PreAmble to The Chasm Within

If you go to Grand Canyon, you begin to understand
life. Looking out over the edge for the first time
you might yell "No way!" out loud. You could spend
a lifetime walking and only tread upon a small
part of what you can see from the rim. Despite
how big it seems, the true wonder of Grand Canyon
is nothingness. The jagged edges of rocks are so
impressive as they rise out of the depths that the
formations are named for ancient gods, and the cliff
walls of the opposing rim beckon like a prelude
to some utopian dream hiding in the lands above.
The passage of time has left a deep scar and out
of that nothingness rises the earth that hasn't yet
weathered away.

No one knows for sure how Grand Canyon came to
be. If you believe the theories, water carved through
rock and over time the scar in the plateau grew wider
and deeper. Eventually it became an awe-inspiring
site. Words cannot do it justice. To understand Grand
Canyon you must go there and experience it. You need
to hike the trails, touch the sun-baked rocks and
relax at pristine waterfalls. I did that for the first
time in 1986 at the age of twenty-two, and after I
left, the great chasm became connected to scars inside
of me -- a bond formed between my inner and outer
worlds. The Canyon beckoned me to come back and
explore, to make sense of its wonder. And there alone
on dusty trails I came to appreciate my improbable
journey in life.

In my younger days I was lost in utter chaos. I
hid it fairly well, but at times I felt overwhelmed
with bottomless emotions and flooded with intrusive
images and dark thoughts. I believed that the
hollowness I felt inside me was the way that life
is -- as my conservative catholic father often said.

I thought I saw signs of the armageddon war from the bible unfolding before my eyes. I imagined that one day I would lead a band of post-apocalyptic survivors through the mountains to some paradise of a place where a great society would be built.

These dark thoughts and ideas stayed with me into adulthood, but I pushed them into the depths of my subconscious. There they lay hidden in a restless sleep, occasionally stirring to sabotage my life. Then I came to know Grand Canyon and something inside me changed. I started to connect with a sense of mystery and wonder about life -- things I once knew and had lost. A great battle erupted inside me as I began this journey of conscious evolution. Secrets from my childhood, generational memories, even the greater secrets of humanity, were poking through the shadows and illusions of accepted consciousness. In the beginning it was a ridiculous thing to believe, but I followed the path. Over time I emerged from the chaos. The whole of my life started making sense.

I'm not saying I'm more enlightened than you, and I don't want to be your guru. If Grand Canyon is mostly nothing then the difference between you and me is that I have a little more nothing to my past than you do. Imagine that the government, in the name of reducing awe and disbelief, decides that changes to Grand Canyon are needed. So they place explosives around Cheops Pyramid, the Zoroaster Temple and against the rocks atop Isis Temple and blow those natural monuments to bits. Appalling? Certainly, but what if it were done in secret before the exploration of the Canyon? Geologists might puzzle over those extra piles of rocks and explain them as natural. They might say that the formations were weak and their flaws caused their collapse. But those piles of rubble would still betray some truth, hinting at what used to be, telling us that a little more nothing only amplifies the echoes of the whole.

What is the worth of a place like Grand Canyon? What purpose does my life have? I've asked myself those questions often while hiking over five hundred miles solo in the depths of the Earth. Would I have come to understand my life journey if the government's plans to dam and flood Grand Canyon in the 1970s had succeeded? Finding the Canyon beneath man-made reservoirs would have angered me, left me lost and defeated in the struggle to understand the forces that shaped my life -- and maybe turned me into a damned soul spreading chaos and terror.

So does my journey hold some greater meaning? Perhaps my words are simply a message to my former self saying I've made it through. This is the story of one pathway walked in the age of terror. The question is, what does it take to change one destiny?

5. THE CHASM WITHIN

I remember one ordinary day in my youth when I found a twenty-dollar bill blowing across the sand dunes of the Outer Banks in North Carolina. I don't recall how I came to be there, and like all my memories I picture myself not as a child but as I am now. At that young age, twenty dollars was a big deal to me. I showed it to my parents and they said I could keep it. When I got home I bought a record player, and with each song played I remembered that fortunate day on the dunes. It stood as a pillar in my young mind.

Even under the best of circumstances, childhood memory can be a tricky thing. Mine became further compromised because of the tactics used against me. In a sense, mole doctors placed explosives around the secret pillars of the chasm within me, blew them up and disguised the entrance to that void as insanity. I used to worry about the logistics. I wanted to prove that the shattered pieces were not my natural state, that they once fit together into an impressive whole. I wanted to show how I got from here to there and back again, but I decided it didn't matter. The remnants of my past still tell the story. The rocks of the exploded pillars claw their jagged edges against the nothingness, and that rubble holds more truth about my childhood than any standing pillar possibly could.

In truth, all of us have holes within us, voids that hide away the excessive emotional pain of our lives. We are drawn into these dark places in our being because we know that exploring them is the process by which we fill them with light and make them disappear. Maybe they are secrets from our own lives, or generational memories from the wars of our parents, or the struggles of our ancestral families. For me, the chasm within touched on secrets that people in power wanted to disguise as delusion. As a young man I bought into that disguise, but as I explored that inner void I came to know the lies and I began to fill my darkness with the light of truth.

My journey stepped on the toes of people in power wanting to maintain their status quo, and they tried to use the state-run psychiatric system to convince me that I was delusional. Under tyranny I may have succumbed, but freedom allowed me the means to rule out delusional illness and escape the clutches of corrupted officials. I found a few brave souls in the private sector who were willing to help me explore the chasm within and reclaim the lost parts of myself. Were it not for them, I imagine the holes in my being may have been filled by the demons of terror running loose in the world, but I caught those demons in writing and they lost their power over me. Over forty-seven years on this Earth, I climbed out of the chasm within.

Back in those dark days of 1993 before I understood the depths of my past, I started hypnotherapy to diffuse the visions of cliff jumping at Apple Orchard Falls. When I first shined a light into that chasm within, the turmoil was great and the overwhelm pushed my mind to its limits. It was like taking an overflight looking for a safe way down into the depths. I kept picturing a pristine white room somehow associated with the government. I called it the white isolation box and *they* were trying to break me. I decided to enter the box under hypnosis.

I'm in a small square room in the middle of nowhere, surrounded by wilderness. It's like a prison cell. There's a green cot, and the walls are very white and clean. I am the only blemish upon the place. It seems there's a loudspeaker there, but I can't recall anything that I might have heard from it. It seems people are watching me, but I can't remember anyone having ever come to the door. Still, I'm scared. I worry about what would happen if they found the place messed up. There's a strange undercurrent of other thoughts and emotions, things that aren't allowed in this room, things distant from me that defile my soul and can't enter my mind because I'm in this pristine white room.

A voice suggests that at some point I must have left this room, and getting out comes to mind.

I wake up on the cot and the door is open. The bright white light outside shines into the room. I had pictured the building a number of places — on a battlefield where a war raged at night, in a green pasture with tall grass to frolic in, in a wooded area far from civilization — but I now see it is surrounded by fallen trees. The sky is incredibly bright, and the terrain is soaked by white light. In every direction I see downed trees that are as straight as poles and stripped of their leaves and limbs. I recognize the pattern of the fallen trees. It's the same as the downed trees in Siberia, Russia, from the unexplained explosion of 1908. Some say that explosion was a meteor, but others say it was some kind of nuclear test. The trees outside the white isolation box match those trees in Siberia. I know it means a nuclear explosion has happened here and that the time is after Armageddon.

I sense my location somehow. I'm in the Blue Ridge Mountains of southern Virginia. Home is to the northeast and I start in that direction, climbing over the downed trees. I know by now that this place isn't real, but I don't know why it's in my mind pretending to be a memory. I soon reach the edge of the blast zone. On one of the first upright trees I come to is the body of a lynched black man, a slave who tried to escape. His face is bruised and his lips are bloated. His clothes appear blackened by oil or grime. Flies buzz around his face. I notice someone is there with me. It seems to be the mole doctor. I am very scared at first, but he puts his arm around me and we look at the body — now seemingly my body — together.

I'm back in the white isolation box and it's a mess. I worry someone will come in and punish me. The undercurrent of thoughts, emotions and images not allowed in this room start to intrude into my mind. I am scared beyond reason and the white light grows brighter trying to block it all out. I feel nauseous and sick.

Sounds come over the speaker. They seem distant and unreal but are also loud and nerve-racking. They are the sounds from another place. It seems to be a dark medieval room where people are being tortured. The sounds get in my mind. The white light grows brighter and a new sound blocks out the other. It's "bird head screech," a vibration in my head like a stuck electric saw. It's too much.

How do I get out of here?

I wake up in the isolation box again. The door is open. I leave, hoping I can get away and find my way home. I wander over rolling green hills, hopelessly lost in the mountains.

I realized that the white isolation box served as a phantasm of the medical room where mole doctors destroyed my memory. As I closed in on hints of the real thoughts and emotions from childhood experiences, they were replaced by a white light and electrical screech vibrating in my head. Clues to my lost past were strewn about the vision like stones near the edge of a cliff, and the landscape in my mind resided near the cliffs of Apple Orchard Falls below Sunset Field on the Blue Ridge Parkway. I figured there was more to explore in that area. I went deeper under hypnosis and found myself headed for emergency surgery at a small medical complex. As I was being wheeled down a hallway, I heard the name of the place over a loud speaker—Darlington—but as an adult I couldn't remember any place called that. I looked on maps and soon found two towns named Darlington, one in Maryland not far from the Aberdeen Proving Grounds and one in South Carolina within flying distance of Fort Bragg Military Reservation. Both could have had medical complexes that treated military accidents back in those days.

More *frozen-moment* images showed up in my thoughts and nightmares, static memories of things that seemed somehow familiar but I couldn't place them. After the white isolation box vision, those frozen moments started to expand, and I began to have detailed dreams about military training scenarios. I remembered army barracks where a bunch of young guys stayed. The lay of the land outside and in some of my other frozen-moment memories looked the same, sand with red clay. For some reason, I associated that land with Fort Bragg Military Reservation in North Carolina, but I had no recollection of ever being there as a child.

There seemed to be no way to get at it all. Lost moments and emotions were jumbled and twisted around each other, and they were also tangled up with images and memories that I knew to be false or symbolic. It felt like a great river had been dammed inside me, and trying to make sense of any of it threatened to destroy the dam and sweep me away. But I realized that the same sense of impossibility can be found standing on the rim of Grand Canyon. The journey begins with a step and the memory lives inside you forever. I saw two ways down into the chasm within me—two places in my frozen moments existed in the real world. The first place was Apple Orchard Falls off the Blue Ridge Parkway in Virginia, wilderness in the middle of nowhere or so it seemed. The second was Fort Bragg Military Reservation, not much more than a name that stuck in my head whenever I heard it.

Two pillars from the chasm within called out to me, each with their own story to tell.

In 1994 I went on a solo road trip to those two places. I thought I might find nothing and prove myself a fool. Even if I found something, I had no one to share it with, no support system to claim the wreckage if my re-emerging past overwhelmed me. I set out to visit my childhood friend Jerrold who lived in North Carolina, and from there I planned to head toward Fort Bragg to face the depths of the chasm within. Alone.

Fort Bragg Military Reservation consists of about one hundred forty-nine thousand acres of land near Fayetteville, North Carolina. Known as the 'Home of Special Forces' and host to a psychological warfare center, it includes areas for live munitions training and surface weapons testing— things my father worked on as a defense researcher for the government. At the time I drove through, there were remote two-lane highways on parts of the reservation lands. From the road there didn't appear to be much of anything out there, but I saw sand with red clay—land that stirred up frozen memories from the chasm within.

Stopping at my friend's house on the way proved fruitless. Jerrold had taken off for a Woodstock anniversary music festival in upstate New York. Leaving Chapel Hill, I drove on through the night and arrived near the Fort Bragg area in the dawn twilight. I picked a road off a map and started driving through the reservation lands at the break of day. I expected there to be a gate or fence blocking my access or military police cruising the area, but I found an open, desolate highway in the middle of nowhere.

As I drove through the red clay terrain that haunted my visions, feelings and ideas flooded into me and an incredible sense of déjà vu overtook me. I wanted to believe that I was picking up traces of other people's experiences or that I was reliving generational memories from my father. As a boy I had watched my father struggle with post-traumatic stress, both the dark feelings and the belief that he had fought in a holy war and conquered evil incarnate. I tried to convince myself that remnants of my dad's war training had been born inside me and I was somehow following them. It didn't make sense that these images and feelings were mine, but the deeper I went into the military reservation lands, the more the haunting notions that flooded into my mind felt like my own. I lost myself in the chaos of remembrance, and one moment associated with Fort Bragg seemed to connect my ordinary memory with distant dramas dammed behind trauma.

There's a branch in the woods that swings back and bushwhacks me. I fall on the ground in great pain and see the branch above me against a bright white sky. It feels as though the skin of my back has been peeled off and I am lying on rough cement. I cannot move. I feel like I'm melting into the ground, bleeding out. I tell myself it's not that bad.

Soon I am yanked off my feet and pulled out of the woods . . . I'm walking toward a reddish dirt road. I am dazed, in concussive shock from some kind of explosion. It seems I got caught in a stinging mist of sand or blood.

This ties in with an ordinary memory from my late teens and early twenties. I used to get boils on my back, and Thérèse helped me drain them. Strange and gross I know, but the boils began to heal after small particles of what appeared to be sand emerged to the surface of my skin. We puzzled over the particles, thinking they were something organic produced by my body, thinking they were from another plane of existence — we joked that the boils contained some kind of ectoplasm left after demons tried to enter this world through me but got reduced to grains of sand. Foolishness of course, but in the face of the frozen-moment memories about the sand on the ground at the military reservation, I considered a different possibility.

Was there an explosion that embedded grains of sand in my back sometime in my childhood?

After leaving Fort Bragg, I caught up with Jerrold and spent a week at his house in Chapel Hill. I didn't tell him what I was up to in the military lands. Jerrold had been my friend since our high school days so he could fathom the inner demons I wrestled with, but we never spoke of that. Our times hanging out in nature and going to music festivals were a sanctuary for me—my new paradigm—a haven from the cruel holy war world of my upbringing. I'm sure he could have followed me down some strange roads, except that I didn't want to burden him with my heavy and confusing past as we chased bliss together. Bringing my darkness into the mixture of our friendship would ruin the place reserved for laughs and light times, so I kept quiet about it.

After catching up on nonesuchness, I left Jerrold's house and headed north on Route 501 toward the Blue Ridge Parkway. As I closed in on the mountains past Lynchburg, night set in and the remnants of memories sparked on the military reservation came back fresh in my mind. I was on the trail of my lost past again, and my awareness heightened as I drove up the winding switchbacks. With no moon in the sky, the forest teemed with life force and the air felt a touch cooler than comfortable. My senses reached out ahead of me for the crest of the Blue Ridge and the Apple Orchard Falls area in the distance. I remembered those visions of suicide I had quieted only months before as the pull of something ahead connected to the chasm within got stronger. When I followed a switchback on the road, I sensed the place off to the side. When the road straightened, the presence pulled from in front of me again. I followed, and the feeling kept getting stronger as I got closer.

I had taken this route because it went near the Sunset Field pullout at mile seventy-eight of the Blue Ridge Parkway. I figured when I got up to the ridgeline the pull would be southward, down toward that area to confront those visions of suicide. I didn't plan to make the thirteen-mile drive to the Sunset Field pullout and go trekking down the trail at Apple Orchard Falls in the dark of night. I figured to get a hotel room nearby and come back the next day, but as Route 501 passed by the Blue Ridge Parkway the pull on my psyche didn't come from the south—it stayed with the James River. I continued on, following the road along the waterway, heading toward some unknown place somehow connected to the chasm within.

The drive brought back spooky feelings from an earlier part of my life, recollections of autumn nights winding along creeks on familiar backroads not far from the Maryland homestead of my youth. I thought of All Hallows' Eve and the haunted woods that the owners of a nearby orchard set up. It seemed that each mile brought me closer to unraveling some lifelong mystery and that my whole reason for being would become clear if I continued following this feeling into the night.

The road took me north along a tributary called the Maury River. I passed through the town of Buena Vista and turned onto a side road numbered 6886 that somehow felt right. There was a radio tower in the distance and I kept on in that direction, following the pull on my psyche. The river split in two, and I took a road following the smaller stream. I felt I was right on top of something from my past. My heart raced and the presence seemed to be all around me, but part of me whispered that I had only followed my overactive imagination.

I got chills driving that road and I felt a call to go back and drive it again. I circled around, calming my racing heart, and headed back up the road a second time, wondering why this place had such an effect on me. I noticed the radio tower off in the distance to the right, but the pull on my psyche came from over to my left. There were several short drives that seemed to dead end at a threshold of tall and dark trees. I went down one of the drives and at the boundary I saw a sign that read "State Property No Trespassing." I parked and walked along the edge of the forest, listening to the sounds of the night creatures. Dark paths led back into the woods and there was no fence blocking my way. I thought of walking down one of the paths, if for no other reason than to prove to myself it was foolish to believe I had found a place straight out of my own past or connected to the generational memories of my father. I told myself that there was no lost military complex or secret training land hidden back there, only spooky woods filled with the sounds of the night.

Along the boundary, I came to a wooden bridge over a creek that flowed into the larger stream. I stepped up on it and stopped in the middle, looking toward the dark wilderness. Images of a possible past in that area toyed with me, tempting me to go deeper into the unknown. Visions of secret buildings, now abandoned, flashed in my mind. I stood on the wooden bridge and contemplated crossing into the foreboding wilderness that seemed connected to my past, but the same intuition that had guided me there warned me to go no farther.

Driving away, I still felt the pull on my psyche. It seemed to beckon me not to leave. It wanted to claim me, engulf me in its mystery. I drove on, wanting to be off the narrow backroad and away from the area. One more thing lured me toward it—a gravel lot along the river that I hadn't noticed the other two times I drove the road. I pulled in and stopped beneath a sign. The words toyed with me, seeming to hint at more than the simple message. "No Trespassing. This project built by the Virginia Game Department in cooperation with the Dominion Military Institute Foundation." I felt a sinking feeling as I read that sign. It felt like part of a great vastness I couldn't quite grasp. I knew I needed to escape the area before all my dark visions became too real. I took off into the night and made a beeline for the nearest interstate highway.

I drove with purpose, running from my past as I had many times before, but in my psyche it was too late for escape. I couldn't deny all that I connected with in that moment beneath the no trespassing sign. I felt the area behind me, pulling still, and it seemed I felt the lure of many other places out of my secret past. I didn't want to believe. I didn't want to feel.

I was trying to rebury it all, to tear down the lines of thinking and memory that had led me to reconnect with a lost part of my being. I wanted to go back into the patterns of denial I had learned from my father—to relive the mystery on some unknowing level, riding the waves of a forgotten history but not making sense of it. In that moment beneath the sign, I felt the power that a desire to reconnect had, and still I wanted to go back into the hand-me-down patterns of broken thoughts and lostness. And I was back. Driving up Interstate 81, I was escaping. I felt it all receding into the distance behind me. I was only half aware of the road, half alive as I had been through most of my life, until the roar of a passing eighteen-wheeler startled me and another wave of *knowing* hit.

I still wonder what lies beyond that bridge near those lands not far from Dominion Military Institute and the Maury River. I have been back in the light of day, and it no longer feels ominous like it did that night so long ago. I found a path through the woods past a cornfield and a farm. Perhaps nothing more sinister lies beyond that, just natural wilderness and state game lands, a place where you might be mistaken for wildlife and shot. I've been back to hike the trail from the Sunset Field pullout on the Blue Ridge Parkway to Apple Orchard Falls. I've sat beneath the cliffs where the visions of my flight to suicide occurred in my dream world, and I've beat on a shamanic drum on the wooden walk below the falls. I think of that night along the Maury River as a metaphor for all the mysteries of life and remembrance. The military intrigue from my childhood could have occurred anywhere—or nowhere—maybe it was a scattered remnant of my father's life, a pile of rubble that was once a pillar. But on that night, all the lost hopes and nightmares of forgotten holy warriors dwelled beyond that dark bridge near an unnamed tributary of Maury River, beckoning me to feel for them and free them.

I like to think that by exploring the chasm within I came to know how indigenous people—the original peoples of the earth—once experienced the world. Not as a classified collection of separate parts but as a living whole. On that night near the Maury River all the trappings I had clung to so deeply, those patterns of broken thoughts I had used to deny my troubles and disbelieve my life, fell away for a moment and the world expanded to its true size. I had been pounded into a form not my own, conditioned to think in limited ways, programmed with the rage of a holy warrior and taught to live a compartmentalized, classified life. Beneath that boundary sign it was like I had a sense of everything all at once—a moment of oneness with the universe—and the limitlessness I felt scared me more than anything.

There is an ancient side to each of us, a second self that contains our animal instincts and knows a wholistic way of seeing the universe. It's not much talked about and often receives no nurturing except punishment. As a child that part of me was cut off by the holy war conditioning and abandoned. When I began to seek answers, my ancient side caught up to me. I felt not only my desire for rejuvenation and integration but also a longing for a deeper understanding of life and mystery. I found ghosts and I ran, and still I run, hoping now that the peaceful primitive feeling will catch me and toy with me before letting me up to run some more . . . to feel the call of the ages, to be a bird of prey learning to fly.

For me, the chasm within holds worth. It contains the remnants of the sense of mystery lost by humanity in our classified world. My mind may not be able to reconstruct it, but my spirit knows what I went through and who I am supposed to be. The war within over my childhood experiences ended, but life's journey begins anew each day.

Except I'm a liar—the chasm within can't be escaped. It can be rationalized and hidden away from view in a multilevel home where the darkest place is the downstairs den, but in those days I was a vagabond not ready to settle. After those road trips to the lands of my past, the ripples of mystery that washed over me became part of a flood that threatened to drown me.

My strange night near the Maury River left me reliving some hazy frozen memories that I called the mind-game stuff. Whether remnants of myself, my father or some lost soul, one haunt became clearer. I envisioned 'ledge dancing' on a building made of black glass hidden somewhere on those state game lands. It didn't feel like part or me, but I knew what the pressure of holding something down inside felt like, and I knew not releasing whatever came knocking might mean a deepening feeling of being haunted. So I gave into shadows of the past, listened to the whispers of truth from beyond a smoky veil, and I realized these were fragments of memories perhaps best described as experiments in psycho-terror.

Over the next four years, I captured the illusory figments in writing and called them 'Voices from the Void.' I knew that my imaginings were not messages from some god or spirit and they weren't true memories—they were notions that held some spectre of truth to my own feelings about the lost experiences of my holy war upbringing.

Scribbling down the words while hiking in a hole in the ground or walking a forlorn mountain trail, with the idea of making the words all neat and clean later, diffused the energy beyond the veil. It felt like foolishness to try to express the whisperings of ghosts or to speak of the spectres of generational memories anywhere else. I saw myself as a peacenik writer—not a spooky, former brain-child—and these remnants only surfaced when I walked alone.

So I captured the 'Voices from the Void' in writing and hid them away, revisiting the words every now and again with the idea that they might get cleaned up. One day, I went back to the homestead house and while poking around in the attic I found a box that belonged to my uncle. Inside it, wedged between pencils and a few blank books, I saw a red Royal typewriter made of wood. I pulled the machine out of the box, and a blank book with a walking dragon on the cover fell down into the void left by it. I grabbed that too, feeling these were gifts from the lost writers of my Irish matriarchal lineage. The typewriter dated back to before the great war—a Royal Vogue refurbished with keys from a Royal Quiet Deluxe—a writer's dream machine even though I hadn't typed on moving keys in years. I fancied the idea that the machine had power to shine the light of word into the dark recesses of the human soul. So I started to clean up those scattered writings that captured the voices from the void, first handwriting them over into the blank book with the walking dragon on the cover and then typing them up on the typewriter.

I folded up the typewritten pages and stuck them in the back of the blank book. Whenever I took them out to reread them, I realized that— like a descent into Grand Canyon takes you back in geologic time—the voices from the chasm within went back in chronologic time. Each was a more primitive expression of the void left by holy war conditioning and my hopes for the future. Over time I came to see them as metaphorical memories, whispers of some medical complex where holy warriors—and genetics passed from father to son—got studied.

Nothing rational. Nothing defensible. The unspoken cries of generations of warriors in my family trying to find peace.

Voices from the Void -- October 28, 1998

I am a survivor of secret holy war trauma. Those
words may seem easy to say, but they're not. Trauma,
by its very nature, is something that goes beyond
simple expression, and when it happens to a child the
overwhelm is magnified. It is seventeen years later
now and I can finally write down the words. I am a
survivor of holy war conditioning.

No, I'm not some gun-toting militant raging
against the government. I don't have a gun and I
aspire to nonviolence. I am not an expert on the MK-
Ultra program or any of the other admitted secret
contingencies that grew out of the Cold War. During
my childhood I was injured, and I was not allowed to
make sense of what happened. I roamed the wilderness
wanting to cry out but not sure what to say. My words
are inadequate, but the voices cry out nonetheless.
It's time to let them have their say....

A Drain Beyond Reason -- October 3, 1998

There are times when I get caught in a spiral of
negativity. My outlook darkens and it seems there's no
way to escape the draining force pulling me down. The
harder I try to swim against the negative current, the
stronger it holds on to me. There was a period in my
life when this spiral of negativity and chaos was the
norm down inside. I was desperate to escape, panicked
to the point of nausea. Things from my past were
coming up, asking me to believe them and I couldn't. I
wouldn't, but truth does not stay buried.

I'd like to believe that the drain beyond reason
is a creation of my imagination or a glimpse into
an alternate reality. Most of the time it seems that
way, but the emotional impact of an imaginary event
does not twist in the guts like the emotion of this
event does in mine. These thirty seconds of shrieking

terror cannot be changed. They are not malleable like clay but hard like solid rock. Logic tells me there is some kind of realness to what I have remembered, but emotionally it cannot be processed. It was either an experiment in psycho-terror, a contorted memory of medical treatment, or some kind of delusion symbolic of the spiral of negativity that I sometimes feel pulling me down . . . a hodgepodge of events circling around the same drain.

As I recall it now, I am on a gurney being led down a narrow corridor with walls made of shiny steel, and I sense I am deep below ground. A door opens and I am thrust into a room. A man in a hooded suit sits at a control panel in front of a window. In the chamber sits another person somehow familiar to me. Their hands are hooked to a steel cable stretched across the room like a power line. A water cannon starts shooting, and the liquid is white . . . acid.

But I'm not really there. I'm sitting beneath a clothesline on a sunny day. There's a bright white sheet hooked to the line. It flaps violently in the wind, and I notice there are bloody handprints next to where the sheet attaches to the line.

Back inside the chamber, I lay on a gurney, I see brown sledge being sucked down a drain beneath me. I know that medical rooms have drains in the floor and that I am now the patient. I'm pulled out into the hallway, knowing there is no one to talk to about this. Ever.

And what could I have done to evade the horror of such a thing? To cover it over, to block it out so it couldn't get in my head? What form of expression might these remnants of occurrence have found if I could not re-associate them and write them down? What power does thirty seconds of such terror have if it remains just below the verge of consciousness?

There is a strange power to believing and expressing. It seems to diffuse the spiral of negativity. The only way to evade the horror of such a thing is to accept it and not include it in my definition of insanity.

Ledge Dancing -- April 20, 1997

Somewhere there's a ledge that I've danced upon. . . .

Somewhere, be it an alternate reality, a government installation or a place real only in my dreams, there's this ledge and it won't go away. It's a place I'd rather not be, but I keep returning there in my mind. The unbelievable happened there.

Far down below this ledge that plays in my mind are the remnants of two things. I look down at them from up high, trying to make sense of what they are. From the ledge, where there are three metal poles, I can see the cool, black glass of the building across the way. Down below are the two unreal things, perhaps what's left of a comedy team.

If you ever lost your head, you might reach up to check for it . . . one last time. That's probably better than being broken in two, eviscerated down the middle. Somewhere, there is this ledge with three black poles anchored into the wall. It seems that down below bombs were going off, the sound of balls on chains hitting the building. Last one left holding the anchor gets pulled inside for leg maintenance.

I had this dream once. In it I was sitting in a classroom at my elementary school, either third grade or sixth. Blood was running down my leg and I didn't want anyone to see. There were these fissures in my leg and the blood, not a whole lot, oozed out of them, but I couldn't let anyone know. It seems this dream left some real scars. As I'm writing this, I feel tightness in my lower back and upper thigh.

I have a memory from elementary school where I wrapped my left arm and leg around the metal pole of the monkey bars or swing set. I just held on and felt the coolness of the metal against my body. I found something comforting in that.

I don't know. Maybe those two bodies down below are just my phobia of falling crystallized into images. I am broken in two about my trauma, making sure I haven't lost my head. What's going on here? I hope you won't suggest that I'm pulling your leg. Dislocated limbs often occur when patients are strapped down for painful procedures.

When I go back to this ledge in my mind or in my dreams I'm dancing like a madman. Everyone's worried, but I don't care. I'm just dancing. Sometimes the dreams have turned nightmarish in the past, but now there's a sense of joy . . . happy to have two legs.

Somewhere, be it an alternate reality, a government installation or a place real only in my dreams, there's this ledge that I dance upon all alone. Care to join me?

Voices of the Rainbows -- December 4, 1995

I'll be dead within ten years but I'm not supposed to say that. It's pessimism. It's tempting fate. It's just not said even if there are good reasons to believe it's true, even if I have a sense in my heart and my spirit that it is true.

I've been seeing a lot of rainbows in things -- sunbeams, moonbeams, those rainbow arcs to one side of the sun or the moon. And I think when I see them, because I notice them in such a way, that it's a message from the Great Spirit. I'm being called home. My time here is short, and it's only natural. People exposed to the level of trauma I have just don't survive, and often as they get older and can't connect or get intimate, things get worse. Bitterness

sets in. I can see that for myself. So I have a good
ten years left before cancer or some disease from
my stressful past claims me. I'll pass on, hopefully
having fulfilled. . . .

Or maybe there is nothing. Maybe it's just a
tragedy playing itself out, ten years of increasing
frustration and bitterness at my draw in life. I
begin to fall into obsolete patterns. I think there's
a miracle coming, that healing will lead me past
the inevitable that should go with my post-trauma
condition. I come back to that way of thinking -- that
all of this must have some greater purpose than to
settle down and live life. But maybe that's all there
is. Isn't that all you can do, live life? And I don't
want that so I convince myself I'll be dead in ten
years unless the Christian God brings me a miracle of
healing. It's a ransom on him -- give me a miracle or
I'll die.

But the voice from the rainbows is different. It's
the call of the ages and it's soothing. Because my
troubles don't mean much in the grand scheme, a life
shaped by things beyond my control, rich people out
of control. The Great Spirit calls to me through these
rainbows to remind me to take it easy, that this too
shall pass. Is it only natural that years have been
shaved off my life by my stress levels and shattered
psyche? All I can do is live life and go when I'm
called. There will be no miracles for me, only what is
meant to be.

Up above, the rainbows tell me I'll be dead in ten
years and I find that comforting. Below, the rocks of
Grand Canyon laugh at me, telling me my time is short.

My writings about those voices from the void seem unreal to me
now—the words of someone on the fringe, a hermit who hears the
call of ghosts. Back in those days, I took off running from myself, took

off into Grand Canyon, but I didn't escape the haunts. It seems that energies left by others toyed with me, as if to scare me back into facing my own demons. So I went back and relived it all, faced them down. Yet it always felt like too little too late, like the rescuer didn't arrive in time.

Down in the Phantom area of Grand Canyon I have visited a grave in an alcove just north of the black bridge over the Colorado River. Under a pile of rocks near the ruins of a pueblo lies Rees Griffith, a crew foreman who was working on the trail in 1922 when a boulder, loosened by a blast he set, fell and crushed him. He survived the initial incident and was taken to Phantom Ranch where he waited for a doctor to arrive from the Canyon rim. The doctor made his way in haste, trekking down from El Tovar to the recently built trail on mule and proceeding by foot over the unfinished bridge up to Phantom Ranch. He arrived shortly after eleven o'clock, about six hours after the accident and a mere fifteen minutes after Griffith died from his injuries.

They thought of packing the body out on a mule and taking him home to his wife, but they decided to grant Griffith's dying wish and bury him near the area where he worked, in the Canyon he loved. The South Kaibab Trail he helped to build became a bypass to the only other way into the Canyon in that area, one that required all who passed to pay a toll.

These days Griffith is sometimes thought of as the phantom roaming the trails near the creek, except phantoms roamed there long before he arrived. The creek got the name Bright Angel because of the cleanness of the water and the way that mist rising off the water caught the light, making angels appear. In the dark of night beneath the moon, that same phenomena can look like a spooky phantom. I doubt Griffith imagined as he waited for the doctor on his dying day that he would become known as a ghost haunting the area rather than a crew leader that helped to build a free path down into the chasm.

I've visited that grave in the night, trying to catch the light that is said to hover over it, trying to spot the ghost of Rees Griffith who died in his forty-eighth year. To no avail. I guess I just can't tune in to that wavelength—or there is nothing real about it—or I have quieted enough of my own demons that the ghost has no interest in me. It seems that the chasm within can be filled with escaping and arriving, with a negative spiral of deviance amid whispers of love and hope, a flow of positive and negative becoming one and the same.

I escaped the destiny conditioned into me as a child, but grabbing hold of a different one continued to elude me. I had gone to Grand Canyon seeking my true nature—what I was meant to do with my life—but there was no simple highway to follow. I didn't understand that the well-to-do people who inherited prosperity while I fought with demons didn't want me to seek my true nature. They saw me as one of their peasants, and they were taking away my freedoms in the name of a war on terror. Life was no simple highway to begin with, and new roadblocks and dams were being put in my way. But the once wild river that flows through the heart of Grand Canyon remembered what it felt like to be wild, and I still felt the pull of my true nature upon me.

FREE WRITING — GRAND CANYON RIM, DEC 26, 2002

Every Grand Canyon hike has a spiritual lesson to learn about yourself. If you go solo, those lessons are deepened and so is the danger that you will never re-emerge from the depths. I do not at all mind the risks. In some ways I like tempting fate — asking the Canyon spirits to take me and living to tell about when they almost oblige. But mostly the spirits walk with me and without using words talk to me. The patterns of my life emerge on my hikes, and more than anything those trials of spirit on the trails of Grand Canyon keep me grounded.

6. NO SIMPLE HIGHWAY

I don't know why I decided to go back to face my nemesis the hermit one more time. Ten months had passed since the dismissal of my court case, and I had settled into a paycheck-to-paycheck existence in Flagstaff doing van tours and working at the university. My end-of-year break gave me a chance to get away, and I decided to try a route I had never walked before into the depths of the Hermit area. I set off on the day after Christmas, figuring that heat exhaustion couldn't get me in the cold of winter. I took the Hermit Trail to the turn off toward Dripping Springs and continued onward, looking for the backcountry trail that followed the cliff edge before descending down to the river.

The Boucher Trail got its name from the man who wandered around that area prospecting and trying to sell a wilderness experience to tourists. He never found much success, became known as *the hermit*, and the route he left across the esplanade didn't draw many hikers in the winter. I went that way because I wanted to cleanse my spirit of my troubles in solitude, and I envisioned myself laughing at my nemesis when I made camp at Hermit Creek on the second night.

The curse of the hermit took hold straight away and I fell behind my planned itinerary. Boucher was the hardest trail I had ever hiked. I began calling it *a route someone stupid once took and now others foolishly follow*. I wanted to get below the Supai layer and make camp in the warmer travertine canyon at about forty-four hundred feet, but as I rounded Yuma Point the sun disappeared behind the upper canyon walls. I came to the brink of the Supai cliffs and saw them covered with snow. The descent required handholds, and I didn't want to be doing that in the dark with a fifty-five-pound winter pack, so I turned back to make camp on the flat esplanade.

I hibernated till morning in my sleeping bag, awaking to find that moisture from my breath had frozen inside the tent and fallen as snow crystals around my feet. I peeked outside expecting to see more snow, but the breaking light of dawn revealed only a barren landscape. I braved the cold and packed up my gear, hitting the trail without breakfast. As I started down the Supai cliffs, I noticed there were no tracks in the snow that hid in the shadows of the canyon walls. No one had come this way in a while, and I knew few would hike this trail till spring.

The way down was slippery in spots and I had to go slower than I wanted. After about twenty minutes of careful hiking, checking all my footholds and using my hiking stick to keep my balance, I came to a narrow washout that dropped straight down about twenty-five feet. Big boulders made for crude steps, and I let my wooden hiking stick hang by the cord off my right hand. This allowed me to make handholds and also have my hiking stick available if I got in a precarious situation. I sat down on the first of the large rocks and stretched my feet down toward the next one. A little jump put me on top of that boulder, leaving me with no way to turn back. I had committed to descending the full staircase. I sat down on the second rock and stretched toward the next landing. My feet dangled in the air, too far to jump, so I slid lower, lost my balance and almost fell. My feet remained dangling a few feet above the landing as my backpack got hung up on the rock behind me. Hanging there, I teetered on the edge of falling. If I moved forward, the weight on my back would throw me over the safe landing head first onto the rocks twenty-five feet below. I looked for a handhold or rock to push against with my hiking stick to move me backward, up onto the previous boulder, but I found nothing within reach. Stuck there balanced on my backpack, hands and feet in the air, I remembered all the warnings about the risks of hiking alone. Realization set in. *No one to lend a helping hand.* I didn't see any safe way out of my predicament.

I wondered if I would survive the fall. Maybe if my pack hit first and I didn't start rolling after the impact, I had a chance of walking away. I looked down and dropped my hiking stick to see what would happen. It hit the rocks and slid to a stop behind a boulder that hid the lower trail from my view. I considered that a good sign. A controlled fall seemed like the best option. *Hitting once might not kill me.* Maybe I could spin around so my pack took the brunt of the impact. I visualized the fall in my mind, practiced the midair spin in an imaginary virtual reality. I filled my mind with positive thoughts, but as the moment to let go arrived I hesitated and reconsidered my options.

Another idea crystalized in my mind, and I saw what I needed to do.

I popped my waist belt and freed one arm from the shoulder strap of my backpack. As I tried to free my other arm, my balance wavered. My situation grew more precarious as I tried to stay focused on what I needed to do—take a jump down while swinging my free arm around and grabbing the boulder beside me once my back faced the fall and I could drop my pack. If the strap didn't hook my elbow while sliding off my arm, I might be able to hold on to the boulder. I saw the whole scene in my mind as one graceful, death-defying move.

I can do this.

I went for it. I jumped down to the step and grabbed the rock as the backpack slid down my arm. For a brief second the strap caught my elbow, threatening to yank me from my perch, before it slid off and the pack fell. I clutched onto the boulder with all my strength as everything I brought with me bounced against the rocks below. I held my precarious position and caught my breath, feeling gratitude for the boulder beneath my feet. After a moment, I climbed down and found my pack wedged against a rock just above a fifty-foot drop. If I had fallen with my pack, hoping for the best, I may have bounced and kept falling. I checked my gear and rested there, gathering my wits for the remainder of the Supai descent.

My two-day trek on Boucher Trail cleansed my spirit—the Canyon felt expansive and new again. My body had taken a beating, and my mind had reached its limits looking for the next handhold and footfall. My legs were sore and stiff and my shoulders were bruised from the straps of my backpack, but I felt grateful that I didn't try to climb down the cliffs the evening before to face my predicament alone in the dark.

The next morning, a day behind schedule, I left for Hermit Creek. While walking along the Tonto Trail, I made peace with the hermit, acknowledging that I was getting too old for solo hiking. After a peaceful rest in the camp thinking about how Louis Boucher used to ride his white mule named Calamity Jane there and tell stories to entertain tourists, I made the trek to Granite Rapid. As I set up my solo camp, I watched river runners playing in the rapid. They rode one boat through and beached it, got out and ran back up to take the next boat through, laughing and yelling all the way. They knew a better way to see the depths of the Canyon, no packs to get hung up on. It seemed like a good way to see the inner gorge without carrying so much weight on my back. I played around the Monument Creek and Indian Garden areas for a few days and hiked out into a new year that felt full of promise. The American dream, that better life I envisioned for myself, seemed just around the corner. *Why would I have made it this far if success wasn't meant to be?*

Back in Flagstaff some harsh realities were setting in. My fight with the government amid meagre employment opportunities in Arizona had taken a financial toll, so I filed for personal bankruptcy. I got out from under all my debts except for my student loan. A banking arm of the Department of Defense owned it, and I didn't want to ask them for relief. The money felt connected to the abuses of power that had been denied in court, and I clung to the notion that destiny would bring financial justice in the form of a major book deal or writing work in Hollywood. If that didn't come, I had a haven in academia that allowed me the freedom of a second job giving tours in Grand Canyon country. I didn't realize that paradigms were shifting and about to tear down the meagre shelters where I nurtured my dreams for the future.

Growing up, I had been taught that earning an education and working hard paid off eventually, but things in America were changing. My college degrees came with a debt that robbed me of possibilities, and there seemed to be no way to capitalize on the sweat of my efforts because people donning suits didn't share fairly with others. I felt that anyone who worked full-time should be able to make headway toward their vision of the future, but everywhere I turned there were roadblocks to realizing my dreams. The budget always lacked when it came to raises for ordinary people, yet the bosses and appropriation hounds always sniffed out more money for themselves. Faced with this disempowerment, I found myself looking back over my life and rethinking my story. It wasn't a journey of personal triumph like I wanted to believe because no one knew of my inner spiritual struggles. From the outside, I looked like either an arrogant, aloof artist or a vagabond hermit who wandered in the wilderness. Yet I saw myself as someone who had organized the chaos within—made my spirit whole—but never turned the corner financially. Sniffing out the next government appropriation by groveling like the money hounds of my generation felt like greed to me, selling out. And even if I wanted to compete in that caught-up world, the happy, shiny bureaucrats had a big head start. They had perfected the greed game, treating all who didn't money-sniff like them with a smug and practiced malicious indifference.

I began to feel a lot of resentment. I saw a selective tyranny in American—not a harsh, brutal tyranny but one where a calculated detachment from the concerns of people who weren't caught up in the grips and gripes of mass consumerism had become okay. The benevolent nation I grew up in seemed to vanish behind the scowls of paper pushers who built lauded lives inside gilded cages. Driven to climb ladders of perceived success in the social jungle, nothing irritated them more than someone with a good education who aspired to be an independent artist or writer. People in monkey suits could not fathom a simpler life free of their clamouring caught-up-ness. They saw me as a backwoods hick ripe for exploitation, or they took my attempt to be a freer spirit as defiance of them. If they had to be in a cage of their own making I needed one too, and they could build it for me.

The disempowerment of being a working stiff in America weighed upon me more than others. It touched on emotions connected to the holy war conditioning of my childhood. I found it hard to hold my tongue or be polite and positive when I knew better ways to do things. In my earlier days, I escaped that to some degree by focusing on a legacy of passing the arts and sciences on to younger people. I felt a sense of purpose in academia that softened the idea of living in servitude to a ruling class that looked down on my life struggles with malicious indifference. Despite there being no simple highway toward a better life, I had pieced together a path against all the odds. But leaving Grand Canyon seemed to switch my fortunes—life began to close in on me. Time and distance took a toll. I had no place of solace from failure, and the dream world felt further away than ever.

Way back in my college days, I wrote a letter to Thérèse about my struggle to capture a better life. I worried that I might never find passion in my work, that I might become trapped in a thankless job living a meaningless existence doing nothing more than slaving away to pay off student loans. As I approached the age of forty, those notions I pondered as a young man were coming back to haunt me.

It's so easy to lose sight of the passions that drive you and to disappear into the folds of skin that are day-to-day life. There are some things that I just can't face and don't want to fathom. Chasing a 'dream' that is out there somewhere — an indefinite being — which at times like now seems very indefinite. You reach for it, and you think you have hold. We gonna rise! Then it slips away and a bit of bitterness sets in, a bit of irritability, dad-itis. By the time you are forty or so you no longer want to push at the folds of skin that have engulfed you. You snuggle a little closer to what you have or whoever might want you and pretend that it's alright. You notice the chaos out there in the world and you wonder what it's all about. Not realizing that it's that dream out there, forgotten, left behind, but still trying to pull you out from the folds of skin that have engulfed you. And I'm sitting here now wondering if I can capture the dream, that American dream to be part of something greater. Can I capture those passions for life and control them, or will I run and hide from them, fearing their power will set me off balance?

* * *

University became my place of solace from the cruel world, a place of purpose to nurture dreams, a place that expanded my mind and helped me shatter the limited prism of a holy war worldview. It transformed me from a lost soul who might make bombs into a man who wanted to write books, but even as a fledgling student I sensed a brewing storm in academia. I saw bean counters clawing their way into the state universities in America. Bureaucratic budget hounds following government appropriations and climbing career ladders started milking the mind machine for money. These wannabe aristocrats invaded the safe havens that the educated and weird had carved out for themselves. By the time I reached forty, the great expansion in education that had benefitted my youth started collapsing, the brain drain came and predatory penny-pinching practices took over everywhere. The money I had borrowed to secure a future became a debt that stifled me, and the banks didn't care because they got paid back quicker by invoking federal guarantees if I defaulted. Caught up in my microcosm trying to make it through another day, all I could do was witness the dying of universities and hope for something better to steal me away and give meaning to my work again.

I had been chasing the ever-elusive American dream all of my life. When I arrived in Arizona in 2000, I felt optimistic about opportunities in the town of Flagstaff. I believed that my money situation would get better, but I learned the whys and wherefores of the adage 'poverty with a view.' I worked meagre jobs that fell short of the promises given when I was hired, and I watched my student loan accumulate more and more interest. All the while I held steadfast to the hope of a full-time job in the distance learning program at my alma mater. I believed if I stayed positive and grateful, karma would deliver me legal and financial justice for past abuses of power against me.

When I moved to the South Rim to work for the corporate regime, I had my eye on a university job in Grand Canyon Village. An interactive television classroom had been built in the community building, and a liaison position was being created. I considered it the best opportunity in the world—an ambassador of Grand Canyon beaming the natural science and stories of the area to people all around the globe. I followed the progress of the proposed classroom, and one day I went and talked to the park ranger attached to the project. She told me that the cost of renovating an old building for interactive television came to almost a million dollars and the opening of the facility had been pushed back indefinitely. The bureaucracy couldn't find the money to pay someone to operate the equipment. Later, the proposed learning center fell off the map of future university sites and the building collapsed amid whispers of insurance fraud. One possible future in academia vanished on me—too many hounds sniffing around.

Back in Flagstaff after my time living on the rim, more budget cuts hit the university. The feel of the place had changed—many of the gifted teachers had caught the brain drain and left for greener pastures overseas. Grey Vonsousa, my former professor who had predicted the death of America's universities some years earlier, couldn't fight the changes. He died unexpectedly just before an academic restructuring changed the study of communication at the university from an "art" to a "behavioral science." A ripple effect spiraled out from that one cost-cutting measure, and a whole legacy got lost. Students began to see communication as an act put on before cameras rather than an art delivered by a science. Professionalism and focusing on informing an audience gave way to a narcissistic idea of celebrity reporting. The camera became friend or therapist, someone to show a 'best face' to or to 'moon' during a credit roll. Journalism ethics courses and history of media courses disappeared, and the graduates set off to assimilate into the channels owned by corporate media.

As the death knell of the working-class university resounded, professors who had spent a lifetime contributing their passions for teaching the next generation were no longer wanted and disciplinarians took their place. The virtual classroom idea that Dr. Vonsousa had championed to save costs and expand education opportunities got cut back, and the spirit of community evaporated as fast as the fancy buildings named for wealthy donors went up. Tuition increased more than sixty percent, and a drive to recruit students from China and other foreign nations took the place of educating Americans in remote areas. The working-class college I had attended turned into a school that only people of money and privilege could afford. Despite my growing frustrations, I bit my tongue to keep my meagre job while looking for someplace else to go.

I found a different sense of purpose in my job as a driver and tour guide. I worked at a small company that allowed me to create my own tours and tell my own stories. It was good, honest work, shuttling river runners to the Canyon, turning people on to the natural wonders of the American Southwest, and sharing the history of the pioneers who ventured out that way before the modern era. After dropping people off, I had time alone to explore wilderness areas and stop at most of the Grand Circle national parks in Colorado, Utah and Arizona. Walking a wilderness trail brought the pathways of my life into better focus. I could hike off the bitterness of my uptight university job by braving the scary jaunt to Angel's Landing in Zion Canyon or by jogging in the heat of the desert out near Horseshoe Bend above Glen Canyon. Alone in nature I had a pretty good grasp of my journey in life—rebounding from an unbelievable childhood—but in the real world, the road never became simple. I kept looking for a place to land, for life to grab hold of me, for some deeper meaning to fill my vocation the way wilderness filled my spirit. I saw the world changing and I knew I had to find a job with a future, but there was no simple highway with road signs to help me along.

After being told at every turn that my intelligence, passion and spirit were not wanted, I took stock of my life and decided to try to focus on a legacy of giving to others. I felt I was becoming a narcissist and not doing anything that reached beyond the fingers of my own hands. So at the age of forty, I started the year-long application process for the Peace Corps. I wanted to change my life because I felt like an animal trapped in too small a cage. My anger at people in power who denied the truth of my childhood and wanted me to live in servitude might lead me into trouble if I stayed a working stiff in America. Seeing my work benefit people less fortunate than me would help me to focus on something other than my own misfortunes.

In applying to the Peace Corps, I was dealing with the government again. I knew that applicants had to clear a federal background check and satisfy a distant bureaucracy. I tackled the daunting application process with vigor, proved all my educational credentials, gathered the many personal and professional references, and wrote about my desire to serve. Upon submitting the paperwork, I got a quick nomination for a position along with a letter saying they needed people like me.

The good feeling didn't last long. A week later the medical office sent me forms to be filled out by my "treating psychiatrist" and primary-care doctor. Being a non-benefit employee at the university and a seasonal driver at a small company, I didn't have health insurance or a regular doctor. I paid for medical care in cash at the local clinic, and I didn't know that admitting I had seen a shrink ten years earlier would trigger a rigamarole of paperwork. Despite passing all the other background checks, my lack of a sufficient health history could keep me out of the Peace Corps.

The medical office allowed me to write my own health statement, and I would have to hang my hopes on that. It proved a tricky prospect to sound rational, balanced and forthright without medical records to back up my claims. They wanted me to tell them how I planned to cope with the stresses of overseas service that would be so much tougher than anything I had faced in my life before. Their questions were so full of privileged-class assumptions that I found them almost humorous, but I knew that I had to take it seriously. I needed to show that my past no longer had a hold on me. I crafted a strong statement designed to help far-off bureaucrats understand the *other* America where I grew up.

I wrote, "I am a working-class person without access to health care, so some of your requests for documentation seem a bit strange to me. I have no 'treating psychiatrist' nor primary doctor to complete the many pages of forms I received." I continued by addressing each of their medical questions specifically, and in closing I wrote, "What are we to do if people conditioned for war as children are not allowed to volunteer themselves to work for commonality and peace between peoples? My ability to organize my own inner chaos with very little assistance is perhaps the perfect prerequisite to serve in the Peace Corps. Though the powerful people in that other America way up on that distant hill have disavowed what occurred in my childhood, that does not make my struggle for peace and self-understanding any less real."

Two months later my application status got changed to "deferred" and I received a letter stating that they appreciated my candor but they couldn't clear me. Now the game had changed. They wanted the evaluations filled out by the health care professionals who had seen me all those years ago. I called and asked how tracking down people I saw a decade earlier could help determine my *current* health status. They had no answer.

The truth was simple—I came from the wrong side of the tracks. Though I deserved a shot at the Peace Corps more than some son or daughter of privilege, I wasn't going to be allowed in because I wrote truth from a *forgotten America*. Even though the recruiter vouched for me as an exceptional candidate, the far-off bureaucrats were now looking for any reason to screen me out.

I wasn't giving up yet. I decided to see if the records from Maryland were still available. I called their 'Department of Mental Hygiene'— the *back-east brain-washing department*—where I received therapy on a sliding-fee scale some ten years earlier. I learned that all the state's community-based health clinics had fallen to the budget axe and my records had been destroyed.

I felt at peace with that, maybe even happy about it. The doctors from my past were lost from me. They no longer had a say in my life. The lack of medical records meant I couldn't serve, but if the Peace Corps was just another choice among the many choices available only to the rich and privileged, it wasn't about helping others anymore. I didn't want to live among elitist people feeling good about themselves by helping communities impoverished due to America's warmongering in the world. I decided to write a letter to the recruiter thanking her for believing in me and withdrawing my application.

No simple highway toward a meaningful life, no future, no way to pay off my student loan—my choices narrowed. I kept writing in the wilds, sending queries to Hollywood and looking for work to keep me busy. I applied to become a nighttime custodian at the university, cleaning up the science labs where test animals were kept. I felt a connection to the legacy of my grandfather as I filled out the paperwork. He had arrived at Ellis Island in 1909 and later worked as a school janitor for over thirty years to give our family a foothold in America. I aced the interview and got hired on the spot, but a few days later they told me the budget axe killed the job. I noticed that the call for applicants continued, and I figured that they lied about the lack of money because they didn't want to tell me the truth. Someone had ruled me out because I appeared too smart for the position—my 'liberal' education mixed with credo discrimination, or *creedism*—made me an animal rights activist in their eyes, a potential liberator of the animals. I couldn't get a simple job in America because of suspicions about my 'liberal' education, but I couldn't expatriate and serve in the Peace Corps due to worries about me being too feebleminded to handle the stress.

Everything kept pushing me back to my calling of being a writer. I knew that becoming an author meant networking and selling my story. For years I had queried agents and publishers, but the literary world didn't answer my proposals to write an academic book about childhood memory and the generational effects of war on a family. Among the scant replies to my reach-outs, I heard the same refrains. "Your education doesn't matter." "Your idea doesn't fit our needs." "We're simply too busy to take on another client." I knew I had to create some kind of buzz about my story and get a referral from a respected author, so I decided to follow the methods of a self-help guru to make myself marketable.

Over a period of about a year, I attended seminars designed to boost my ego and sell myself as a writer. I needed to change from being a quiet man who felt at home in nature into an outgoing, marketable luminary. I took life-coaching sessions and developed strategies for getting people interested in me, but nothing gelled. I finished a draft of my nonfiction book about how the promise of America turned me away from a darker life, saved me from becoming a holy warrior or hatemonger, but I couldn't get published because the literary establishment saw me as too introverted and not *positive-thinky* enough. No one understood how getting a master of arts degree and hiking Grand Canyon healed me from sketchy military abuses in childhood. But it was more than the story—again I saw a kind of discrimination at work, a type of creedism. The image of the American writer had changed to a well-kempt hack who rarely ventured out of doors. Authors recreated ideas from forgotten books and schmoozed their way to financial success, filling the place once held by more eclectic souls. To the literary gatekeepers in suits, everything had already been written, and I didn't appear writerly enough to regurgitate what gruff scribes said first.

Not writerly enough? My vision of myself began to change. Being a writer meant sharing my story as a triumph over my past—exorcising spooks that once haunted me—but after so much rejection I began to fall into doubt again. My eidetic memory seemed more an inability to let go, my dark wit a shield to hide behind, my sense of humour a lance to cut down others. Making it in the real world required denying my true self, burying my emotional pain and dumbing myself down— the opposite of what I believed a writer should be. I knew that if I did that to fit in, the inner resentment would fester into racism or creedism or some other -ism where I projected my dark-side doubts onto others and hated them while wrapped up in positive thinking about myself. *Become ordinary?* I felt trapped in this spiral of chaos, and the rage of that cage welled up inside me. Fantasies of violence gripped me again, visualizations of revenge on a system that denied the real me and wanted me to be simple and normal. I knew that acting out those fantasies was just a futile effort to escape past trauma by layering drama over top of it, and yet these very ideas of violence grew out of my hidden experiences. Marketing myself and creating a mass media face led my rational mind to an unexpected conclusion—the most honest and logical way to express my rage at the denial of my life journey and my true nature as an introverted writer meant perpetrating an act of personal armageddon.

I felt trapped in a stark dichotomy of fate. Personal armageddon for failure stood opposite the idea that success brought with it a personal utopia. I clung to the notion that a major book deal meant justice, meant that the spirit world heard me and cared for me, but as the years passed a deepening crisis of faith devoured me. I had spent my life moving back and forth between extremes, caterwauling out of control, stuck in alternating beliefs of blissful triumph or hellish descent, personal utopia or personal armageddon, the rise and fall of my own creation, all of it ridiculous.

Turning to intellect to solve a deep emotional hurt made me more aware of the hurt and the duality of human nature. So the inspiration behind my writing changed again. I realized I had lived a life free from the editors and critics pawing over my every word, reviewing my every thought, and dragging me down into mediocrity. I had lived as a free writer, and writing for myself allowed me to put my inner being in order. I decided that my measure of future success meant writing more of love, of nature and of Grand Canyon than about the spectres of my childhood. I let go of the mass media version of myself and let the amok shadow run loose—someone else could catch it.

Writing is for the soul—you win it or lose it with your words.

I tried to be grateful there was no simple highway toward riches. I had taken a road less traveled. If I had settled into a corporate type of life, one of those roads more traveled, I may have never come to understand the truth of myself. Maybe money didn't find me because I attached strong negative associations to it. I always managed to earn enough to live humbly and no more. With most of my energy going into making my way and healing myself, I didn't have time to think about fulfilling that dark-side destiny nurtured into me at an impressionable young age.

This left me reduced to one of the stranger ideas about creating wealth—wishing for money to fall into my lap. I came across a notion that, if all else fails, visualizing a financial windfall and fixating on a specific dollar amount could create some sort of magic. I read stories of people doing this and having some fortune befall them out of nowhere. So I came up with an amount and concentrated on it while trying to deny my skepticism.

A short while later, I got news of a windfall coming my way. My dad's younger sister, Rafaela, had died with an unexpected sum of money hidden away in the stock market. After probate, I would be inheriting an amount equal to half of what I had wished for, a low six-figure amount . . . enough to cover my student loan debt. A lifetime of conscientious work had left me broke, but a foolish wish seemed to deliver the possibility of financial freedom from a more prosperous time in America.

I can't say I was elated. I thought of declining the money because taking it meant inviting my family back into my life. It didn't seem fair that my windfall would go to paying off student loan debt when my siblings had their tuition paid for by my dad before he died. I decided that taking the money might be a means of reconciliation, maybe some feelings of alienation could be resolved and the rumours about me might stop. If nothing else, my godmother's money might give me the freedom to build a writer's life in some small town free of student loan debt that stifled my future prospects.

During the process of settling the estate and splitting things evenly, we never talked about our good fortune or what we were going to do with our cash. At one point I told my siblings that I needed some emotional support, needed help getting into a different situation as academia waned. Dead silence ruled the other end of the line, followed long moments later by promises of a list of resources sent by email. I was on my own after that. We never laughed together about our windfall, never shared anything fun. Family felt dead to me.

The money from my godmother seemed to bring some kind of curse upon me, as if the ripples of the past that I had outrun for so long found me again. I started looking backward—not out of nostalgia, not deliberately—more out of fear that the ghosts of family didn't like my choices in life and were exacting retribution from beyond the grave. I didn't take to this idea right away. I welcomed the ripples at first, believing that all my conscious efforts to change myself into a different kind of person—to escape *the curse upon my family to always be holy warriors*—were on the verge of paying off. So I accepted the changes coming into my life with excitement, but I couldn't deny a lingering sense of being haunted by ghosts bent on crushing my luck and pulling me backward.

I had achieved a weird kind of balance living near Grand Canyon, and the money from a distant godmother threatened to knock that off-kilter. My Aunt Fae led a solitary life and never married, remaining a devout catholic waiting for a knight in shining armour to bust down her door, but no one ever made her an honest woman. Instead she played the stock market, got rich and hid the money away. She could have retired and traveled the world, but after all those years living in the same apartment and working for the government in military support services, the world probably seemed too big for her. Taking her money brought with it energies that pulled me backward into those family patterns—I felt the pull of archaic religious thinking all around me.

I knew I could never fit back into the confines of the archaic belief system that ran in the shadows of my family. I had escaped the holy warrior curse passed down the generations—I wanted no part of a life where men fought wars and came home to pure women who had waited for them, pined away for them, and they trapped each other in a cage called The American Dream. I took the family money thinking that having a cash cushion might allow me to make a shift that other people couldn't make because they didn't see the effects of generational memory like I did. By knowing the patterns, I could defeat them. But my arrogance got the better of me, my prospects for the future dried up—the curse found me anyway.

Paychecks at my driving job started bouncing and higher-ups at the university began eyeing more cuts at the department where I worked. That made me happy—I believed all my conscious efforts to change myself had reached my core and these jobs mired in lack were leaving my life to be replaced by things I always wanted. I could move now from a place of wholeness to recreate my life while the former me became a memory.

Except the ghost of my former self lingered, held on while I let go.

My driving job disappeared, leaving me to file a lawsuit to collect my remaining pay, but the troubles at the university festered over a period of months. My boss announced his retirement, and all us employees were stunned. We couldn't understand why he quit just as the position of head director opened up. It turned out a university administrator had plotted a money grab and our piece of the pie was in their sights. Each year a department was targeted for cutbacks so that some of the diminishing budget money could be rerouted into the pockets of the higher-ups to fulfill their goal of keeping up with their peers at other institutions of learning. They wanted to force my boss into taking on a different position in addition to filling his previous one without a raise. Insulted by the idea, he announced his retirement and took his accumulated leave, telling those closest to him that he might be joining a seminary somewhere in Idaho. His abrupt departure left the university in a bind, but the bureaucrats wouldn't figure that out for months. No one else knew all the specs of the studio he had built, so the whole thing would have to be ripped out and redone. While my former boss packed up and left, word came of a meeting to be beamed across Arizona to tell us about our futures.

That day, I took my place in the middle of an interactive television classroom. Rumours had swirled around the department for a few weeks about what kind of cutbacks were coming and how many jobs would be lost. We all knew that the president of the university got a forty-thousand-dollar raise each year as part of his keep-up-with-the-joneses contract. No one knew how much more money got routed to his friends, and as we entered the room there were four dressed-up bureaucrats waiting to tell us our fates. Sitting there I had a feeling my part-time job would be axed.

A man in a suit stood at the podium and said in an ingratiating voice that a human resources administrator was taking over as department director. A woman approached the podium as a name echoed through the room. "Candie Apple Baconey." A few of us stifled honest laughs. The moment felt surreal, and one of my friends whispered "baloney" to me. I grabbed pen and paper and wrote, "I'm getting fired by someone named 'sweet pig-meat'?" Up at the podium, Candie broke into a gleeful smile, accepting our stifled guffaws as good-natured murmurs. She began her unctuous talk by thanking the absent president of the university for his great friendship over the years. She told us not to worry about the fact that she had no experience in television because she had plenty of experience supervising people and we would be doing all the work. She conveyed the sense, without meaning to, that all her power-playing had paid off and now she got to take the place of someone who had real experience and knew what he was doing. If we did the same for her, we could stand at podiums and smile with glee too.

After her self-aggrandizement, the lights in the room flickered and some sort of dark-side persona took over her being. She displayed a despicable spectacle of hypocrisy and greed, telling us that our great institution had made some decisions. Major job cuts were being implemented in the department to part-time and low-wage employees.

A sense of quiet consternation filled the room, but I didn't want to play along. Layer upon layer of disappointment had been built up over the years, going all the way back to my student days at that university. Rage at a lifetime of being taken advantage of took hold of me. I felt that my final chance at building a future was being crushed. I took to a mic in front of me and blasted the whole charade.

"This is what we get? This is what we get after years . . . a lifetime of giving ourselves to a place of learning? I have been passed over for fifteen, FIFTEEN full-time jobs that fell to the budget axe or went to unpaid students. Now I sit here taking baloney from a candie-appled baconey?" My frustration grew and I added "MAYBE I should buy some weapons and carry out my childhood programming . . ." as the cameras found me and beamed my image across the state of Arizona on the interactive television system once lauded by the now dead Professor Vonsousa.

The room fell silent for long seconds, and no reply ever came. I said this before the Virginia Tech tragedy, and there was no intent behind it. The words came out of the ghost of my former self, an honest expression of my generational memory mixed with the collective anger bounding around university campuses in those greedy days.

Others take more militant routes, but I voiced my anger in words—thinking *listen to me now or listen to others later*—each communication from the ghosts of our lost souls gets a little more dire, a little louder, more challenging to make sense of. I used words and no response came because the shiny, happy people were caught up in a power play and didn't want to stop to listen. Another American university fell to greed and stupidity, moved on without a response to those who felt the pain of being left behind.

Later that evening I was detained by police for questioning. They claimed I had made a threat, to which I pointed out that I used the word "maybe" and quipped that "a university is a terrible place for a rhetorical statement." One officer said he was sticking his neck out for me so I could keep my job and not get a permanent mark in my record. At that point I didn't care—I believed in good riddance, better things were coming, and the ghosts of the past couldn't stop that. I didn't need a part-time job without benefits that provided me no future while *sweet pig-meat* mucked in her pen. The police had nothing to hold me on, but an edict from Candie said I couldn't leave my job—I was suspended from work pending further review.

A week later I met with a bunch of overdressed university bigwigs who assumed I didn't know what I had done, but I did know. I spoke provocative words over a communication system, and they had to report that to men and women in suits who monitor such things for the federal government. I spoke out of frustration, but I knew I could be prosecuted for what I said. I had decided to make a stand again, to bring my life experience out of the shadows for serious discussion. I would have more rights as a defendant than I ever got as a plaintiff. So we sat down to talk and the bigwigs stifled due process, cut me loose to go make trouble in the world on someone else's turf. I lost my job and got banned from walking on campus for life.

I didn't let it lie. I took up the issue with the university president in a formal letter. I wrote, "At the age of ten, I was trained to kill by the Department of Defense and conditioned to believe that I needed to sacrifice my life to the great armageddon holy war. At the age of twenty-four, I enrolled at your university and the education I gained was an important part of turning my childhood conditioning around. Now I watch as you and other greedy administrators scuttle the university that I love so that you can keep up with your peers at other institutions." I asked him to resign or face a future where "your retirement years will be filled with news of the tragedy of increasing terrorist attacks upon our once great nation."

A few days later I was again detained by university police and questioned. In the interrogation room, a sergeant named Missy told me that writing another letter would violate Arizona laws on harassment and intimidation of public officials. I asked how telling the truth to public officials or sharing opinions in writing could be grounds for arrest. *Isn't that the basis of the democratic process?* Sergeant Missy had no answer. She just repeated the consequences of writing letters to public officials. I knew they didn't want to arrest me—my adversaries in the U.S. Attorney's Office of Arizona were calling the shots. After some coerced picture-taking and threats to call my mother, I was released from questioning and locked in the back of a state-owned sport utility vehicle.

The older male officer in the passenger seat looked through the metal screen separating us and cleared his throat. "You understand that if you come on campus you'll be arrested . . . or even shot on sight?"

"Shot on sight? All because the feelings of a rich bureaucrat to my words in a letter are oh-so-serious, but no one cares about the child militia abuse in my life."

"Child abuse!" He paused. "No one wants to hear about what happened to you when you were ten years old."

"Yeah, I get that. Shot on sight for writing letters." I looked out the window and decided those were my last words in this conversation.

He began to ramble on as I waited for my ride home to end. "These are different days. Writing letters could be a violation of the patriot act. . . ."

The whole thing seemed ridiculous. Why would a university police officer be talking about the patriot act? Was that their jurisdiction? Why did he say "ten years old"? Had he heard that somewhere else? I knew this was intimidation from the federal government filtered through the lowest common police force. I felt I had handled myself well, but I didn't want a life like this. I didn't want to be caught up in *why-so-serious* situations or endless discussions with armed officers and people who could take away my freedom because uptight bureaucrats were too scared to have an open discussion. I didn't want angry confrontation, and trying to reason with candied-apples was folly. I snuck onto campus and spent a day at the university library studying up on methods of hunger strikes during detainment. Later, I asked a hypnotist to help me get past my pattern of seeking answers from the great system of silence on what actually matters.

I didn't realize that I had attained a measure of freedom few people ever experience. Having the windfall of family money and no job meant that I didn't have to find work right away. I decided to default my student loan and follow the invite of my bohemian friend Jerrold to *come out to paradise* in California. I needed to chase some personal utopia for a while. I would live on the central coast near Santa Cruz and visit Grand Canyon for annual river trips.

So in October of 2005, I made my escape and followed another ripple in my life, one that led me back to my deadhead days. I packed my stuff in a rental truck and left Arizona for California, where I would live among the redwoods and begin contemplating the question *What was I meant to be?*

Grand Canyon gave me more metaphors for this time of my life. My impetus to move to California came out of a week-long trip to Clear Creek in the last week of 2004 before I ever heard of a bureaucrat named Candie Apple Baconey. I was unhappy in Arizona, and I wanted to change my life. I planned the Clear Creek trip as a last solo hike in the Canyon where I would make decisions about my future and finish hiking all sections of all the trails between Grandview and Boucher. I followed the South Kaibab to the Tonto, cut across to the Bright Angel Trail to close off that loop, and spent the first night at the campground near Phantom Ranch. Like always, I contemplated life while walking and wrote down my thoughts in a journal afterward.

On the nine-mile trek from Phantom Ranch to make camp at Clear Creek, I thought about the waning spirit of America. My nation, the land of the free and the home of the brave, seemed neither. Freedom to me meant only one reality, but I had to live under two. I couldn't speak about my upbringing. I had been selected for tyranny, left licking my wounds, a would-be hermit. I had been brave enough to stand up for the truth, and I consoled myself with the idea that the lack of support or caring from others wasn't my fault. In camp that night, I went to sleep feeling I had done good in my spiritual journey.

The next day I bushwhacked my way up a dry creek bed to Cheyalla Falls. I crawled over twisted heaps of dead wood and hiked through dense brush that clawed at my clothing and skin. No formal trail went to my destination, and words of self-doubt and self-ridicule filled my head while ideas of annihilation ran in the shadows. I got to the falls to find them not much more than a trickle, and I saw that as a metaphor for my struggles in life. My real-world accomplishments left me dissatisfied. I felt unable to manifest anything I wanted. All the big plans and dreams of my younger days had fallen by the wayside, amounted to less than a trickle. I bushwhacked my way back to the campground at Clear Creek and went to sleep that night feeling alone and misunderstood.

The Canyon spirits threw a storm at me the next morning. Winds starting gusting as I packed up and prepared to hike back to Phantom Ranch. The rain came in horizontally before being swept vertically up the Canyon walls. By the time I walked up the trail out of camp, I was soaked to the bone with no other option but to continue my hike exposed to the elements. I remained warm in my soaking wet fleece as the cold winter storm challenged me all along the way.

Despite the weather, I found pleasure in the hike. I thought about the mood of the Canyon, how it made me focus on each step and enjoy each vista a little more. I felt the storm mocked me, and I stopped to write about how I always faced a blustery disposition and a damp outlook on life, always fighting a storm of my own making or one forced on me by others. The harsh weather motivated me to keep striving for my final destination of Phantom Ranch, where I envisioned a warm dorm bed waiting for me. My plan called for making camp at Bright Angel, but with everything soaked and the temperature near freezing, I needed to get a bed in the dorm of the always-booked lodge or spend a miserable night freezing in a tent.

Six hours later when I got to Phantom, I learned that the main trail had washed out and beds were available. I felt good about my day because of the storm I had overcome. In the dorm we all talked about our weather experiences. I got to be an ordinary person with the same struggles as others, not a disavowed American who shouted into deaf ears.

Over the last days of that trip in the Canyon I created a detailed one-year plan to change my life. I wanted to break out of Flagstaff, get a real job and start a great financial and emotional expansion. I even thought of finding someone to fall in love with for the first time in a decade. I didn't want to be the hermit anymore, the odd man out living a life where no one relied on me personally or professionally. My time at the Canyon had made me whole, but I felt a little too free. I liked that I had followed my heart as a young man and stayed true to my spirit into my forties, but I knew that the time had come to move away and hatch those eggs of delayed success.

Looking back on it, those Clear Creek plans to change my life were more like some kind of naive conjuring spell. I asked for expansion, and an incredible storm came and knocked my life out of balance. Seeking to collect on my *well-deserved good karma* invoked a wrath upon me. All the dark emotions that I had avoided during my years of becoming whole came back to challenge me, cursed family money found me, and the militant patterns came alive again. My Arizona life collapsed in deceit and confrontation, and I saw my move to California as escaping that negative spiral pulling me down. I believed in the best of times, an age of rebirth, but those days on the left coast proved to be a season of great emptiness.

"We are, as a whole, still in that low state of civilization where we do not understand that it is also vandalism wantonly to destroy or to permit the destruction of what is beautiful in nature, whether it be a cliff, a forest, or a species of mammal or bird. Here in the United States we turn our rivers and streams into sewers and dumping-grounds, we pollute the air, we destroy forests and exterminate fishes, birds and mammals—not to speak of vulgarizing charming landscapes with hideous advertisements. But at last it looks as if our people were awakening."

~Theodore Roosevelt

7. ECHOES OF A MIRACLE

I abandoned Grand Canyon to make my life in California. With the family money to sustain me, I took a break from day work. I wanted to embrace the artistic side of my being and rediscover my true nature lost beneath the latest upheavals of life. Jerrold set me up in a basement apartment down the street from his house and found an eighty-six Volvo wagon to be fixed up. The driver-side door of the purple clunker creaked, and on some mornings the engine remained silent when I turned the key, leaving me stranded at home to write or daydream while watching six-inch banana slugs crawl around my patio. I lived above the San Lorenzo River on the edge of a mossy, forested gorge not far from Boulder Creek and fell into a crunchy-granola state of being. My hair and beard grew wild, and I believed that good spirits had my back, replacing those demons whispering of personal armageddon left behind in Arizona. I embraced this lifestyle hoping for the best and waiting for a new calling to give me a direction to go.

The Santa Cruz Mountains can be a haven for weirdness. Alfred Hitchcock kept an estate in the area for many years, Jerry Garcia lost half his middle finger in a wood chopping accident while vacationing there as a kid, and Ken Kesey's Merry Pranksters may have started their electric kool-aid acid tests near there, though no one seems sure. I felt I was going back into a bohemian phase of my life. I wanted to feel rejuvenation again, chase personal utopia, but one last demon from the past lay in wait. A forgotten milestone in my healing journey drew nearer, and echoes of a miracle haunted me.

> I've been seeing a lot of rainbows in things —
> sunbeams, moonbeams, those rainbow arcs to one side
> of the sun or the moon. And I think when I see them that
> it's a message from the Great Spirit. My time here is
> short. I have a good ten years left then dis-ease will
> claim me. I'll pass on, hopefully having fulfilled. . . .
> I'll be dead in ten years unless the Christian God
> brings me a miracle of healing. . . .

Almost ten years gone since I wrote those words and death never found me—that meant a miracle of healing had occurred in my life. I didn't want to believe in miracles, but the spectre of death I wrote about all those years ago had other backers too. A medical record unearthed while applying to the Peace Corps showed that doctors from my grad school days didn't see me reaching age thirty-five. Their prognosis called for a diminished life both in years and my ability to connect with other people, but somehow I survived the long road from militant christian upbringing to educated scribe without reverting back and being born again into religious thinking.

So this ten-year milestone forced me to consider a self-proclaimed miracle of my own re-creation. I wanted to believe that I was a great spiritual warrior, but telling my story came off as arrogance and left people thinking I wanted to be their guru. Spiritual journeys—like most everything—had been turned into a commodity, even a competition, and my experience pushed the limits of credibility in the minds of most people, so I kept quiet. I decided to mark the passing of my ten-year miracle date alone hiking among the redwoods.

As I set out into the forest, sun high in the sky, I told myself I needed to change my approach to life and stop believing in miracles. Momentous shifts or big breaks were folly, epiphanies of spiritual insight could not take hold of me anymore. It was time to work on my ego, to move away from the intense spirit-reclamation work that filled my days in Grand Canyon country. I wanted a more ordinary life, but I had spent too much time alone in the wilderness to feel at ease among trendy

Californians. Social elegance eluded me and my life defied stereotypes. I didn't fit. I wanted the past to let go so that the future could arrive. I needed grounding. I needed to grow deep roots like the giant redwoods in the mountains around me. I needed a different face for the world of people, but I felt trapped behind a mask that hid my true self.

Late in the afternoon while hiking the loop trail out of the mountains, I had a weird experience near an abandoned logging camp. I saw a swirling green light in the darkening forest—a case of tunnel vision that felt like a vortex pushing me away. Drained of energy, I collapsed and sat down, wondering if this could be one of those whimsical manifestations of the Santa Cruz lights or will-o'-the-wisp faerie fire. *Piezoelectric energy? My eyes adjusting to the twilight? A patch of shrooms giving me silly sideburns?* People had turned less into extraterrestrial visitations or messages from the gods. The swirling light reminded me of the tunnel from my shamanic vision back in Carolina many years earlier. I began to wonder if the spiritual connection that saw me through my Grand Canyon days had closed—this negative spiral opposing that inviting positive one. *Was I being abandoned for not believing in my miracle?*

The strange light faded away, and after a few minutes of regaining my strength I got up to leave the area. Twilight set in and the forest grew dark, winds off the ocean began to pick up. I still felt disoriented, and I wondered about the trail beneath my feet. Had I made a wrong turn? Did this path take me back to my clunker or deeper into the woods and the growing darkness? I quickened my steps beneath the clattering of branches and the creaking of tree trunks, remembering similar sounds from the woods behind my childhood home. I told myself not to be scared, the trees weren't alive like in some fantasy book. I spoke aloud in whimsy, asking for calmness, not believing the trees or wind could hear me but thinking the sound of my own voice might soothe my nerves. The wind howled again, and I reckoned that the trees might be talking back in their own language of creaking wood and rustling leaves—voices from the wilderness expressing anger at my presence, unhappy with my intrusion into their world.

I didn't fancy myself a man to talk with trees. Anthropomorphizing the great redwoods of the left coast felt a bit silly. I knew that wood, living or dead, didn't have human feelings—that's what made talking to the log on the North Rim of Grand Canyon so funny. I thought of tree huggers as simple-minded folk, and yet I *talked* with the spirits of the Canyon, and here in the forest I talked out loud thinking it might calm the forces of nature. The Canyon had served as a deep reflection of my inner thoughts and feelings, a place to deal with the chasm within, but I also believed in something more—the whimsical notion that spirits watched over me there. These redwoods seemed to be reflecting back my inner turmoil, and I needed to calm the storm within to calm the woods around me.

But the wind grew worse. I broke into a slow jog, watching out for roots and dodging falling twigs and pine cones as I rushed through the fading twilight. My mind raced like my feet beneath me, and the world felt split in two. I ran hoping to see the edge of the forest and my car waiting in the parking lot. Contrary ideas from two divergent worlds fought each other in my thoughts—spirit and earthly plane, small town and metropolis, solitude or desolation, personal utopia or personal armageddon, creator or destroyer, secrecy or openness. I tried to merge these two sides, but the angry forest had no end.

Cali-duality—a culture shock of fitting in while pretending not to care—gnawed at my sense of freedom as I made my way through the woods. The journey to a *normal life* seemed too far to go and required a level of superficiality foreign to me. Canyon trails came with an unwritten goal of becoming *whole* while walking them. The left coast came with a plan to *be somebody* worthy of friendship, love and maybe even envy. Lots of people lived in their own little worlds complete with their own declared miracles, some of which seemed ridiculous to me.

During my darkest days there had always been esoteric intuitive clues to move me forward on my inner spiritual journey, but in chasing an ordinary life that spiritual guidance eluded me, or I forced it upon decisions I made asking for a sign. When things didn't go my way, I felt forsaken. I couldn't understand why I had made it through so much darkness only to end up feeling alone and alienated among people. Seeking human connection and an easier life robbed me of my faith and drew up a great rage inside me. I saw people caught up in pettiness trying to perfect a *lifestyle* and convince themselves that their choices were the best ones, and I envied what they had—their large houses, friends and life partners—but I watched them create unhappiness through deceit and manipulation of those they claimed to love. And these people were trying to make me like them, to hone me into a form not my own and use me as a tool in their schemes, to get me caught up in their caught-up-ness.

No amount of words could free me or answer the questions people had about me, and I didn't care to explain myself. After forty-some years of living and writing and remembering, the amount of information coursing through my mind stymied me at times. I appeared slow or confused as I tried to sort through all the possible faces to present to the outer world, and showing my intelligence only served to get me labeled as *the man who knew too much*.

All these thoughts seemed to create the storm in the forest surrounding me, and I realized I had to let it all go, give it over to God so-to-speak. I couldn't merge my two worlds, so I gave up a piece of my soul to the notion of impossibility, and that seemed to calm the winds around me and placate the redwoods. I found my way out of the forest and back to my dilapidated clunker of a life. I didn't dare tell anyone about what had happened that day. People saw me as a bit strange already, and some story about lights in the mountains and angry trees didn't seem like a good impression to spread around. Wunderkinds valued their ability to size up others, every word taken as a microcosm of a bigger worldview or a statement of a credo. The seriousness attributed to my whimsical notions among civilized folk often surprised me. Talk of miracles, spiritual journeys and strange lights in the forest could prove alienating . . . or inviting to others who saw such things everywhere.

I knew I needed to find natural power spots for alone time to ease my mind, but hiking under the redwoods didn't seem the answer. Driving and looking for isolated wilderness areas along the coast proved futile, people were everywhere. And when I found a spot of public land, the force of nature seemed weak—nothing compared to the feel of Grand Canyon for recharging myself. Seeking time alone away from redwood trees that might start talking to me, I took to finding open land along the beach where I could run.

I kept looking for longer stretches of seaside where I could run and let go of my troubles, and one day I found an area north of Santa Cruz with five miles of trail. I set off jogging next to a cliff where mist from ocean waves crashing in the distance occasionally sprayed me. The openness of the water felt similar to the open gorge of the Canyon, and my lungs were conditioned to higher elevations so running at sea level didn't make me tired. I felt like a super-human as I jogged and contemplated my long strange trip in life. I looked back over my journey with arrogant eyes—re-imagined my life story and fancied some crazy, convoluted notions.

As a boy and a creative soul in my militant catholic family, my gifts of imagination got praised as blessed from God or shamed as cursed abnormality. I took in that dysfunction, and I became *keeper of the craziness*. As long as my kinfolk could see me that way, they didn't have to face their own feelings of inner chaos. I had the role assigned to many youngest sons of religious families—to be crazy and die first . . . the grief of my death creating a somber place in the hearts of others to allow them to reach for the American dream. Long into adulthood, siblings continued gossip that I was *schizophrenic* without talking to me about it or checking the facts. I became the 'crazy uncle' for the next generation of WyKliffe descendants, left to roam the wilderness for death to find me. Except that the Canyon spirits didn't take me. I survived the intended fall, came full circle in my life, returned in touch with my true nature as a storyteller and scribe in a world that didn't have a place for freethinkers anymore.

I saw things others missed and didn't want to talk about. Many of my generation had gotten sidetracked from the revolution of thinking for one's self. They had arrived at a place of comfort and looked to the *gov'mint* to make sense of their reality, to feed truth to them as easy-to-swallow candies. Working for corporations and raising kids had made them retreat into hand-me-down notions of *us and them*—always on the lookout for a lone wolf who might disrupt their haven. I had run off into the wilderness and continued the revolution in my mind. I had seen the world's dysfunction from a vantage point on the rim, lived a momentous paradigm shift in my isolation, but my insights were too much for a plodding world. I became a voice crying out in the wilderness—more like the howl of a lone wolf—a spook.

Long ago, when I shattered the prism of my limited worldview and faced down my inner demons, I learned that the stories we tell ourselves shape our lives. If we focus on the negative or the futile, we feel depressed and helpless. If we focus on growing and learning, and we celebrate our life as a story of triumph, we move toward triumph. Telling life events from a place of freedom and strength, and developing meaning for our actions, transforms us. I knew that and believed that. I lived waiting for the day when my story could take flight, but it seemed others had used those same techniques to delude themselves, to get caught up in clinging to fantasies of grandeur that others could not see. And so my story of rising from the ashes of a dark childhood ready to take flight looked like just another delusion. My wings had been clipped long ago, and that left me the odd man out, a voice crying out in pain, another one of the humdrum-vanilla folk trying to escape from a backwater.

Rebirth couldn't find me because *the mole doctor* knew the power of storytelling too. He devised a plan to corrupt my true nature, to cripple me inside and isolate me from others. The secret medical conditioning created a repeating loop of disempowerment. I lost the ability to fulfill the unwritten expectations that create deeper friendships. Whenever I started to get close to others, I felt the overwhelm of past conditioning weighing down on me. I retreated into my mental wilderness, thinking I was defying the group consciousness, defying my martyr role, but actually I was gathering up all the repressed anger and resentment of people rewriting their personal histories into stories of triumph. I tried to ameliorate my sense of isolation with a dream of bringing a great truth back to the masses and shattering their delusions. The mole doctor had made me into the keeper of the craziness for a whole world who never did their spirit work, a whole world playing kick the can.

I could run free along the beach filled with the repressed thoughts and fears of people living in their suburban homes. I saw myself as a hero who had outlasted all the chaos society could muster. I had defeated the mole doctor in every way that mattered. I held on to my true nature, but the conflicts from my childhood still existed. And that made me *keeper of the craziness, the one with their foot on the can calling out the hiders*. My true nature as a scribe put me in conflict with the powerful who sculpted society for their own means. I called out for truth in a land where everyone played kick the can. I had spent my life trying to capture patterns of thoughts, striving to awaken dormant emotions, hoping to rejuvenate a sense of mystery and wonder—being a creator rather than a destroyer. *A scribe mind . . . in a world that wants word tinkerers perfecting pidgin prose.*

And I wondered about the mole doctor, this phantom from my past. What kind of man was he? Did he know his true nature? Did he know happiness? I pictured him as someone who reveled in aristocracy yet worried about a coming paradigm shift that could send civilization into another dark age. A man who spent his life caging the scribe minds of children, destroying their gifts of imagination and insight that might shift paradigms too fast.

Running along the beach, my mind raced faster than my legs. I tried to figure out how I might fit into this society along the left coast, and I cycled through all this craziness creating a revisionist version of my history. As I turned back to retrace my steps and run another five miles, I hoped for silence in my mind. I knew that all my convoluted thoughts needed a place of solace, of calming. I had some money to buy that and I thought of Grand Canyon river trips, but one getaway a year wouldn't be enough. I had no answers, no place to go, but I believed a new calling would find me.

Back at my starting point, as I wound down from my run, I saw a strange waterfall creating rainbows up in the coastal mountains. It didn't make sense being so close to the top of the ridge with no way for a creek to feed it. The place seemed like paradise, a natural power spot, and the glass walls of a silver temple building next to the waterfall glimmered in the sun. I didn't want to join a religion, but this felt like destiny calling—my racing thoughts calmed by these rainbows up above. I needed a place to belong, and there on that beach the distant waterfall seemed to whisper of fate, providence and karma—a path to follow.

A few days later, a woman working in a metaphysical book store told me about a temple for 'the goddess' down a road off the mountain highway. The retreat was shrouded in mystery, hidden behind a black gate that remained locked until the 'secret word' got spoken into the speaker phone—a word given out only after paying a tribute. *No doubt a situation rife with disappointment. Another sham religion, but also my new calling in this strange land off the left coast.* I decided to give it a try, thinking that maybe a woman as disillusioned with life as me might find me there and drag my whole world toward bliss.

I made contact and talked my way through two phone calls with a *matroness* whose gentle voice massaged my ears. I mailed a pledge and made a sincere promise of my desire to learn the ways of the goddess. We both knew we were leading each other on—pretense being the first lesson of following this particular manifestation of spirit. I didn't fret. Having been raised in a strict patriarchal religion, I always thought my life path required balancing that out, moving in the direction of matriarchal spirituality. Thérèse had shared this idea with me in our rebellious teenage years, and I had explored it with other women along the way. I had studied comparative religions in my prism-shattering days, and I went to energy healers during those dark times of confronting my demons from the chasm within. I knew the power of true mistresses of light and the potential shams and scams of the shadow side—*nothing can lead me too far astray.*

The initiation gathering happened on the winter solstice—the darkest day of the year serving as a chance to celebrate returning light. I drove the ridge highway looking for the turnoff but missed it three times before seeing a winding drive that took me west toward the ocean. Arriving at the black gate, I buzzed the speaker phone and spoke the word "resurrexī" (rhymes with sexy) as the matroness had told me, a Latin root related to resurrection. The gate clanged to life, receding away from me, and I drove in. I saw a mansion to the left with shiny Audis and BMWs out front, but the turnoff was blocked and the road went around to the back. I parked my Volvo wagon next to a few other hand-me-down cars and made my way to the temple. The glass walls of the round building allowed a clear look out to the ocean, and a stream feeding the waterfall I had seen from far below ran out the back of the building. The doors opened as I approached, and three women in shimmering white dresses guided me in, one of them telling me to make myself comfortable.

I walked about the place and noticed three groups of people—mature women who were the temple regulars, young women who seemed to be the daughters of the older women, and mediocre men who had been invited to the initiation. The mature women were dressed exquisitely—clothes, hair and skin calling to mind ideas of angels or goddesses, each with their own unique style. Some felt dark and daring, a negative vortex that might be inescapable, while others radiated a sense of light and calmness that could tempt and tease a man into wanton, hand-fed bliss. They were all knockouts in a way that pulled knees toward the floor and they knew it. The younger women, twenty-something neophytes, wore matching white dresses with a heart opening below the neck. The fabric shimmered in a rainbow of colours, and a frill of lace teased the cleavage of their breasts. The light that bounced off the dresses played tricks with my eyes—it seemed to both puzzle and mesmerize, making me stare to try to figure out why the shimmering happened. I got caught staring more than once and apologized politely.

When not looking at the women or trying to solve the mystery of the shimmering dresses, I noticed the men in the room. Most seemed about my age, an unimpressive lot, past their prime courtship years and dressed for business but pulling at their collars and clothes uncomfortably. With my full reddish beard, a maroon pullover and black jeans, I didn't fit in and I didn't care. I never did like dressing up for church.

Lights came on and a hush fell, followed by the soft clicking of shoes across the platform that extended into the room. The enchantress of the goddess, or some such priestess, approached to give us a welcome. Her feet were hidden by the frills of a robe-like dress made of shimmering fabric in a rainbow of colours. My eyes followed the slit up the dress that spiraled to the left around the knees and ended thigh high. Her belt had an oval buckle made of silver and adorned with green snakes climbing upward, and that directed my gaze higher still to sheer fabric that grew thinner and ended where multiple curved slits teased the top of her breasts. Platinum blonde hair too good to be real hung about her shoulders and extended down to the middle of her back. He lips were full, round and pouty, but the rest of her face didn't matter because a man alone with her probably remained on his knees. She arrived at the circle at the end of the platform and waited, as if knowing that the men were still processing her entrance.

She began speaking in an accent that sounded Scandinavian or Russian, a twinge of iciness that brought to mind snow falling on a frigid day. As to what she said, I only heard echoes of it across the chasm that exists between men and women. She welcomed us into an exploration of the mysterious and described three pathways to choose from, each with a different intensity and no doubt a different price tag. We could enjoy energy sessions with masseuses and body workers, talk sessions with counselors and spiritual guides, and more intensive outings with companions after jumping through some hoops and proving our devotion to the ways of the goddess.

She told us that a group of women initiates had already pledged to join the temple, and we would meet them during the weekly gatherings. If we proved our devotion, we could 'graduate' to be invited into the mansion healing rooms, *extra special places with kittens and other exotic purr-y creatures to play with.* She may not have said that out loud, but those words spoke in my mind as if they had been sent by telepathy— or that's my best excuse. I didn't buy into it. I felt amazed at how much the whole idea of following a healing path had changed since I lived my supposed miracle a decade earlier. I wanted to believe that somehow, some way, happiness waited for me beyond my skepticism, so I hid my disillusionment hoping for the best.

After the talk, a few of the young women guided the men along a path next to an indoor creek fed by a fountain. The water meandered through the center of the temple and flowed outside to a patio where shirtless teenage boys spackled over a wire framework, fixing holes in the mock rocks of a plaster canyon. As I walked beside the fake waterway, I thought of the dam on the river at the head of Grand Canyon, and a twinge of disillusionment danced on my chest. The creek flowed over a precipice creating the waterfall I had seen after my run on the beach. I stepped to the edge and saw a small pool below where the water got sucked down a drain and recycled back to the fountain in the temple to start the same short journey again.

The women guides lured some of the men to the edge of the balcony to stand in the spray of the falling water. The light of the setting sun shimmered off the silver metal surfaces, and the women talked about how the guys glowed with Shakti and radiated life-force energy. I wanted to believe, but I saw mediocre men in a mist of water and refracted light. The other guys ate up the attention while I stood back thinking over my twenty years of healing. I had met magical mistresses of light and traveled the cyclical pathways they presented, navigated the spiral of deepening mystery that kept me coming back for another session seeking my miracle of healing. Except that the magic got lost somewhere, evaporated into mist and mirrors.

The healing path had become big business. Birth trauma, childhood hurts and normal adolescent growing pains got turned into challenges to be explored and overcome. Listening to your breath and heartbeat, and being grateful for them, got turned into proof of miracles in the world. The whole connection to healing true trauma had been lost, and touching upon anything too deep brought a potential 'referral' to a practitioner of psychiatry or some other dark art.

I wondered if I had been gullible in my younger days, an obvious introvert fooled by women into chasing miracles out in the wilds. And I took it too seriously, set out and found a real canyon, dreamt up real miracles, which made living in metropolises feel too confining. I felt sorry for the water trapped in its short run down an aluminum creek on a balcony—bubbling out of the fountain filled with life and hope, flowing down the plaster canyon with anticipation, only to freefall into a pool of disillusionment where it learned its whole journey had been preordained long ago. I had reached the waterfall in my life, a time to get cycled back through for another rebirthing full of the awesome pretense of admiration for women married to corporate guys and teasing other men's hankerings.

I straggled along at the end of the pack feigning a level of enthusiasm. Spirit had led me here, so there had to be some payout, some connection waiting to happen. I decided to give the goddess temple a few weeks and see what came of it. I set up counseling sessions, scheduled a therapeutic massage, promised to attend some social gatherings— hoping to see my skepticism wane and miracles bubble forth. *Or maybe there is nothing . . . a tragedy playing itself out, increasing frustration and bitterness at my draw in life . . . falling back into old patterns.*

* * *

A week later I returned to the temple for my first of four sessions with a spiritual counselor named Pru. She told me the curls in her hair held wisdom from the male god Krishna, the eighth avatar of Vishnu. If I followed her rituals, magic could happen. I never told her that the strange introduction made me think of Vishnu Schist at the bottom of Grand Canyon—a billion-year-old igneous rock and a better listener than her.

I delved into my background, told my story with arrogance as if taunting any dark demons or forgotten ghosts to come out of hiding and play kick the can again. Pru wanted me to detach myself from my words and see what I spoke as false origin stories that kept me in a never-ending spiral of the past, robbing me of being in the now. She raised the idea that I had picked my life path with all its hardships, as if I had seen it on a shelf somewhere before birth and said, "Please, give me that heritage." She didn't know I had been through this before. I had let go of my past and lived in the 'now,' but somehow the ghosts of generations gone returned and destroyed my haven. I felt trapped in a bounding curse, as if listening to echoes of a miracle fading into the distance and dying out.

Every time I entered a social group, I sensed an undercurrent of backbiting. I believed that I saw more of the true spectrum of experience while other people viewed the world through a limited prism, and a negative spiral of self-obsession overtook me. Joining the temple had me living all those patterns again. It seemed to me that the self-professed spiritual warriors of this age focused their lives on the bettering of one's self as a pathway to accumulating riches, lovers and even worshippers. Their stories of *awakening* and their personal experiences with *miracles* seemed simple compared to my journey, like following fairies in a forest. I felt they were mocking true spirituality, packaging it in self-published pamphlets as mainstream messages for a caught-up middle class. *Buy my seminar and bring more utopia into your life. You deserve to have others serve you.* And I wondered. *Had they forgotten all the lessons learned from the sixties to the eighties about being creative and weird and grounded? Had we all gone off on our own paths, forgetting to check back in with reality?*

The rise and fall of my own re-creation suffocated me. Pru told me to wait for magic to happen—a shout could make echoes and create magical coincidences. But I knew I couldn't follow those ideas anymore. I didn't believe. I remembered the magic of the past, the mistresses of light, those feelings of opening my heart—and I couldn't deny that my heart had opened. I had changed, but these same actions now felt fake somehow, like going through motions, an echo without a shout. And I still wondered if the magic I felt in my younger days had been a mirage too, like a will-o'-the-wisp in a dark forest or a trail that existed only in the mind of the walker. Did all those mistresses of light dupe me? And in that duping did they save me from fulfilling a dark-side destiny? The mist and mirrors, the irrationality, my miracle of healing, the running from demons and chasing ghosts, all of that kept my mind from falling into defunct holy war patterns, but now I needed something more.

And Pru didn't have it. These ideas bounded off cliffs in my mind while she talked about self-love and finding others who can see my divinity. The people drawn to the temple were a new tribe all brought together for a reason, she said. If I followed them and dedicated myself, magic could happen. The same notion I had heard so many times before but it never worked out, so it didn't feel right anymore. I didn't like pretense, hobnobbing, dancing the dance of high-society niceness.

After two sessions with Pru, she convinced me to come to one of the weekly temple gatherings to meet the women initiates. I didn't expect much, but I stifled my disillusionment enough to walk through the temple doors on the first Friday of the new year. I almost left after a few minutes of mulling around, but I noticed a woman in the group with the same look of skepticism behind her eyes that I felt in my heart. We were the contrary ones, the ones running in the shadows of feigned enlightenment. I wondered if the call of fate had worked to bring this woman into my life. She hid her disillusionment well, feigned a lightness of spirit, but somehow I sensed the depths of her disenchantment. I wondered if I had finally found someone who could 'get' me.

Her name tag read Sienna MacLeland, and her red hair betrayed Scots-Irish ancestry. In her obligatory background story to the group, she told of a childhood bouncing around with her parents on philanthropic missions, from Britain to Australia to the West Indies. Her mother had once worked to save *mermaids*, Sienna said with a hint of mischief before laughing and admitting she meant manatees, or dogs of the sea as her younger self called them. When she turned eighteen, she escaped the confines of her parents and came to America as a nanny for a couple in Utah. She got into saving earth dogs, first those of the prairie variety, then coyotes, and finally she took up spreading awareness about the misunderstood lobo. She admitted to loving a lost cause—she even adopted a rez dog from the backblocks of New Mexico and dragged him with her as she followed her heart to a dream job in California at the Golden State Wolf Preserve. She had reached the age of thirty-seven having never married, sold out or grown up— and she didn't intend to grow up, though she hadn't ruled out marriage. That was her story, no doubt refined over years of stringing together a stopgap existence and having her parents bail her out when things didn't go as planned.

I dismissed any notion of her at first blush, vaguely aware of her listening to my quick story of seeing a waterfall after a run on the beach and deciding to check it out. Sienna seemed too full of pep and glee to be a match for me, yet she stayed in my thoughts after the gathering, and I went back a week later wanting to see her again. She showed up dressed to the nines, donning a long-flowing blouse that had sleeves that looked like bird wings. Seeing her swooping about the place full of smiles took me back to my thunderbird walking days—a healer had said *a bird spirit who runs with wolves is the one who holds your fate.* So my heart took a flight of fancy seeing Sienna in wings. I figured that an introvert like me needed an extrovert, so I cornered her next to the fake waterfall and asked her to come see a real waterfall with me.

I told her about Julia Pfeiffer Burns State Park, a lone spot of paradise about a hundred miles down the coastal highway that had a picturesque waterfall and the remnants of a homestead on a cliff overlooking the ocean. Sienna had never heard of the place, but she accepted my invite while shying away from my piercing gazes into her greenish eyes.

The next day, early in the morning, she climbed into my car wearing blue jeans, an outback hat and a button-down shirt. She had no cleavage to speak of, couldn't create it if she wanted to, and that suited me just fine. We took off down the coastal highway in silence and after a few miles agreed to stop to get some coffee to drink along the way. Back on the highway, we fell into some repartee.

"Is your mocha okay?" she asked while finishing a sip of hers.

"My moksha? It's fine."

She caught my play on words. The term moksha had been used at the temple, the only new idea gathered from all the talk there. Pru had brought it up first, and I just figured it as one of those foreign words that guru types use to stop people from thinking rationally.

"Mocha, not moksha," she said. ". . . But on second thought, how's your moksha?"

"It killed my karma."

"A bloody, well-deserved death I hope."

I smiled and swerved to miss a pothole. "My moksha ran amok all over my karma."

"I know the feeling. I have an amok shadow too."

"Amok shadow . . . what does it do?"

"What does my amok shadow do?" she laughed.

"Yes, Sienna. What does your a-mok-sha-do?" I said with serious pretense.

"My a-mok-sha-do fights with my a-mok-sha-don't."

"And who wins?"

"My karma loses."

"Ahh, the end of the ego. No more rising and falling. No more stories," I said, feeling I had killed the moment.

"You can never claim to achieve moksha because that is an ego thing."

"Moksha fills the gaps in our mojo," I said, and took another sip of my coffee.

"Yes, I have gaps that need filling," she said, ". . . I need a gap filler in my life."

I felt stumped as my mind wandered into thoughts of sex and filling gaps.

She laughed, "I think I'm going to shut up now!"

The silence didn't hold. We were two people riding the same wave that day, moving in and out of each other's thoughts in a way I hadn't felt since my teenage days. We got to the park and checked out the waterfall, played around in the remnants of the homestead on the cliff and took a hike along a forest trail. Whenever a little awkwardness came between us, we fell back into trite talk of moksha, karma, filling gaps and maybe jumping off cliffs together.

I am sure when we left each other that day, after a late drive back up the coast, we both felt as if we had found a little magic, found someone who *got* us, and thought that our days of being alone were ending for a time. Except that we hadn't escaped karma. Maybe inwardly we believed in moksha, but the world hadn't arrived there yet and fate decided to throw us a curve.

I couldn't reach Sienna after our outing and I became worried. I thought of Ally's motorcycle wreck and Devi's disappearance from my life as I waited for Sienna to get back to me. A couple days later, I tracked her down at a cafe she had mentioned, snuck up on her unannounced with two mochas and met a harsh face filled with hurt. Seeing the look in her eyes, I sat down next to her waiting for an explanation.

"I suppose you heard that I lost my job," she said.

"No, I had no way of knowing."

"I learned that night. It happened the day we were together."

I didn't know what that meant, and I tried to look on the bright side. "Something will turn up. This could be a blessing."

"No, I'm leaving."

"Leaving, for where?"

"Australia, my parents are . . ."

I didn't know what to say as her voice trailed off and our eyes fell upon the two cups of coffee on the table between us.

She looked at me with bitterness. "If anything I said made you think I had feelings for you, I'm sorry. I don't feel that way."

"Oh come on. You don't have to be like this. Let's stay in touch and see what turns up." I tried to catch her eyes and poke a little humour at her. "Maybe I will show up on your doorstep some day with a coffee."

"I could totally lie and make things up to make this easy for the both of us, but I'm not going to. The truth is I feel creeped out that you might have feelings for me. I don't feel the same way. I fooled myself and you. And showing up at my doorstep . . . no. . . . I'm sorry if there was anything I did to make you feel or think that I was interested in you." She grabbed one of the coffees and got up. "Look after yourself, Thomas."

She tossed the full cup in the trash can and walked out the door.

The next weekend, I went back to the oceanside park alone to think about lost possibilities. I told myself that my feelings were ashes before rebirth, that some greater meaning lived beyond my experience with Sienna. My days in California had led me to a deeper understanding of karma, or so I wanted to believe. I kept expecting to see Sienna there running toward me with arms open and lips speaking an apology, but I knew she was gone for good. Our story had been written. We had no way back from the words spoken in the coffee shop.

I left that sliver of paradise, drove up the coast, and late that afternoon I hiked into the redwood forest of the Santa Cruz Mountains. Alone near where I saw the negative spiral of green energy on the ten-year anniversary of my miracle, a revelation in thinking beguiled me as if some spirit was whispering into my ear and taking me back to the time when I wrote about the calm muck. *We're all trying to find bliss, but we fail to see there is both 'ignorant' bliss and 'knowing' bliss. Many seek the 'now' moments of ignorant bliss and call that enlightenment, but there's a knowing bliss where 'living in the moment' takes us beyond darkness. It's not everlasting, darkness returns, but 'knowing' bliss spawns freedom while 'ignorant' bliss creates a cage.* There in the forest I imagined helping people move from ignorant bliss to knowing bliss and creating moments of happiness for myself along the way.

I saw back over my whole spiritual journey, and I realized that I had replaced the concept of good and evil with a watered-down sense of karma. *Putting 'good' out into the world means that bliss returns to you in the future?* By age forty, I knew this couldn't be true. Sometimes bad things happen to good people—sometimes random chance changes possibilities and destroys happiness. Out of that arises the notion that there is evil in the world trying to destroy good . . . and because evil exists, holy warriors are necessary.

But isn't true karma about living in the moment? I remembered a saying that claimed *all karma is instant, and once you understand that you hold the key to happiness.* Up there in the mountains beneath the redwoods all these ideas swirled around me—the notion of moksha, release from cycles of ego death and rebirth, the rise and the fall, and realizing we never arrive but we continue to strive—it all hit me at once. *Karma is instant. If you seek the bliss of each moment, you achieve moksha and move beyond the continual rising and falling of your own self-creation and destruction.*

The revelation went further—I felt myself getting to the root of my patterns of suffering and disillusionment, and a faux calling began to materialize out of the moment. Instead of following others and sharing my life story to be accepted into a group, I could say I met with a spirit in the Santa Cruz Mountains who gave me a mission to take people on retreats near Grand Canyon. Somewhere off in the remote wilderness, when people were loopy from a long hike, I could share wisdom gathered from an eclectic life lived on the edge of society. Americans with lots of money from working too much loved connections with nature and eccentricity. They could escape their corporate cages on vacation, and I could make my way in the world as a superficial guru with no real training.

I sat there proud of my revelation, believing I had a future, until a twig from a redwood hit me in the head. A laugh came up from inside me and started resounding through the forest. Sitting under those living trees, my cackles echoed just like they had next to a dead log on the North Rim of Grand Canyon. The laugh seemed to chase all the spirit voices away, and I felt happy and in the moment. I realized I could never pull off becoming a guru. *I am a scribe, a dreamer, an idealist, not a Sage. I don't clean up well, and I've spent too much of my life alone to ever find lasting love or connection again.* My whole story of rebirth from the ashes of lost possibilities rose and fell in the lush greenness of that redwood forest afternoon.

I had nowhere to be in the world, and I started feeling ill in California. An aching crept into my bones, my life force became weak. Migraine headaches split my head, and my neck and shoulders hurt. Pollution clogged my lungs, infesting body and spirit. My intuition told me that the stresses of all those years of going unheard and unloved had caught up to me. The disease I believed should have arrived in ten years showed late, but only a little. I needed no doctor to tell me what the feeling in my bones meant.

I had no where to turn. My distant siblings were lost to me, and Jerrold didn't need my burdens dragging him down. I didn't want to spend my final days fighting against an illness, living under hospital arrest, a subject of study, caged in a way to make others comfortable with my dying. My fighting days were done. I wanted to embrace this final earthly mystery in the way I had embraced life—with no simple roadmap made by the hands of other men. I had but one question awaiting an answer. *Do I stay out in California with an old friend or go back home to Grand Canyon?*

Jerrold loved the area around Santa Cruz and often referred to it as paradise. One day while playing disc golf we came to the top of a hill overlooking the forests some twenty miles to the sea. He stood there taking it all in, said it was his favorite vista. As I looked out, I noticed a brown cloud hanging in the air over the ocean. I didn't say anything about it. I didn't want to ruin his moment. I figured baseline definitions for paradise had shifted. The clean air and wilderness of less populated areas had spoiled me. I needed power spots like Grand Canyon to feel more alive. In California, I had found only one spot— Julia Pfeiffer Burns State Park—and now that held bad memories and feelings of loss. I took drives up into the mountains past the temple gates I didn't enter anymore, seeking but not finding solace. More and more I missed the clean air of Northern Arizona and the solitude of nature that rejuvenated my spirit.

I saw the world on the left coast as being shattered into a great duality of those seeking their personal utopia and those caught up avoiding a personal armageddon. All the hard work I had done to recreate myself didn't matter because I arrived too late to the party. I knew I couldn't hide my true story without falling back into darkness. I couldn't manage the great duality with the gigantic scar down the middle. I had made all the changes necessary inside of myself, but it seemed to be a time of increasing expressions of personal armageddons in the world. The chasm between the two sides felt wider than ever, the crossing took too long, and it weighed too great on my mind and body—*too far to go in one life.*

I tried to hang on to my optimism in California, but I slipped back into darkness. The constant pull between extremes drained me. I lost what I liked about myself, and I was dragging down a friend. The economy teetered on the edge of a crash, killing the hopes of people like Sienna, and all the luck and miracles had drained out of my life too. Arizona had my favorite natural haunts where I could rejuvenate my ailing spirit—and some kind of rebirth *might* happen there.

So I said my goodbyes, packed up my Volvo wagon with everything I owned piled high on the roof, and I headed east for the Tehachapi Pass out of California. Up there somewhere overlooking the Tehachapi Loop Railroad that runs in the gap in the mountains, I pulled out my journal book. The pages in the refillable leather binder hadn't seen much use in California—my writing days and love of words seemed to be over.

FREE-WRITING – TEHACHAPI PASS, CALI

How did I arrive at disillusionment? It's been a long strange trip not of the good kind. It started with illusions of course – false notions that I believed to be true. You might think that getting rid of false ideas is a good thing, that disillusionment could be a good thing. And maybe it will be after a time, but right now it doesn't feel that way.

Some of that is the nature of the illusions that fell over these last eight years. As Mark Twain is rumoured to have said, "Don't part with your illusions. When they are gone you may still exist, but you have ceased to live."

I lived an illusion of a path to justice that started on my thirty-seventh birthday. I believed in it with all my heart. I signed on to that path all alone with hope, and even when the path forked off I still believed in justice of another kind. Now, so many forks later, there is nary any hope left. Still I tell myself that at least I am not as lost as so many others who are devoid of hope in their hearts, but the illusion of justice, of being heard, of being able to make a difference on something, is now placed at fanciful. One more note to a new administration to review something that the last one crushed. But we know that justice delayed is justice denied. I'm done with the illusion of justice.

I lived an illusion of arriving at a healed self. I took to that path thinking a day would come when things got easier, when my wisdom could make the path easier for others. Instead I arrived to a place of dense brush, for not many have been this far before. Those ideas that were once easy, that uplifted my heart, have taken a turn. There's a place where karma meets moksha and they do battle, but how can you describe that battle other than to say maybe you should go another way. Not much peace of mind here. All karma is instant, when you know what that means your path will be overgrown too. Healing is a path, first one you follow and then one you hack out of the growth. I'm done with the illusion of arriving at healed.

I lived the illusion of carefree happiness in a relationship . . . for life is enhanced when you share it with another. I thought I knew that once and could capture it again, that a woman would see past this ugly exterior to a kind and open heart. It's a rare thing, sharing a path. Mostly the attempts to connect beat you down, the illusions fall as the most inviting path dead ends. You lose the way back to your own path. Animals keep coming out of the woods to play. Should you give in to the mundane, the meaningless, and try to assign it great meaning? Or does that only make the disillusionment greater later? Another dead end. Where did I put that machete? Life is work and love is folly. We put our best face on it, hide our disillusionment. Why didn't I ever settle? I'm done with the illusion of carefree happiness in a relationship.

I lived that age-old illusion called love. Quite a fanciful notion. It's an exotic ornamental flower or some crazy-coloured reef-dwelling fish. So beautiful in the wild, in its natural surroundings, but we want to take it home with us. I can build a terrarium or fill an aquarium and look at it every day. Check the soil and humidity, fertilize it, learn to take care of it . . . check the water and oxygen, feed it, learn its needs. And the damn thing dies anyway. Where can I ever get another one like that? Is it more trouble than it's worth? Russian bride? Why can't I get rid of the illusion of love?

I lived the illusion of disillusionment. Here love comes again in the most impractical form of all. She's a most fanciful female, smiles all the time, as if daring someone to put a stop to that. Full of hope. Can conquer any darkness. If she's into dogs and lost causes, she's bound to fall for me. The only thing that trumps disillusionment is fancifulness, and this feels unreal.

Will I ever be done with illusions?

Those were the last words I ever wrote by hand in a journal.

Upon re-entering Arizona and getting closer to the Canyon, I felt defeated and rejuvenated. Rising and falling in equal amounts. Ready for the best of times or the worst of times. I still had some family money—money that seemed to curse my prospects, money I wanted to spend—and maybe enough to see me through what remained of my life, years forty-four to forty-seven.

My first days back in Arizona came with an adventure paid for some months earlier, a sixteen-day river trip through the heart of Grand Canyon. And I wondered about my fate. *Did some unexpected rebirth await me? Or would I become one of those voices from the wilderness of Grand Canyon toying with people who hiked there?*

"In the Grand Canyon, Arizona has a natural wonder which is in kind absolutely unparalleled throughout the rest of the world. I want to ask you to keep this great wonder of nature as it now is. I hope you will not have a building of any kind, not a summer cottage, a hotel or anything else, to mar the wonderful grandeur, the sublimity, the great loneliness and beauty of the canyon. Leave it as it is. You cannot improve on it. The ages have been at work on it, and man can only mar it."

~Theodore Roosevelt

8. A TALE OF TWO RIVERS

The purple clunker cruised up the Mogollon Rim and got me to Flagstaff on the eve of my river trip. I put my stuff in a storage unit on the edge of town and found a cheap motel room off old Route 66. My whole life for the next two weeks needed to fit into a dry bag to be carried on a raft through Grand Canyon. I spread my river gear out on the bed—paddle jacket and pants, Aussie sun hat, three pairs of sunglasses, a duffle full of clothes, a backpack for hikes, a waterproof river guide, a hydration pack, sneakers, hiking shoes, Teva sandals, Keen flip-flops (with the big toe cover), a stash of food, other items from the checklist—and it seemed like too much.

As I pulled clothes from the duffel, a reflection of my crunchy-granola self in the wall mirror caught my eye. I realized having a beard down in the hot inner gorge of the Canyon might be unbearable, so I went into the bathroom and found my trimmer. After cutting my beard short and shaving, I looked at my bare face in the mirror and noticed the hair on top of my head. *Might as well get rid of that too.* Entering the Canyon clean and leaving with only new growth felt right somehow, so I ran the trimmer along my scalp, letting my locks fall in the sink. With my head bare, I turned off the razor and looked up. The face in the mirror jumped out at me and I staggered backward, feeling a punch hit my gut as I noticed the heap of shorn hair covering the drain in the sink. Feeling faint, I fell onto the toilet. Memories of sitting in a chair as a child and getting military buzz cuts coursed through me. I dismissed the notion that an end-of-life parade was flashing before my eyes and got up, threw the heap of hair in the trash and went off to the pre-trip meeting.

In a conference room at a hotel, the river guides handed out maps and started to describe what to expect on the trip. They told us that the river through Grand Canyon alternates flat pools with steep rapids— slow-moving, lazy flows with heart-pounding, downward rushes. There's time to daydream while floating between the steep walls, but when a side canyon breaches into the inner gorge, the rocks form rapids that pull boats in and spit them out the other side. The rapids have personalities that try to trick the boat pilot into trouble, to catch them in an eddy or vortex, to strand them in a backwater or maroon them on a rock protruding out of the stream, to turn them askew and flip their boat sending everyone for a swim. There's a preferred path through a rapid, a line to hit that makes for the littlest effort and the least danger, but that line changes based on volume of water, location of rocks, and the strength and tendencies of the boater.

At the beginning of a trip, the group of strangers has no idea what sharing a sixteen-day adventure on a wild river means. As the days pass, a sense of camaraderie forms, playfulness follows and mischief ensues. *Wry smiles beget sham rebukes, I'm-with-you laughs follow folly with nature, in-the-moment yells echo far beyond pretense.* A feeling of sharing a wilderness journey with fellow adventurers takes over, but the solitary moments in the womb of the earth stay with you forever.

The Canyon keeps you on your toes while reminding you to remain light of heart. The thrill of riding a rapid may give way to swimming in frigid water, waiting for rescue and worrying that the Canyon spirits are 'calling you home.' I knew about this before the meeting. As a driver years before, I dropped people off for river trips and picked them up on return, and I saw the change in their faces from sheepishness to wider awareness. I wanted to believe that hiking hundreds of miles solo below the rim made me a natural for a river trip, but I knew that running the Colorado River through the heart of Grand Canyon could turn sage to jester.

The next day, I took a seat on a paddle boat with six other people and set off from Lee's Ferry. We dashed through Paria Riffle and floated along a smooth stretch of water where we got lessons on using our paddles. After mastering the basic commands and learning to turn the boat in circles, the lead guide called for us to meet in the middle. We tied the cargo boats around the paddle raft and floated together down a calm section of river in Marble Canyon.

We had a good mix of people—locals who had saved up for the trip of a lifetime, people from back east who took the adventure every year, a couple from Denmark on holiday, and a group of friends from small-town America who always wanted to see Grand Canyon. As we passed under the spans of the Navaho Bridge, it became my turn to speak, last of the runners to tell his story to the others. I talked about being a Grand Canyon solo hiker and said that these yellow boats were my only home for the next two weeks—all my stuff sat in a storage unit in Flagstaff—and when I left the river, a harsh reality waited as I tried to figure out what comes next in my life. A murmur of support met my ears, and after a pause the guides started their repartee, ribbing and teasing each other as they gave their introductions.

I sat back and stared at the sky between the canyon walls, seeing each of the guides as echoes of ideal river folk that lived in my imagination. Ethan, our trip leader and a gentle giant of a man, had run the river for more than a decade. Glenda, the 'old lady of the Canyon' and an expert on birds, expected to be a grandmother by the end of the trip. Finny, an auburn-haired siren with a cackle that echoed into the heart, warned us that she liked to play flute in caves and alcoves. Jed, a slender fellow with a beard, seemed like a quintessential reincarnation of a Powell-expedition boatman. And Jacinth, our paddle boat captain, looked out of place, but the red streak in her blonde hair hinted of an edgy spirit wrapped in a diminutive form. These were the five people taking care of us, cooking for us, guiding us downriver and on hikes, and delivering us back to the world above the rim if all went according to plan.

We headed off downriver and I kept looking for signs of magic along the way. My life jacket had the name 'Hayduke' on it—the saboteur from *The Monkey Wrench Gang* by Edward Abbey—and the others took to calling me that. I humoured them, but the nickname made me feel like the odd man out, trapped in the lone-wolf, rebel role again. I figured my shaved head didn't help first impressions much, but my beard and hair started growing back in softer and redder than before, leaving me looking more Irish.

On hikes I straggled behind and sometimes wandered off to spend time alone. It never lasted long because the 'cleanup' guide trailing the pack forced me back into line. While the others hiked and camped with their partners or friends and used a buddy system to look out for each other, I wandered around solo, stopping to look at things on impulse. I noticed Jacinth keeping an eye on me, sometimes outright following me like a personal escort, making sure I didn't wander off. I figured the older guides put her up to it, asked her to buddy up with the loner, *charm him* and make him feel like part of the group. So to make things easier I started to hang out around her, buddy up with her.

After returning from a day hike up to the Nankoweap Ruins, I found Jacinth resting at camp near the river reading Abbey's *Monkey Wrench* novel. I sat down across from her, pulled out my river guide and started making notes. She looked up from the pages and said out of nowhere, "Hey Hayduke. It's real," as if answering a question or continuing a conversation I started.

I guessed what she meant. "The red streak?"

"Yes. I know guys wonder about it. Think it's some kind of trendy . . . cry for attention."

"Never crossed my mind. Honestly."

She looked back at her book. "Not sure I believe you. But if so, can you keep a secret?"

"Maybe."

"It's real, but not so bright anymore, like when I was a girl. So I add a little colour before each river trip." She ran her hand through her hair and smiled.

"Your secret is safe with me, mostly because no one listens to what I say anyway."

She closed the book and looked at me. "So, Hayduke, what's your secret?"

I gave her a blank look.

"Something you've never told anyone before? The Canyon is a place to tell secrets."

I laughed. "I kind of hate the Hayduke nickname—I like the book but not the name."

"What's a good nickname for you?"

I thought for a moment. "It was given to me in a dream, and it's funny. Wouldn't want anyone to call me that, so can you keep it a secret?"

She nodded.

"ThunderBird Walking."

"Really?" She laughed.

"Remember, I've never told anyone that before."

"Your secret is safe with me," she said, laughing a little, ". . . mostly."

After that, we began having moments on hikes sharing secrets and dumb stories about ourselves. On a hike up to an inner gorge overlook near Cremation Creek, she told me she grew up in the boondocks, a Midwestern farm girl, to become "the smallest Grand Canyon boat woman ever."

"But pound for pound the toughest?" I mused.

She laughed. "Ethan, big as he is, is still pound for pound the toughest. If I get into trouble in a rapid, I'm at the mercy of the river spirits."

"Except that you commune with the river spirits before each rapid, so that you don't get into trouble."

"Yes, Hayduke, being blonde and a woman, I talk with river fairies rather than knowing how to read the flow and hit the perfect line."

"Ha, sorry. It's just that I talk to river spirits, so I thought you did too," I said, redeeming myself.

Our flirtation had no legs, she being too young for me with a ". . . sort of boyfriend." She didn't seem the type who wanted to domesticate with anyone, least of all a man in need whose life above the rim sat in a storage unit waiting for rescue and a place to belong.

On day eight, we set off to meet the hermit monster—my nemesis reborn. The flow of the river hit an all-time high that morning and Hermit Rapid had changed recently, so the guides didn't know what lines to run. As we beached the paddle boat upriver from the rapid, Jacinth told us that a new rock had appeared out of nowhere a few weeks earlier and it created a huge fifth wave that could swallow a boat. There were no signs of a rockfall from any nearby cliffs, and a boulder that big couldn't have just floated downriver on its own, but it was there nonetheless. So we needed to take a look at the rapid and decide if the monster could be conquered.

As we closed in on the roar of the water, we saw another group standing there with their gear. They looked dejected and a little spooked. After seeing the river they had decided to walk the shore rather than risk taking on the raging waters. Standing next to them, I caught my first glimpse of the monster and understood how they felt. One of their guides had lined up his oar boat to take a run at the rapid alone. The blue raft looked like a speck in the middle of a torrent, totally at the mercy of the river. The craft hemmed and weaved, and a wall of water knocked the boatman sideways and almost pushed him overboard. He got back on the oars and with the grace of nature—being at its whim— he fought through the rest of the waves and arrived at the lower end upright in the boat, drenched, shaken and stirred. The river looked too daunting to run in a paddle boat, and I figured we would grab our gear and walk the shore too.

Jacinth started milling about trying to recruit people for *the ride of a lifetime* with her. Ethan warned her to be careful what she wished for, but three muscular guys stepped forward to answer her call and a fourth joined soon after. A woman stepped forward to make it five, saying she could sit in the back and hide behind the men. No one else made a move, and Jacinth's gaze fell upon me.

"Come on Hayduke. I've got all the big guys I need. You can ride in back next to me."

The others turned toward me with pleading eyes—none knowing that the *hermit* lived in my mind as nemesis. I conjured up some courage. "I guess . . . if little Jacinth is willing to go . . . and rescue me if I fall in . . . I'll make it a full crew." A yell echoed through the Canyon.

Back at the paddle boat, as we checked the straps on each other's life jackets, the guides got in a huddle and worked out the order of the boats. Two oar boats set off ahead of us to wait on the river below the rapid for anyone that fell off. The seven of us in the paddle boat lined up next, to be followed by Finny's oar boat. Ethan brought up the rear, carrying three people who could pull any trapped stragglers out of the water as he powered through.

So I took off into the rapid, one of six paddlers with captain Jacinth, our raft a mere speck in the middle of a raging river. Me, facing my nemesis—full of fear of death, and of life, love and acceptance—

thinking that sometimes God lifts you to greater heights so that the devil can smack you back down.

As we entered the monster, a wall of frigid water swamped the boat, but we were all still there, digging and pulling and heaving forward, doing whatever the woman with a red streak in her hair said as if life depended on it, because it just might. We rose and we fell and we lost our seats only to paddle standing in a watery grave of a boat before it came up and smacked our ass and sat us back down. We got thrown about in wave one, screamed through the second wave, faced our fears of loneliness mixed with thoughts of death on wave three, and powered our way over wave four. As wave five approached I dared to be happy we might make it through unscathed.

The raft rode up and up and up, and at the crest I looked down to see a void below us. If there were time to ponder, I may have thought that the fifth rock embodied my rage in the form of a hole, a chasm, a vortex into some land of the lost—but we began to fall with no time to think. Jacinth yelled for us to dig hard, and we ripped our paddles though the air while riding on the back of a beast. I thought we were lost, but water swelled back beneath us and we lurched forward still intact, knifing our paddles into the spine of the monster. We broke over the wave and came careening down the other side, cutting the perfect line and shooting out the lower end still one crew—happy and all the worse for wear.

We screamed and cheered and accepted applause from other boats while smacking our paddles together. Finny pulled up beside us and spun around, and we all looked for the last boat. Ethan flew up over the fourth wave and powered toward the fifth. His raft disappeared into the trough and we waited for him to reappear. Jacinth gasped as he came into view—his boat emerged on top of the monster skewed a slight ways left and faltering. She yelled out, "You've got the power to get out Ethan," but the roar of the river swallowed the sound as Ethan fell to the side. His raft got swamped and swept away. Flipped. Tossed. Four people lost in the water.

At Jacinth's urging, we began paddling back toward the rapid. We gathered up two drenched, shivering runners and kept moving toward the upside-down raft as it came washing out of raging waters into the gentler flow. A third runner splashed about near the toppled boat, a look of gratitude in her eyes as we pulled her into our raft—shaken but not hurt. Ethan gave his okay sign as we made our way to him.

Jacinth called out tongue-in-cheek, "Hey big man, what happened there?"

Ethan held up a broken oar. "Damn monster, snapped it right in two."

Jacinth laughed as we pulled up beside him. "I could never snap an oar in a million years."

I nudged Jacinth and whispered to her, "I'm sure glad the spirits guided you to the perfect line."

We worked together to right the swamped boat and made camp a few hundred feet west of the rapid. As we unpacked the gear, a storm passed to the east, leaving in its wake a brilliant double rainbow that lit up the Canyon.

I realized, looking at the double rainbow as the sun faded into a golden glow, that we were at the halfway point. This journey had already changed me but not in any way I expected, not in a way I could put into words or make into a story. I had let go of myself, let go of all my ego constructs—not to live in a 'now' moment, but to find a non-moment outside of time and feel the cosmic dance of Shiva again—to get back to being that rocking child. And like the rainbow, I knew the feeling would pass. Every day on the river brought me closer to the end and farther from the beginning.

That night at camp we celebrated our victory over the monster. *An old nemesis conquered again. A celebration of thanks to nature for showing us her power and sparing us. A toast to the news from Phantom of a grandchild born. A magic moment all around.* And I knew that the world above the rim waited to claim me again after eight more days in the heart of Grand Canyon.

A few days later, as we hiked up the trail to Thunder River Falls, Jacinth joked about revealing my secret nickname to the group, saying, "There's a ThunderBird Walking up to Thunder River Falls." I reminded her that I knew about her red streak, and we came to a truce. While walking the switchbacks and closing in on the thundering sound of the water, Jacinth led me into a private alcove of trees next to the flowing stream. A waterfall crashed down over rocks, and she pulled me to a specific spot and stepped back. I looked at her, thinking maybe I should kiss her, but that didn't feel right. She stepped forward and moved me a few inches to the left, and a cool breeze shot up from below . . . natural air conditioning coming off the water.

I laughed and reached out my hand, wanting her to take it. As she stepped closer, the couple from Denmark stepped into the alcove hugging each other. Jacinth dropped her outstretched hand and turned to them. "Come feel the cool air coming off the water here."

I moved aside and let them take my spot, thinking back to the moment at the California temple next to the fake creek. It seemed dumb to make a big deal out of cool air coming off of a waterfall in an alcove, but after going so long without air conditioning it reminded us of the comforts of home. I wanted to believe there was some deeper meaning to the moment, that it healed the hurt of California and signaled the beginning of a new life with Jacinth, as improbable as that seemed. But after snapping a few pictures, Jacinth and the couple walked out into the hot sun together. I waited, thinking she might come back in to pick up where things left off when we were alone, but she called to me and asked if I was coming with them.

We hiked the rest of the trail and stopped for lunch next to the falls cascading down the cliff from the North Rim. Sitting there, Jacinth poked me and feigned yelling out my secret nickname to the group. I ran my fingers through my scruffy hair to warn of my revenge. The afternoon ended with our secrets intact, and we walked back and got on the river to run the remaining miles of the trip.

Over those last days, my greatest strength—of creating stories and seeing the Canyon as a metaphor for my life—turned into a burden that I took downriver with me. I wanted to capture my experience and bring the feeling of rebirth and rejuvenation with me to reinvigorate my life. I kept revisiting Canyon moments from the trip, weaving them together into stories, but those stories became like the weight of time gone by. I carried that weight downriver through the largest rapid at Lava Falls, where I watched the guides share a hidden hug thanking the Canyon spirits for a safe run. And I carried it into the feigned fall from the paddle boat to swim one of the gentler rapids on a scorching hot day—and I remembered the weight during the celebrations at camp in the waning nights, and I took it onto the beach at Diamond Creek for breakdown and our last lunch together. And as the bus to the surface world waited, I wanted to capture some of the magic to take back with me.

I found Jacinth sitting by herself. I wanted to thank her for being a Nightingale to Hayduke. At the start of the trip I saw her as a girl of privilege whose parents pulled strings to get her a job as a Grand Canyon river guide, but now I knew she had earned it. So I sat down next to her and tried to get her to look me in the eye.

"I think you're an amazing woman."

She had nothing to say. I felt my words hanging there and realized she heard them as a come-on, a cliché for a river-runner woman at the end of a trip. Up above the rim we could only be an awkward couple, star-crossed lovers, people who had met in the wilds outside of time and tried to turn that into a relationship. But my surface life sat in a storage unit, and we didn't have a realistic chance. So my words hung there in the air of Diamond Creek, nothing more to say as the magic of the Canyon let us go.

The creaking in my bones that had disappeared on the river trip came back as I moved into an apartment in Flagstaff. In those first days setting up my place, the cool air from the vent smelt stale and the hum of the fridge made me miss the natural sounds of the Canyon. I bought my first real bed—the kind that comes from a bed store with a special sheep—hoping that good nights of sleep might slow the advance of the creak. The full mattress with box spring and frame became my symbol of hanging on to the middle class. I placed the pink, number forty-four sheep next to my pillow to watch over me as I slept, and I gave myself a year in this place to see what might take hold.

I filled a bookcase with my handwritten journals—my life in twenty-eight volumes—roughly two-and-a-half million words. *Fodder for a fire? Let the smoke and the ashes join the journal I burned years ago on the rim of Grand Canyon?* I couldn't bring myself to write anymore, and I couldn't face a calling that never bore fruit. I knew an epoch of my life had ended, and whether anything might rise out of the tattered remnants of broken dreams and false promises, I could not see. The void between what was and what could be left me feeling lost, and reading through those pages again might only serve to remind me how many dreams I wrote down that never became real.

None of it fed the future. A journal of personal writings might be a treasure for my future kids or kin, but it didn't look like my life led that way. It seemed that letting go of journaling might open a void to be filled, might seed a transition into some kind of paid writer, and the old standard of 'write what you know' came to mind. I could write about Grand Canyon—capturing moments from hikes and river trips—and out of that maybe become a travel writer trying to get people to take on adventures for themselves, to lose their ego in the wilds and experience true freedom. But I realized that other writers already had a foothold there. They would see me as a pretender arriving late to the party, a straggler. And I knew that so many years of writing only for myself made me too undisciplined to write for anyone else.

I had sunk a whole life into writing, and I wondered if condensing all those words down into one ultimate, loose-bound journal of the peaks and pillars of my experience—ignoring the voids and chasms—might lead to rejuvenation. If nothing else, it could be a personal project to see me through the waning summer and into the darkness of winter, maybe onto another spring. But I also knew that the more time spent trying to define the moment, the less remains of the moment. Letting go, getting into the flow, feeling the waves of the universe roll over me and rocking to it, maybe that is all I ever needed. I could let go of journaling and let every word I ever wrote and all those dreams of being someone fade away if it meant having more non-moments away from civilization. So summer waned, fall closed in and nothing took hold except reading through a lifetime of journal entries and taking out pages to put into one ultimate binding never to be read by another person.

I picked up the ceramic star in two hands and held it with the rays sticking through my fingers like spikes. The sculpture had a sense of motion and a feeling of impossibility to it, and it drew me in for a closer look. The blue paint glittered in the light as I turned it over trying to find a starting place to count the points. It had six rays around the center, each with four triangular sides, and four more rays above and below, but as I turned the star in my hands and counted, I lost track of where I started. Some of the rays were missing, as if the star didn't shine there. I laughed as I held it, feeling a whole lifetime might pass before I could understand it, but it was only a crude, ceramic star put up for silent auction to benefit kids wanting to take a river trip.

As I set it back down, I decided to post a bid on it. I had just set up a Christmas tree in my apartment and it needed a star. This ceramic sculpture wouldn't work as an ornament—it would crush the tree—but I could put it underneath for the holidays and keep it as a 'work of art' after. I looked at the bid sheet and saw the words "The Heart Star" followed by a blurb about the healing power of sacred geometry. The unique shape affected the tantric heart center in a person and helped heal loneliness and isolation. I added a bid of forty-four dollars at the bottom of the list and dropped the pen. It rolled down the page and came to rest beneath the name of the sculptress. *Jacinth.*

Earlier, when I entered the room, I saw Jacinth rushing about the place getting things ready. A look of distress crossed her face when she recognized me. We hadn't seen each other since that awkward moment at Diamond Creek months earlier, and I wondered if she remembered telling me about her work with the Canyon Kids Foundation while we were on the river. I didn't approach her right away. I went into the auction room, found the star and waited for the right moment to talk with her. After making my bid, I saw Jacinth standing with a group of river guides, a few of whom I knew, so I went over to say hello.

Jacinth looked different out of the Canyon. She seemed older and closer to my age, not the diminutive woman from the river. She stood next to another outdoorsy woman who looked like her. They flicked their hair behind their shoulders in unison as I stepped into the circle, and I thought of Jacinth's words from the river—"sort of . . . boyfriend."

After the hellos, I felt like an outsider on the group's conversation. They were talking about a fellow river guide who had died recently, but it didn't happen on a trip in Grand Canyon. He had been rock climbing with friends when a hold gave way and he fell fifty feet onto a ledge. He survived the fall but slipped into a coma and died a week later. The community of river guides began a collection to pay his medical bills and funeral costs.

As I stood there listening, I kept looking at Jacinth trying to figure out what had changed since our time on the river, but my staring came off as flirtation and that made her uncomfortable. I stepped away and went back to check on the heart star. Someone had bid a dollar more than me and someone else five more than that. I raised my bid to fifty-five dollars and decided to end it there—more than that for a crude ceramic sculpture seemed ridiculous even if it had some magical power for healing.

Jacinth and the heart star both felt like enigmas to me, strange bookends that trapped me between them that night. I kept going back to check on my bid, saw that it remained untopped, and I tried to find Jacinth alone to tell her in a corny voice that I had a bid on her heart. But the right moment never came. At the end of the evening I collected on my winning bid and saw Jacinth across the empty room as I headed for the door. I held up the star for her to see and mouthed the words "I won your heart." She shook her head, and I sensed a hint of remorse in her, a feeling that she hoped to see someone else with her sculpture.

After the holidays, the heart star became a pedestal for sheep number forty-four on the corner of my bed. Together they reminded me of my precarious hold on the middle class, one that might slip away as the family money from my godmother dried up. Over the months of winter and into the spring, I dreamt up a future for myself, trying to cling to the fading notion that everything happens for a reason. My healing path had led me to Jacinth—all the signs pointed me toward her, and I figured that before long she had to see it too. Everything I wanted still waited for me if I could eke out a living in a small town near the edge. I believed there had to be a reason why she seemed as enigmatic to me as the healing heart star she created.

Every path I might take toward a writing life or a creative life had dead ended. I had lived too free and gone too deep into the wilds to ever make it back to being a commodity. I still wanted to believe that abandoning my journaling opened me up to new possibilities, that instead of trying to capture fleeting thoughts in words and being a creative writer, I could morph into an extroverted wordsmith in line with a new world order. I could learn to write articles in first person plural—*we're all in this together or get the hell away from me*—or I could swallow my pride to become a technical writer of government documents preparing for—and creating—a zombie apocalypse. Except in my heart I knew I could never live that dichotomy.

I rejected the whole mythos built up around becoming a successful writer. Thinking inside the box, hanging out with a success story and compromising my vision to meet the market didn't sit well with me. The de facto design of the literary world is to miss the great trees deep in the woods for a sapling near the edge of a meadow. But the great writer walks a path all their own, creates in isolation and ask others to come into the wilderness with them. I had wandered too far and too long and became a haunt of a tree too deep in the woods.

True writer dues are earned in solitude, and their words entice longing souls into the deep woods past where a simple path exists. Most are too scared to go that deep. They keep to the trees that are planted in straight lines, the planned forest, getting harvested over and over again.

My soul dwelled too far from where light might penetrate, but I held to the hope that healing from some witchy source might still find me, rays of light piercing beyond the planned forest and the craggy trees to find something unique if not forlorn. But my lifetime of writing sat never to be shared, and I found myself still taking up that project of reading through all my journals and choosing pages for one ultimate chronicle. Organizing my life seemed to organize my mind and domesticate my soul, giving me hope where no hope existed.

I got in the habit of taking my ultimate journal out to a ledge on the rim of Grand Canyon and letting the wind flip through the pages like some forlorn spirit sifting through the scattered remnants of a life. And I got to thinking about my nickname, ThunderBird Walking, wondering why my life never took flight, why all those hopes and dreams never manifested.

The world I envisioned in my younger days never materialized. Just as it seemed possible, the negative spiral took hold, and I couldn't turn that around save for one river trip in the heart of the chasm. Out there on that ledge with pages flipping in the wind, all sorts of reasons why came into my mind, but mostly the failure had to do with not evolving, not believing, not going further. A whole different world waited if I could brave the fall from this one. I could walk another earth, one aligned with my true self, one where the thunderbird took flight.

Standing there on the ledge, pages flapping in the wind, I thought about the story of a shaman who fancied himself a sorcerer next to an abyss. He believed that the chasm lived within him and outside of him, and if he took the leap of faith—braved the fall—all his fears and all those obsolete patterns of thinking and all the haunts that held him back would evaporate and flee, making him light in spirit and giving him wings. He could fly down to the ground to walk on a new earth that matched his dreams, forever living in a world aligned with his changed self. If only he dared.

I kept going back to that ledge with more pages culled from writings across a lifetime. The book grew thicker, but my prospects for the future didn't brighten, the futility of life on the edge of the chasm remained. I thought about taking the fall, knowing the folly of it and yet still wondering if maybe the wind might carry me. I couldn't make it in the real world, trading my freedom for more belonging, settling into ordinariness and letting go of the growth path. All my miracles felt used up.

The next river running season I got a driving job at the company where Jacinth worked, and I bargained to get a river trip at the end of the year as an assistant to the guides. I got to see Jacinth as she breezed through the warehouse before and after her runs through the Canyon, and she warmed up to me again. Resistance fading, I thought. The impossible heart star sat on my bed, and the impossible life that I wanted seemed to be coming together.

The light of summer faded back toward fall and a sense of somberness came over me. My time in canyon country felt short, and I hoped getting back on the river might bring magic to save me. I knew, like all writers and artists, that outside of making it big in your twenties or thirties, you had to let go of those dreams and join the branded masses, make yourself like the harvestable trees. For things to work out with Jacinth, I needed a more practical way to make a living. Working odd jobs, driving for a river company and waiting for the reward of a free river trip each year wasn't sustainable. The time for my second river trip arrived, and I needed it to be magic.

The flow coming out of the dam hit at an historic low on the day we departed, leaving the river only a shadow of its true nature. The guides told us that rocks usually hidden beneath monster rapids would be standing like sentinels above well-worn channels, but the smaller rapids would be more dangerous. Rocks usually hidden deep below the water would be lurking near the surface, creating tricky currents rarely seen on the mightier river.

On the first day I rode on an oar boat with Jacinth and tried to learn the part of assistant and servant. She told me about the guides, my masters for the journey. The leader of the last trip—the gentle giant of the river—had moved on from the company, taking his years of experience with him. The new leader, touted as an improved breed of river runner, had learned from lecture and books, so he lacked the sense of sureness that comes from a few years as a protégé. Two of the older guides had gotten married on a river trip before moving back east, and they came back about once a year to rekindle the magic. Two young male guides rounded out the crew. Rumour had it that one of them came from a family of privilege—his parents held a fortune—and Jacinth joked that if she were twenty years younger she would throw herself at him and marry into money. After saying that she fell silent, and we rode under Navaho Bridge into the Canyon. Me, a nowhere man—neither guide nor passenger—with decisions to make about my future in the world above the rim.

On the third day of the trip I took an unexpected tumble into the river first thing in the morning at Twenty-Four and One-Half Mile Rapid. I was looking backward riding on Jacinth's boat when she hit an awkward wave and I fell overboard. The cold water took my breath away and a strange, crushing feeling surged through my chest. Flailing in the water, I thought about second chances. *Had life passed me by? Were there any miracles left for me?* I felt like I was somewhere else for a moment, being chased by peaceful primitives.

The evening before, most of the group had taken off for a hike while I helped the lead guide set up camp. He told me that I needed to watch out for Jacinth. Word around the river community was that she intended to settle down at the ripe age of thirty-five, finally find a man to marry. So my innocent flirtations could lead to something more than I wanted. *Except it might not be more than I wanted. Canyon magic giving me a second chance at love with Jacinth?*

Late in the afternoon we made it to Buck Farm to set up camp for the night. After gathering our gear on the beach near the river, the lead guide called us over to look at the remnants of a wooden boat. It once belonged to Bert Loper, a man who had died long ago running the rapid where I fell in. He flipped his wooden vessel and his lifeless body floated away down the wild river never to be seen again. The boat came to rest at Buck Farm just past the site of a proposed dam that never got built. Bert had told people that he wanted the Canyon to be his final resting place, and he got that wish for a while, but his skull and bones were discovered by a hiker downriver many years later. The pieces of him got moved to a cemetery in Utah—leaving boat, man and skeleton scattered in many directions.

I had fallen into the river at the same place Bert did. As we started to get dinner ready at Buck Farm that night, I felt haunted by that, felt the presence of a ghost that spoiled the calm of the Canyon and seemed to get inside the people sitting around camp as we waited for dinner. The trip leader and the bureaucrats got in an argument about the true nature of the river, the city folk saying taming the river was inevitable and the guide saying it was better wild. As the back-and-forth lingered on, I felt angry that talk from above the rim intruded here—anger that seemed not wholly my own, anger of a ghost unable to speak out loud.

The wind began to pick up, pots and pans started to clang, and sand swirled around. A metal table fell over and people scrambled to pin everything down. After securing the camp, the wind raged on, and it seemed like the words of a ghost echoed inside me.

You lost your true nature. You lost your future!

We got our dinners on covered plates to take back to eat in our tents away from the blowing sand. As I walked up the path, the wind grabbed at my plate with a howl, sending it flying from my hands. I felt a whole other realm of thoughts descending upon me, and a howling on the wind seemed to say that we get only one sweet chance at life, or one magic run down the Canyon, or one real shot at love. *Why do I deserve a second?*

I ran away, abandoning my tent and scrambling over the dark rocks of some forlorn side canyon, but the haunt followed, beating me down, mocking my life. And a vision of those last minutes of Loper's life came into me. I saw him running the rapid at twenty-four-and-a-half, looking backward over his life, not looking ahead at the river but facing upstream trying to remember what he had lost. Except looking back only rekindled his doubts, his fears, his lostness. And that is when the rapid flipped his boat and took him. Washed him under, crushed his heart.

I ran up the side canyon trying to escape the vision, but the wind screamed after me. I felt the storm outside and within me. I ran like I ran from the peaceful primitives off the road near the Blue Ridge Mountains—Apple Orchard Falls. I heard voices from the wilderness and felt a beast rising up inside me, and I heard echoes on the wind.

Two rivers live within. One conjures dreams and hopes laced with fears and darkness, a cauldron of spirit that challenges us to be something greater. The dirty waters can wash us clean and test our mettle, rock us back and forth till we feel the ripples of the universe taking us over like some kind of dancing Shiva—letting us rise and fall in the moment without creating a story of triumph or defeat. But the other river within is dammed by man into a riddle of stagnation. It tears us down as it builds us up, moves us forth as it mires our mojo. Instead of finding and releasing our troubles, it confines and amplifies them, dares to trap a piece of our soul in a backwater while letting on that everything is normal and natural.

I saw my hands like paws scurrying over rocks amid flashes of matted hair and shining moon and swirling sand—and again the peaceful primitive feeling of knowing everything at once flowed through me. Scattered moments of my life flooded into me, drowning me—*a life spent hiding from my true nature*—and as that feeling of lostness haunted me, Jacinth's face appeared hovering over me like an angel peering down through a watery surface, deep concern on her face.

But she's not actually there. I realize I'm on some other river, some other flow, stuck in a dream until all is black. I wake up in the night, cold but none the worse for wear. The storm has passed. The haunt has left me, but my mind feels jumbled, back from the brink. And I wonder if I will ever be the same and if I will get my second chance.

Three nights later I stood on a rocky sandbank near the turn of the river below the Desert View Watchtower. The open expanse had me feeling like the eyes of the universe were upon me, and I thought this might be the night to move things forward with Jacinth. I had promised the group a brief tale about Grand Canyon hauntings at the Watchtower, but the haunt of old man Loper still had me rattled. I fell into 'um's and 'ah's and lost my way. I felt Jacinth's eyes upon me the whole time I fumbled through the story, but no one else looked at me. The stories I used to tell people up on the rim had faded into a backwater in my mind, my gift seemed lost, so I drew my talk to a quick close and let the group leave.

Alone on a rocky outcrop, Jacinth came over to talk to me while looking up at the starry sky. "Oh T-B-W . . . all I've got is 'ah's and 'um's. I hate when I don't know what to say."

"Yeah, telling my story, I felt like I was two places at once. Up on the rim in the Watchtower and down here where my words were failing me."

"What happened to you?"

I paused, not sure what she meant. We seemed to be talking past each other. I walked nearer so she could see me. "Actually, I think you are partly to blame."

She forced a smile. "How?"

"Do you know how to tell if a guy is into a woman? He's all ums and thumbs around her."

She shook her head, not understanding.

"If the guy is calm and collected, always saying the right thing, he might just be playing you. The guy who is fumbling about probably gets you at a deeper level."

"So you are all thumbs too?" She turned and walked to the boats, her poke at me still hanging.

The other guides were getting ready to sleep, and I figured she was calling it a night too, but she grabbed a few things and went looking for a spot to lay her stuff on the shore. Her actions seemed halfway between indifference and invitation—I couldn't tell which—but I had already started a flirtation, so I needed to take it further. I went to her.

"Do you want to, um, *sleep* together under the stars?"

She pursed her lips as if tasting a bitter lemon and shook her head no. As she turned away, I realized I had said 'sleep' rather than 'sit,' and the idea of sex with a grungy man six days into a river trip had turned her off. I laughed and called after her.

"Jacinth, I meant to say we should sit and talk."

She dropped her sleeping bag and started spreading it out on the ground, not looking at me. "I don't feel *that way* about you."

"I thought I saw . . . or felt something between us."

She finished laying out her sleeping bag and faced me. "I need to be more practical. I can't have another relationship with someone I met in the wilds."

"Practicality over passion? Doesn't seem like you."

"Oh T-B-W, I'm finally letting go of the romantic idea that those two rivers—practicality and passion, tamed and wild, whatever you might call it—will ever meet."

"So you're giving up on synergy . . . on following your passions and making the best of whatever comes your way?"

"What? You're forty-six . . . forty-seven . . . and you're still hanging on to those silly ideas? For me, the feeling of security with a man beats the feeling of passion for the wild side. We flirt here on the river, but it could never work in the real world."

As I watched Jacinth get into her sleeping bag, a hundred ideas of what to say and how to say it came to mind, from pleading with her to yelling at her, but I knew that words would fail me. Sometime between the magical trip last year and this one, our moment had passed. We were two very different people, rocking to our own rhythms. Two rivers so divergent that they could never flow as one. Time had closed in on us. We were star-crossed and nothing could heal that, so I walked away and left her there alone.

For the rest of the trip I felt like a man trapped in the middle, caught between the bureaucrats and the guides, between moments alone in the

Canyon and being servant to others—running the clean, cold, tamed river while memories of the muddy, wild river flowed inside me. Jacinth remained friendly to me, no hint of anger or resentment between us, but the deeper connection felt severed. I wondered if it had ever been real. She had the power to rescue me and end the star-crossed affair that raged in my mind, if only she let me back in.

The days moved by and on the last night of the trip, the guides lit a bonfire and passed a talking stick, giving each of us a chance to say what this trip meant. As the stick started around, the bureaucrats all talked about how the canyon would serve as their *go-to place* when work got them down. I listened and waited, and by the time the stick came to me, a whole rant had built up inside me—ideas started flowing out of me like some dam within had given way.

"I sometimes fear I don't have much time left in this world. And I dream of a grander Grand Canyon, one that is three times longer than this one. Its headwaters come down gorges born out of majestic rocky mountains and forge together in the midst a wide, meandering plateau. Through these canyonlands a great river flows beneath arches and cliffs and buttes, carving ever deeper in its channel, till it gives way to a gentler canyon filled with glens of cliff-hanging flowers and seeping waterfalls the likes of which are unknown through all the worlds. And then it opens up again into a true Grand Canyon, one where a wild river flows beneath formations named for gods and goddesses, a place greater than this one around us because it is all natural.

"And imagine taking all of one summer to run that grandest of canyons, over six hundred miles to ponder life, to rise and fall with creation, to sleep beneath the stars. Can you imagine?

"The thing is, this grander Grand Canyon exists, but the caretakers of it could not fathom something so great. So they broke it in three— put up a tombstone that drowned the gentle glens of the middle third of it—and left a clean, cold, utopian river running though the lower third. That tombstone might as well have my name on it . . . put up the same year I was born.

"In my whole life I have never known the grander Grand Canyon, and I now believe I never will. I used to think that somehow that dam, that tombstone, would be breached or fall or be decommissioned in my lifetime, or at least the same year that I die. It seems a cruel twist of fate to be born in a time when I will never know the true nature of Grand Canyon. I wonder what that does to my heart.

"Instead, we as a generation wait for rescuers to heal us, to carry us from our forlorn ledge. We spout gratitude for what we have instead of striving for something greater, instead of recognizing we have been tamed from our true natures. We look back feeling we have lost something, but we only bring back those things we were better off without—stagnant ideas and backwater notions—instead of free-flowing rivers.

"If this generation had half the vision and gumption of the people who built the tombstone at the head of this canyon, it would be gone. Instead, we live in gratitude of our domestication, give up our free-flowing hearts to be boxed in between tombstones marring and marking our birth and our passing. All of us ghosts waiting for rescue from our chains."

As the words from within stopped flowing, I looked down at the stick clutched in my hand and passed it on. Silence, except for the river, reigned for thirty seconds . . . into a minute. Finally I broke it by saying, "Maybe no one can follow what I just said."

A few laughs broke out, and the man next to me started talking, finding his story. I looked around the circle and tried to catch the eyes of Jacinth, but she wouldn't look my way. Our adventure ended for a second time, and I wondered if someday we might share that other river again—or if all possibilities were lost.

WHERE STARS FALL . . .

Coming off the river I knew that my time living on the edge had ended. To make my way in this world, I needed to let go of my dreams, snuff the smudge and deny connection to nature—let the smoke and mirrors go.

The purple clunker had sat as a fixture in the parking lot outside my apartment. I turned the key and heard a click and a sputter, more than it had given me in months. Maybe it needed to be junked, but I hoped enough spirit remained to get me to Salt Lake City or back east or to wherever life waited. The bicycle that got me around town and all my furniture were going to charity. Everything else needed to fit inside and on top of a car. If the Volvo's engine came back to life, I could make my escape in the box car from the eighties. If not, clunkers for cash and a rental would do.

I checked under the hood, cleaned the points and broke encrusted corrosion off the battery. I turned the key to a chitty and two coughs before the engine revved to life. I thanked the aging machine and drove it around the parking lot till the engine settled down. Needing to make sure it had more than a short drive left in it, I thought about heading to the ledge overlooking Grand Canyon—to set my journal on the rock and see if the wind might support my ideas of flight—but instead I headed east across the reservation toward a distant calling, the dam. I wanted to see that grand tombstone one last time before I packed up all my stuff and took off to places unknown.

I parked the clunker above the gorge and perched myself on a familiar rock overlooking Glen Canyon Dam. I sat there daydreaming about an F-16 shooting a couple of missiles into the concrete wall and releasing a great flood to restore the true nature of Grand Canyon. I stared at that tombstone and concentrated my thoughts on widening imaginary cracks in the concrete, as if my mental power could make it so, as if the water might get angry and ugly with my negative energy and breach the aging dam. No luck, again.

Sitting there about a hundred feet from my Volvo, I watched as a white sedan came speeding along the road. Two men got out and made their way up to my perch. They looked like police types, plain-clothes division, and they questioned me about terrorist intentions. I promptly denied any connection to George W. Hayduke and explained my presence by pointing at the purple clunker. "I'm just an old peacenik who lost most of his hair and comes here to dream about having it again." They laughed, took my name plus a few other details and went away.

I left soon after but I kept thinking about the dam—that concrete headstone—and I recognized connections between myself and the river in Grand Canyon. Both of us had lost touch with our true natures. We were living a great duality. I knew the dam's history, and when I got back to the apartment I found my magic typewriter hidden away in my pile of belongings. I hadn't opened it since my California days, but after popping in a ribbon it worked like a charm, and I wrote a lament for a once free river.

Give Me a Free Winding River

I have never known the true nature of Grand Canyon. On the year I was born, Glen Canyon Dam closed on the Colorado River fifteen miles above the starting place of the world's greatest natural wonder. Over ninety percent of the sediment -- the rich lifeblood -- that once flowed through Grand Canyon now gets trapped behind the dam. There are drastic changes in the vegetation and aquatic life of the river, and ancient archeological sites are eroding because floods no longer bring sediments to replenish beaches.

I wonder if I have ever known the true nature
of myself. As a child, a great wall was built in my
psyche. The free part of me got drowned and after
that I believed in a clean, cold, utopian picture of
my emotional self. Like sediments trapped behind the
dam, my passions and emotions -- my rich lifeblood --
got stunted behind the wall in my psyche.

The dam builders admit that the river below the
dam isn't natural anymore. It's clear and cold, rising
and falling to fulfill demands for power. At any
time, about one hundred forty people are involved in
studying and managing the Colorado River below the
dam. The job of these 'Psychiatrists of the Canyon' is
to try to restore the ecosystem to what it was before
the dam was built without pointing to the concrete
headstone and the absurdity of the evaporating fake
'lake' in a desert as a problem.

In 1981, as I reached the age of adulthood, a great
flood rushed forth within me. I was overwhelmed
almost to the point of destruction. Like the great
flood of 1983 at Glen Canyon Dam, the wall in my
psyche got saved among hushed whispers. Somehow I
remembered the feeling of true flow, always seeking
to recreate it, to become vibrant and alive again. But
just like pointing to the dam on the river and saying
it's a problem, pointing to the great wall built in my
psyche that changed my true nature from peaceful man
to holy warrior isn't allowed.

So I am caught in a drought of belief. I wonder
if I can live my true nature and fulfill some of the
original promise evident in my childhood. I know that I
am part of something greater than myself, but there is
fear in fully reconnecting and realizing that. It seems
easier to live day to day and not care about a legacy.

I am not someone great enough to leave behind a
massive structure built by the hands of men. I want

no great wall or paved highway to bear my name. It
seems right somehow that the best legacy to leave is
natural canyons and wilderness rivers stretching for
miles across desert. Only nothingness lasts forever,
and only the awe of nothingness can contain my
true nature.

Give me a path to follow, no simple highway but a
free winding river that unveils some of the mysteries
inside of me.

Like everything ever written it needed work, and not just tinkering
with the words but a weaseling into the cadre that acted as gatekeepers
on anything related to Grand Canyon. Those people who had let the
dams be built wanted to be the ones who got rid of them . . . or died
trying. And they were wrapped up in tit-for-tat arguments about
evaporation in a desert that ignored the larger emotional truth of
damming rivers and damning spirits. Only emotion can take down
such walls, and words can shine a light on those emotions and the
folly of building tombstones that break apart natural wonders. But *they*
owned the ground, so I had nowhere to go with my emotional plea for
a free river. I chunked it in with the writings in my ultimate, never-to-
be-read journal and thought of going back to that ledge one last time
to take flight into the world I dared to dream about. Except I needed to
pack up my stuff and make my escape.

The next afternoon I finished tying the last of my belongings to
the roof of the clunker. I felt a sense of foolish pride that everything I
owned could be carried by one dilapidated, hippie vehicle—probably
the last time in my life that could be true, especially if I ended up back
east. The charity truck arrived and took all my furniture including my
bed, that symbol of clinging to the middle class. I didn't mind letting
the bed go, mostly when I laid on it I felt the creak in my bones and
thought of death approaching or an angel easing me into my last
night. I needed to escape that pending tomb. I walked into the empty
bedroom and saw sheep number forty-four looking dumbfounded on
top of the heart star on the floor. I spread out my sleeping bag and let

Jacinth's creation and the sheep watch over me as I drifted off to sleep in that space once last time.

I dreamt of being a bird of prey swooping down over Bright Angel Canyon, and I felt myself in all those places again. On the ledge with the pages of my ultimate journal flipping in the wind. Standing on the cliff at Plateau Point looking down on the river. Walking though the tunnel toward the black bridge near Phantom. Playing in a hidden waterfall, running the Hermit monster rapid, swimming in the Havasu waters at the magic moment, feeling the cool air of the private alcove at Thunder River Falls, and flying over it all. Falling . . . falling . . . falling into that world of my imagination.

I woke with a start, into darkness.

I packed up my sleeping bag and took it along with the heart star to the car. The nip in the pre-dawn air made me abandon my plan of tying the sheep and sculpture to the roof to watch over my exit. I put them in the passenger seat next to me and fired up the engine. I drove route 89A, crossing the Navaho reservation in the morning twilight, and turned into House Rock Valley. All the while sheep number forty-four looked at me as if to ask, *What are you going to do among the branded masses?* I had no answer and I got sick of the question.

As I approached Navaho Bridge, an idea came to me . . . let sheep number forty-four and the heart star fall into Grand Canyon. I pictured the hollow star floating through the heart of the Canyon after it made a big splash from the bridge. DOWNRIVER! Two hundred seventy-seven miles of wilderness to be explored, and maybe one day the heart star would get back to Jacinth, letting her know the way I felt. *Star-crossed*. Denied a one in a million shot of finding a life with connection and fulfillment and love, a free-flowing river with dreams fulfilled. So I resolved to drop the star with sheep tied atop from the bridge before escaping House Rock Valley, but as I got to the parking lot with the sunrise, people were already there. If they saw me throw something in the Canyon, they might think I was polluting the place and throw me in after it. So I drove on, turned toward Lee's Ferry and went down to where the Paria River cuts into the Canyon.

Mud from rains in Utah had turned the Paria brown, and the dirty river mixed with the clean, cold water flowing from the dam. I stepped out into the muddy current and threw the star with all my might. It splashed into the water and disappeared, swallowed by the river, but a moment later it came back to the surface, pink sheep and blue star running the riffle, off for adventures unknown. I laughed as it stayed afloat and rode out of sight, and I imagined the look on Jacinth's face when it hopped into her boat while running a rapid—or when she stepped into the alcove near Thunder River Falls and found it there.

I got back in the clunker to escape House Rock Valley and all those broken promises of a dream out there . . . waiting.

Every spring, as the river runner season starts, I find myself back on the same ledge overlooking Grand Canyon, the pages of my journal flipping in the wind. I feel like I can see everything from here, and I wonder where that blue star got to. Did it fill with water and sink soon after it rode the Paria riffle? Did it get swallowed by a rapid downriver, or get shattered upon a rock leaving curious shards to be mistaken for ancient pottery? I feel trapped here on this ledge till I know the fate of that star. If it returns whole to Jacinth, will my dreams be reborn? Or if the hands of another pull it from the river, will possibilities flower anew? Or maybe it waits at the bottom somewhere, wedged between immovable rocks until the dam fails and releases a torrent, caught in a backwater until the tombstone breaks and all the ghosts of the Canyon run free with the flood of rich lifeblood. I wait here, trapped on this ledge until the star is found.

And I think of seeking out an angel, a mistress of light, to talk me into that final good night—to make me give up clinging to this earth, to give up the ghost. But I'm not ready to see all the truth yet. I want to keep calling out the hiders, whispering to them to join me here in the wilds, enticing them to run a river or hike a trail before life slips away. Before the concrete comes. The heart star lies hidden somewhere in the Canyon, and I think of shouting out onto the wind, creating echoes that bound from cliff to cliff and heart to heart. But my voice fails me. I wait for a rescuer to find the star, and I call out with all my might—that amounts only to a whisper . . .

Olly olly oxen free!

www.ingramcontent.com/pod-product-compliance
Lightning Source LLC
Chambersburg PA
CBHW071251250626
47163CB00002B/413